HAIRPIN BRIDGE

ALSO BY TAYLOR ADAMS

No Exit

Our Last Night

Eyeshot

TAYLOR ADAMS

WILLIAM MORROW
An Imprint of HarperCollins*Publishers*

HAIRPIN BRIDGE

A NOVEL

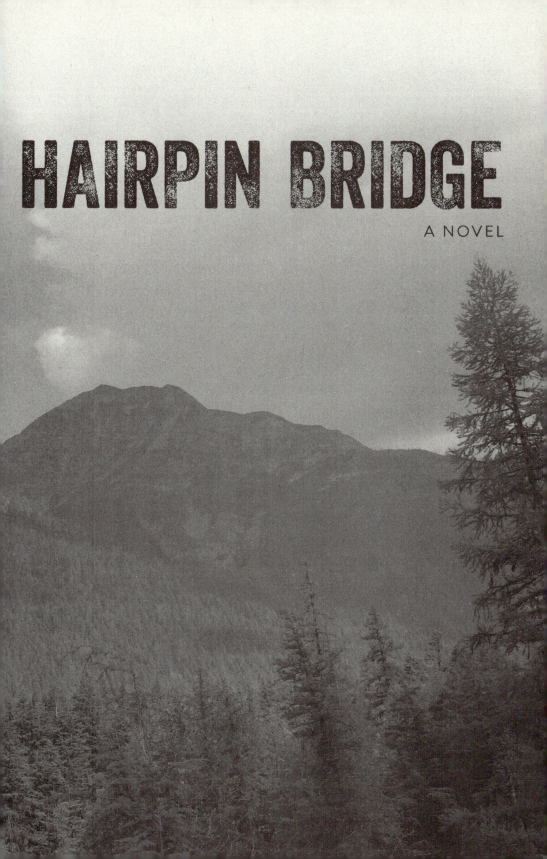

HAIRPIN BRIDGE. Copyright © 2021 by Taylor Adams. All rights reserved. Printed in the United States of America. No part of this book may be used or reproduced in any manner whatsoever without written permission except in the case of brief quotations embodied in critical articles and reviews. For information, address Harper-Collins Publishers, 195 Broadway, New York, NY 10007.

HarperCollins books may be purchased for educational, business, or sales promotional use. For information, please email the Special Markets Department at SPsales@harpercollins.com.

FIRST EDITION

Library of Congress Cataloging-in-Publication Data has been applied for.

ISBN 978-0-06-306544-4 (hardcover)
ISBN 978-0-06-306635-9 (international edition)

21 22 23 24 25 LSC 10 9 8 7 6 5 4 3 2 1

FOR MY PARENTS

HAIRPIN BRIDGE

FOUR SMALL FIRES

CHAPTER 1

LENA

"YOU LOOK . . . *EXACTLY* LIKE HER."

Lena Nguyen had heard this, many times before. It never got any less upsetting, being someone else's walking, talking ghost.

"And you were twins?"

She nodded.

"Identical, right?"

She nodded again.

Something changed behind the state trooper's eyes, and he looked regretful. Like he'd already committed an offense by not starting with this: "I'm . . . I should say, I'm so sorry for your loss."

Another greatest hit. Lena made polite eye contact.

"I can't imagine what it's like to lose a sibling."

No one ever could.

"Just try to take it one day at a time."

The oldies kept coming.

"You'll never get over it. But someday you will get *past* it."

That's a new one, Lena thought. She'd add it to the list.

Corporal Raymond Raycevic had agreed to meet her here

in a gravel parking lot shared by the Magma Springs Diner and a Shell station, sixty miles outside of Missoula. An exodus of wildfire evacuees fed a constant stream of passing traffic, and the highway hit a dangerous junction here under two blind corners and no stoplight.

Corporal Raycevic himself was a gorilla-like man stuffed into a tan-brown highway patrol uniform pulled taut to contain him. All shoulders and biceps and a gentle smile. He'd shaken Lena's hand with earnest delicacy. He had bags under his eyes, the soft color of bruises.

"Thank you for doing this," she said.

"Of course."

"I really appreciate it . . . you know. With you being on the clock and all—"

He half smiled. "My shift is over."

He studied her again for a long moment, still transfixed, and Lena felt a familiar impatience. Discussing her sister with strangers always felt like this; a choose-your-own-adventure book she'd memorized ages ago. She knew exactly what Raycevic was thinking before he said it, his words arriving right on schedule: "I'm sorry. I just . . . I can't get over how much you look *just like* her."

You should try it, she thought sourly. *It's awful, grieving for someone while seeing her face in the mirror every single morning.*

"It must be awful, seeing her face in the mirror every morning. Every day, anything with a reflection, even a car mirror, can just . . . blindside you."

She looked at him.

"You have my sympathy, Lena."

Yeah? And maybe I underestimated you, Ray.

A squealing hiss startled her. She turned—an eighteen-wheeler had taken the turn too fast. For a stomach-fluttery moment, ten tons of rolling cargo skidded directly at them on locked tires. Then the truck swerved back into its lane, and Corporal Raycevic watched the tinted windows pass, as if expecting the driver to apologize.

He didn't. The engine throttled up and the rig thundered on, a wash of displaced air tugging their clothes. Lena swept her bangs from her face and watched the trailer's stenciled letters hurtle past like film in a projector: SIDEWINDER. In another moment, gone. Just a ring in her ears and the gritty taste of dust.

"Idiot," the cop muttered.

I'm really here, she thought. *I'm really here, doing this.*

The dust in her teeth made it real. After months of waiting, twenty-four-year-old Lena was finally here in Montana. Miles from home. Moving forward. Making progress. Another voice, just a faint whisper in her mind: *Don't get comfortable. Don't let your guard down.*

Not even for a second.

She caught herself twirling a lock of her hair with her index finger and tugging—a tic she'd had since elementary school—and stopped herself. It made her look nervous.

Raycevic didn't notice. He was squinting into the distance. "Hairpin Bridge isn't far from here, but there's zero shade once you're up there. The sun becomes a spotlight. Saps your energy. Before we go, do you need anything from the diner? Water, maybe?"

"I'll buy something."

"All right." He pointed. "I'll start my vehicle. Follow me."

She hurried back inside the air-conditioned Magma Springs Diner. She'd already waited there for hours today, sipping black coffee as groups of firefighters talked shop over plates of greasy eggs. She pretended to waver at the mini-fridge stocked with energy drinks and bottled water, and once she was certain Corporal

Raycevic was occupied inside his cruiser and not watching her through the front windows, she returned to her booth.

There, she had a laptop on the table. She triple-checked the power cable, the Sony unit, and the connection to the restaurant's router. All good.

"Thanks again," she said to the lady at the long counter. "I'll be back soon."

"Is that a college project you're downloading?"

"Something like that."

SHE FOLLOWED THE COP CAR EAST ON HIGHWAY 200, FIFTEEN minutes of fresh asphalt under a horizon banded with smoke. Then Raycevic veered sharply right, crossing two lanes, as if the turnoff had surprised him. Lena had to stomp on her brakes, grinding rubber.

He waved out his window: *Sorry.*

This new road hadn't been maintained for decades. Weeds sprouted through fissures in sun-bleached concrete. The lines were faded. Over a locked metal gate, an equally faded signboard read: PUBLIC USE PROHIBITED. Corporal Raycevic had the code memorized. After relocking it behind them, he drove on at seventy-five, fifteen over the speed limit. She wondered if he was testing her, trying to goad her into a ticket. That would be a dick move.

She matched his speed. She would test him, too.

She drove in silence. No music or podcasts since she'd left Seattle this morning because she didn't have the correct dongle to connect to the speakers. She was afraid to touch the CD player or radio presets because the car wasn't hers.

It was Cambry's.

Had been Cambry's.

Driving your dead twin's car is a jarring experience. Their father had urged Lena through teary eyes to accept the vehicle, insisted that this lived-in 2007 Toyota Corolla was one of her sister's few remaining possessions and it would be wrong to sell it. Maybe so. But today's journey to the dry foothills of Howard County, Montana, was the longest Lena had ever driven it.

She hadn't altered anything. Every detail was a freeze-frame. The empty thirty-two-ounce fountain drink in the cup holder was Cambry's, sporting a superhero who'd already come and gone at the box office. The red cooler full of rotten food. The backup battery, the air compressor, the dirty tool bag. The minimalist living quarters in the back seat—a duffel bag of folded clothes that still had her scent, separate Ziploc bags containing deodorant, toothpaste, and mouthwash. In the trunk, a two-person tent, an electric grill, and a perfectly rolled sleeping bag. Lena could never roll a sleeping bag that tight. Ever.

I'm not just driving her car, she'd realized with a hollow pang, somewhere between Spokane and Coeur d'Alene. *I'm driving her house.*

City girl that she was, Lena couldn't help but marvel at her twin's spartan lifestyle. The duct tape on the steering wheel. The exposed wires betraying the handmade repairs to the cigarette-lighter adapter. The scattered dryer sheets (to fight odors, Lena guessed). To change or discard anything here, in this intimate space where her sister had lived capably for over nine months, felt like a profound insult.

So it all remained.

Even the moldy food in the cooler. Even the fountain drink at her side, sweet-smelling in the sunlight. Cambry's lips had touched it three months ago. Maybe her DNA was still on it.

You look exactly like her.

She was surprised Corporal Raycevic hadn't recognized Cambry's car. He'd found it the same night he found her body. Wouldn't he remember it?

His patrol car was still forging ahead—approaching eighty now—so Lena pushed the gas and matched his speed as the road climbed into the foothills. Tires jostled over rough concrete. The land dropped away in places to an alarming vastness on her right, and for a moment Lena considered how close you are to death on most roads. The buffers are mostly imaginary. You're only a swerve away from an oncoming lane or a ravine. She tried not to think about it.

The lodgepole pines grew taller up here—sixty, seventy feet. Frayed branches cooked brittle in the sun, standing over floors of brown needles and crunchy juniper. A million acres of tinder waiting for a spark. And beyond the changing terrain, rising in the distance . . .

She felt a knot tighten in her throat.

There it was. The structure was already taking shape over the sloping hills, jagged and unwelcome and thoroughly man-made. An ancient fossil emerging from the land.

Oh, Jesus, there it is.

She felt her chest tense up as the rust-brown form came into clarity, rivets and girders drawn toothpick-sharp in the sunlight. Becoming real before her eyes as the cracked road pulled her closer. She knew she was committed now, that her and Corporal Raycevic's fates were entwined here. She couldn't possibly turn back.

As it drew closer, momentarily obscured by another hump of dry pines, she tried to calm her nerves. No battle plan survives first contact with the enemy, right?

Still . . .

It looks so much bigger than in the photos.

BEFORE I GO
Posted 9/20/19 by LNguyen

It starts with a bridge.

A precarious steel monster with a fierce turn on its south ramp, spanning six hundred feet across an obscure valley on the fringes of a bankrupt silver-mining town, all rendered perfectly obsolete by the interstate. Seventy miles from Missoula. As far as bridges go, it's a total fuckup, and it knows it.

It's also where my sister died.

Allegedly.

Sorry to be heavy, dear readers. I know this blog post isn't my usual writing for *Lights and Sounds,* and that may upset some of you. And I appreciate the kind words and FB/Insta well-wishes over the past few months I've been AWOL (obvious reasons). Yes, I'm back in the blogging saddle, but not quite how you may expect. And I have a doozy of a post here, so buckle up.

But before you read further:

This is not my normal blog. This is not a book, movie, or video game review. This is not a political rant (God knows this has been a great year for that). Nor is this poetry, humor, photography, or the long-awaited part eleven of JustRetailThings. This—whatever THIS is—is something I need to post here, on *Lights and Sounds,* to my modest but engaged readership (that's you) for reasons that will soon become clear. By the time you finish reading this, depending on your time zone, I might just be national news. So, sorry in advance if this ruins your whole day. Good? Good.

Here we go.

I'm spending my Saturday at Hairpin Bridge. Tomorrow morning at the ass-crack of dawn I'm driving Cambry's car seven hours east to the town of Magma Springs, Montana, and meeting up with a local highway patrolman named Raymond R. Raycevic. Yes, that's really his name (apparently R's were on sale the day his parents named him). Via email he's kindly agreed to show me, the grieving sister, the exact spot where he discovered Cambry's body three months ago.

As for Hairpin Bridge . . . well, dear readers, did that name sound familiar? You might have heard of it. It's a bit of an architectural anomaly, given its odd shape (the valley walls necessitate that the road take a funny corkscrew turn on the south ramp before looping back over itself, like driving over a giant metal hairpin). It has another name I won't repeat, because honestly, I don't like the associations it now has with Cambry, and I don't like how her name has become forever linked with it on the search engines. So I won't use it.

Hairpin Bridge is haunted.

Allegedly (get used to that word).

It's a hot spot for paranormal activity. They say space and time are malleable around the hallowed bones of Hairpin Bridge, and as you cross it, past and present can intertwine a bit. The way light refracts through a dirty lens.

I know. I'm not seriously suggesting my sister was murdered by ghosts. But I had a phase in July when I considered it. For a time, I devoured all the user-submitted accounts of corrupted time and glimpsed apparitions. I listened to every EVP audio recording where people claimed to have captured disembodied whispers: *Help me* or *Leave this place.* I even read the self-published book written by the Rupley guy who spent the night camping under it (spoiler: he lived).

It's ridiculous, but that's the hole I fell into after my sister's abrupt death. In the terror of free fall, you're not yourself for a while. You grasp for explanations, no matter how far-fetched. They can be myths, criminal conspiracies, **anything** to assign sense to the senseless. Any answer is better than nothing.

And now I think I finally have one.

(No, it doesn't involve ghosts.)

So that's where I'm going, dear readers. That's why this latte-sipping Seattleite is setting out tomorrow to a butt-ugly bridge in God's Country. That's why I'm writing this. And that's why I won't accept anything less than the truth from Corporal Raycevic.

I'll pay any price for it.

I have to know.

What happened to you, Cambry?

————————

HE WAS WAITING FOR HER ON THE BRIDGE. HE'D PARKED HIS black cruiser on the right, alongside a low and blistered guard-rail, but Lena knew it didn't matter where they parked. Hairpin Bridge served a dead highway. There was no traffic to block.

At the south ramp, just past the bridge's eponymous hairpin twist, a sun-bleached sign stated something illegible about the structure being unsound or uninspected. It had failed to discourage scores of amateur ghost hunters. More recently, someone had spray-painted in black: ALL OF YOUR ROADS LEAD HERE.

Strangely apt, to Lena.

She parked a few yards ahead of the cop car to allow herself a quick escape route. She left the Corolla's engine idling for a moment, took a breath and held it. The drive from Magma Springs hadn't taken nearly as long as she'd planned. Now she was here. She felt unprepared.

I'm here, Cambry.

She studied her sister's bent eyeglasses on the dashboard. The hairline scratches on the lenses.

Oh, God, I'm really here.

In her side-view mirror, Corporal Raycevic stood by his car, elbow on the door, pretending he was picking at a scab on his wrist and not waiting on her. Considerate of him. He'd surprised her with his sensitivity already. On one hand, it was his job—he'd certainly delivered his share of bad news to grieving families—but Lena suspected there was more to it. He had lost someone, too. He wore the mark like she did, another member of that terrible unspoken club. A wife? A young kid?

Her lungs ached. She realized she'd been holding her breath.

She cut the engine and immediately regretted it. She could have delayed longer, and wished she had. Raycevic wouldn't have minded. Now he was staring toward her through his jet-black sunglasses, noticing—yes, this was Cambry's blue Toyota Corolla that Lena had driven out here. The victim's twin sister, driving the victim's car. Arriving at the site where the victim perished, like a ghoulish doppelgänger.

If it disturbed him, he didn't show it. He gave her a gentle nod—*This is the place.*

Obviously.

She climbed out. The sun blazed hotter up here. Mirages shimmered off the bridge's cement roadway in watery ripples. The air was windless.

"You can see the fire from here." Raycevic pointed north. "Four thousand acres at Black Lake, still growing, still uncontained—"

"Is it coming toward us?"

"Not unless the wind changes."

Lena didn't care, then. She had enough on her mind. But the mile-high thunderhead of smoke was commanding. The world seemed to end on the horizon, a slow-motion apocalypse.

"You know, I never understood why it's called Hairpin Bridge," he said thoughtfully. "I see the sharp turn over there, I guess, but it reminds me more of those Marbleworks toys kids play with. You know what I'm talking about?"

"Yeah."

"The straight piece with the curved hook on the end." He pointed. "Right? That's what it looks like to me. Not a hairpin."

Marbleworks Bridge. Somehow it just didn't have the same mystique.

"You play with Marbleworks a lot?"

"Everyone needs a hobby."

For a moment, he was a normal person. It was nice. It was also completely false.

He finally said it. "You . . . drove her vehicle."

"Yeah."

He studied the taillights wistfully. "I recognize it."

"Do you mind if I record you?"

"I'm sorry?"

She'd waited until now to ask, because she suspected it might be harder for him to say no on the spot. She pointed to the car. "I brought a tape recorder with me. An old clunky thing, you'll laugh. But my counselor recommended that I . . . I record everything significant."

He said nothing. Thinking.

"Not just this." She flashed a wounded smile. "I filmed her funeral, too."

"Did you watch it?"

"A few times."

He made a sour face. *Why?*

"You don't really die when your heart stops. You die when you're forgotten. My sister isn't a person anymore—she's an *idea.* I carry her. So every trace I have left of her, every word and smell and sound, needs to be preserved."

"Even the negative things?"

"Yes."

"Even her funeral?"

"I feel close to her. Like she only just left." *It's like picking a scab,* she wanted to add. *Soon you start to feel nothing, and that's terrifying. The pain brings her back.*

It keeps her real.

Raycevic sighed. Then he nodded once. "Go ahead."

She retreated to the Corolla, worrying she'd already blown her cover by using the word *counselor*. Was it *therapist*? What's the difference between a therapist and a grief counselor? She didn't know, but Raycevic probably did. She leaned into her sister's car and pulled it out—a chunky black Shoebox recorder.

She inserted a cassette tape. Clicked the shoulder button. "Testing."

"They still make those?"

"It was Cambry's. When we were kids."

That shut him up. He watched her set the gadget on the Corolla's hood. Through the plastic cover, the cassette's spokes turned. "Thank you," she said, louder for the mic: "Corporal Raycevic."

"Call me Ray."

"Thank you, Ray." She looked at him. "Start with how you found her body, please."

"I was responding. Someone took bolt cutters to the chain on that gate we passed."

"Is that unusual?"

"Happens a couple times a year. Truckers use this route to shave an hour off their runs. This was the night of June seventh. Around eleven. And I came up on that bend there, approaching the bridge, and I saw a blue Toyota parked here."

"Parked where? Can you be exact?"

"Actually . . ." He paused. "Exactly where you have it parked right now."

She felt a tug in her stomach, but quickly dismissed it: *Coincidence.*

"I almost rear-ended it," the cop said. "I slammed my brakes, splashed coffee all over my radio. You can see the skid marks still."

Sure enough, faded markings on the pavement, right where he pointed. Ropy, licorice-black.

"At 11:44, I approached Cambry's—*your*—Toyota Corolla on foot. It was abandoned. No occupant. No signs of disturbance. Driver door was left wide open. Dead battery. Empty tank." Raycevic wavered, as if he felt foolish. "But you're aware of all this—"

"Every detail. Please."

"I checked the rest of the bridge, scanned the trees for camp-fires or flashlights. Then I sat back in my vehicle and called in the plates. Eleven fifty-one, now."

He knows the times too well, Lena noted. He'd studied up.

"I remember standing by while Dispatch ran the plates, gath-ering my thoughts. Wiping coffee off my slacks with a napkin, looking up at the starry black sky, and being struck with a terrible feeling of . . . wrongness, I guess. I don't know how else to de-scribe it. Like being here, on this bridge, was the equivalent of sticking your right hand into a garbage disposal while feathering the on switch with your left. Does that make sense?"

No—but Lena nodded anyway.

It's not just past and present that get scrambled in Hairpin Bridge's prism, she remembered reading. *So, too, are life and death.*

"Somehow I just . . ." He chewed his lip. "Cop's intuition, I guess. Something told me I should step back out into the cold air, cold for June, and look down over the railing. That the woman who abandoned this Corolla would be . . . down there."

"The Suicide Bridge," Lena whispered.

"What?"

"Hairpin Bridge's other name."

"I don't understand."

"According to the ghost stories, I mean." She twisted her hair, embarrassed to have brought the word *ghost* into this. "People on the internet, paranormal nuts . . . they say drivers used to jump to their deaths off this bridge. Five or six suicides back in the eighties. Enough that it became semifamous as a place where solitary, troubled people are drawn from all over to end their lives."

"Huh." The cop shrugged. "Never heard of that."

"Like the forest in Japan."

"Never heard of that, either." He walked to the railing, and Lena followed. He put both palms on the guardrail. His big hands were knobbed with calluses. "I was standing exactly here," he said, "when I saw Cambry."

This gave Lena a shiver.

He pointed straight down, to the mosaic of pale boulders far below. The arroyo was a bed of loose rocks tilled by the turbulent seasons of Silver Creek. Flash floods in March, drought in July.

"Where?"

"Right there."

She joined him at the railing and tried to visualize Cambry's body down there as part of the mosaic. Crumpled, limp, doll-like from two hundred feet up. But she'd been trying for months. She wanted, needed more details: "Was she on her back? Or her stomach?"

"On her side."

"Right or left?"

"Left."

"Was there any blood?"

He turned. "Excuse me?"

"Did you see any blood on her?"

"How is this helpful?"

"I want to know everything." Lena tried not to blink. "All the upsetting, nasty details. If I don't have details, what I imagine at night when I can't sleep is far, *far* worse. It's unfinished, and I can't stand unfinished things. It's a problem I have. My brain works relentlessly to fill in blanks."

She wasn't sure he was buying it.

"It's . . ." She tried this: "It's like a monster in a movie. When you can't see it, it's terrifying. But seeing the monster plainly, in full daylight, takes away its power. Makes it known."

"Depends on the monster," he said finally.

"I've got a hell of an imagination, Ray."

"And your . . ." He squinted. "Your *counselor* signed off on this?"

"I know what I'm asking."

"You're sure?"

"I'm certain."

"A hundred percent?"

"A million."

He sighed and looked away. "You're making me uncomfortable."

"*You're* uncomfortable?"

"The fall killed Cambry," he said abruptly. His voice rang in the thin air, and Lena instinctively shrank back. Hearing men raise their voices had always frightened her. "I don't have any gory details to share about the state of her body after her suicide, because I don't think it's appropriate. Is that okay?"

She felt like she was being scolded. Her eyes watered, despite herself. *Hold it together.*

"After I saw your sister's body, I called EMS and descended on foot to render aid, if possible. As I expected, I found she had no pulse. No breathing. Her body had been down there for at least a day."

Don't cry. She bit her lip.

"Dying in that way . . . it's fast. Faster than the brain can experience pain. It's like an off switch inside you, flipped in a microsecond. Whatever her problems were on June sixth . . ."

He exhaled and glanced back at her, softening. "Your sister didn't suffer, Lena."

She bristled, like an icy fingertip had stroked between her shoulder blades. This was the first time Corporal Raycevic had used her first name. She wished he hadn't.

She didn't suffer was a new one, too. Because when someone decides to jump off a bridge, no one has the audacity to claim they weren't suffering.

She tried to focus on the moment. On here, now, herself and Raycevic. But to be here and stand where it happened was to be plugged into a strange energy, and her restless mind kept whipping back to it, trying to reconstruct details: *It's June 6. After dusk. The air shivers with electricity. Cambry Lynne Nguyen is driving alone on this closed road. And after driving an unknown distance, from an unknown origin, she reaches this bridge. And she stops her car here.*

Right where Lena had unwittingly parked it, in an eerie coincidence.

And she steps out into the cooling night, nine o'clock now, leaving her engine running, her door ajar. And she walks to the bridge's edge, right here—Lena gripped the guardrail with both hands, perhaps in the same places Cambry had three months ago—*and my sister hoists herself over this railing one leg at a time. Then she steps off, or maybe she hangs by her fingers before letting go, or maybe she takes a reckless running leap into the void, like how she seemed to leap into everything.*

She plunges two hundred feet.

She impacts the rock floor at the speed of—

"Fuck," Lena whispered.

What else can you say? Raycevic had stepped back to give her space.

And now the questions. Endless questions in Lena's mind, racing, scratching, clawing, begging to be let free: *What were you doing out here? Where were you driving? Why did you stop? Why did you get out of your car here, of all places, on this remote bridge?*

And of course, the old classic, a terrible refrain: *Why did you kill yourself?*

Why did you do it?

"I'm sorry," Raycevic whispered behind her. But his voice sounded oddly tinny, as if filtered through a distant phone line. All Lena saw was the voided space beneath her feet, the ravine far below, the vast gravel bed of Silver Creek littered with fallen white trees.

Cambry . . .

In your final hours, what was going through your mind?

CHAPTER 2

CAMBRY'S STORY

I swear to God, *Cambry thinks*, I better not die today.

Seeing an owl in daylight is a dire omen. She can't remember where she learned this.

He's perched in the branches like a brown lawn gnome. A great horned owl. His tufted feathers, the eponymous horns, form a devilish silhouette against the blue sky. These horns are the hardest to draw without overdoing. She's using ink, not pencil, and it's already botched—this poor guy looks like Batman. She wants to tear off the page and restart.

If you weren't the harbinger of my death before, *she thinks,* you probably are now.

Downhill, the campground is silent.

Or it was—until thirty seconds ago, when the couple in the Ford Explorer arrived. Now she hears the crinkle of nylon, zippers, car doors opening and shutting, murmured voices. She tries to focus on her sketch. The owl cocks its head, perhaps equally annoyed.

The couple is arguing. From Cambry's spot in the sagebrush fifty yards uphill, she can't discern words, but she recognizes the tempo of their voices. The rises and falls, the whispered cuts, the reflexive snaps. The music of conflict. She knows every note.

The man slides a cooler out of the Explorer and lets it hit the dirt with an emphatic thud.

Cambry sticks out her tongue as she draws—habit, since age five—and keeps shading the owl's outline, Batman ears and all. Sometimes you can rescue a sketch. With enough crosshatching, she makes the exaggeration look intentional. Her subject has lost interest in the couple and now stares back down at her with bright yellow eyes. Unsettling in their alertness.

The Explorer's cargo door slams. The couple is leaving now for their campsite. Their voices fading into the pines.

Now she remembers—an eighth-grade museum trip, where a curator told the class that Native Americans considered owls to be harbingers of death. Guardians of the afterlife, venturing into daytime hours to meet the souls of the soon to be departed. Sure enough, this one is still studying her with those binocular eyes, a strange and powerful attention.

Silence again. The couple is gone.

Finally.

Cambry claps her notepad shut and quietly hurries down to the road. She unslings her backpack beside the couple's Explorer, pulls out a three-gallon fuel can, and gently pries the vehicle's gas cover open so she can feed in several feet of plastic tubing.

The owl watches her the entire time.

When we were kids, I always promised Cambry I would write a book about her adventures. This—what you're reading now—is not what I had in mind.

Obviously.

But there's some painful catharsis in telling my sister's story. Reconstructing the facts of her final hours feels like setting a million fractured bones. Every word hurts, but my parents deserve to know what really happened to their daughter on June 6. And I'll be up-front: I've taken liberties in imagining certain details, as no one can claim to know a dead woman's thoughts.

But who better to try than her twin?

And before we proceed, a special note to Cambry: Here's your book, sis. At long last. I'm so, so sorry that it's fifteen years late.

And that you die at the end.

———————

Cambry's spiral notebooks are a hand-drawn history of her past nine months.

September is Oregon. Through the concrete and chain link of Portland to the watery evergreens of Crater Lake. Then Medford, home brews and couch surfing with one of her boyfriend Blake's friends—an easygoing guy who shared a potent hallucinogen he'd grown in a shoebox. Hairy tarantulas had dropped down on her like paratroopers for the next three hours. Eventually they stopped being frightening and she just swatted them away.

October is California. Highway 101 down past Eureka to Glass Beach. The neighboring residents of Fort Bragg used to dump their trash into the ocean for decades, unintentionally creating the world's largest reserve of sea glass. Blue and green glittered wetly among the dark stones. Pencil and ink couldn't do it justice. She took a handful and stored them in her console.

November is foggy coasts, slick docks, and bridges. The biggest: Golden Gate.

December and January are New Mexico, Arizona, Texas. Things were still good between her and Blake, the money lasting on pace. They played Frisbee in an apocalyptic expanse of bleached desert called White Sands. Pale waves whipped into fifty-foot ripples. One night under a galaxy of stars, Blake asked her what she'd do when this grand pilgrimage was over and they'd finally looped back to Seattle.

Her answer: Kill myself.

He laughed uncomfortably.

February and March are Louisiana, Georgia, Florida. She drew white mansions with half-mile driveways, lightbulbs in trees, scaly alligator heads. She and Blake fought more frequently, their arguments coming as fast and fierce as the storms. Around Fort Myers, hailstones cracked the Corolla's windshield like gunfire. Things were souring now. At the repair shop, Blake sullenly told her he was walking to the gas station to buy cigarettes. She waited thirty minutes, then went after him—and the 7-Eleven clerk said he saw a man matching Blake's description meet a friend and drive away. He'd stolen four thousand dollars and their palm-size .25-caliber pistol. Cambry had seventeen dollars in her purse and a freshly repaired windshield.

She kept going.

Why not?

She would find her way back to Seattle without him. The entire year-long journey had been her idea. Not Blake's. She'd find her way back home—if she even wanted to—and get there on her time.

April is the Virginias, and then through the deep green Ozarks, under the decayed smokestacks of rust-eaten paper mills and factories, and northward to the Dakotas. The sketches get more numerous without Blake touching her arm like an impatient child. She downsized without him and sold the trailer. The Corolla's mileage got better. Odd jobs refilled the money. She didn't like to steal, but she did on occasion. Mostly food.

Now June. Montana.

Her last notebook is almost full. From Magma Springs, Seattle is within a tank or two of gas. Her old life beckons, and she misses its comforts. Running water. Electrical outlets. Her toothache has gotten worse this month. She keeps seeing blood on her toothbrush.

But she'll make it to Coeur d'Alene tonight, she estimates. If she leaves now.

On the hike back from the Dog's Head campground, she takes the public trail before cutting through thick and hilly forest. Her backpack is heavy now with sloshing gasoline. When she siphons this far into the boonies, she takes only a gallon or two. She doesn't want to strand anyone.

The temperature is pleasant in the late evening. The sun orange behind the pines, the sky a bruised purple. No more feuding voices—just the buzz of crickets and the crunch of yellow grass underfoot. She likes the quiet, the smell of pine needles and berries. She's on the final leg of her hike, maybe five minutes from the highway where she parked, when she notices the column of smoke.

My car is on fire, she thinks.

Her mind roils lately. Since Florida, she's lost control of her anxieties—her *furies,* her psychologist used to call them. An owl means impending death. A toothache is cancerous. Smoke means her Corolla is a flaming husk.

The smoke, it turns out, originates a short distance off her path. Several plumes rise in smeared trails against the white-capped Rockies. She's curious, so she stops and squints through a screen of branches.

A grass fire, maybe?

She spots the source a quarter mile downhill: a naked cement foundation, as white as bone. Like a building that never was, now choked by weeds. A trailer and a rusted-out truck. A dried-up well. Heaped lumber and gravel. The soil is raw, dark, freshly churned.

The smoke trails emanate from four fires. They're arranged in a perfect row across the bare cement floor, and each fire is caged in a pyramid of stacked rocks. Like little hearth ovens. The flames are contained to cracks of trapped orange.

A man walks between the fires.

Seeing another human gives Cambry a shivery jolt—fires or no fires, she'd been certain she was alone out here—and she adjusts her footing, disturbing loose rocks. At this distance, the stranger is just a pacing speck. He looks shirtless. He crouches by each fire, as if prodding with a stick or poker. When he reaches the end of the row, he turns and checks each fire again.

Slow, patient, methodical.

She wishes she hadn't left her binoculars in her trunk. She doesn't dare approach any closer. Even a quarter mile feels too close.

The obvious explanation is that he's just burning brush, as many landowners do before the summer burn ban. But the fires are too small, and the stone pyramids appear too purposeful. Maybe he's smoking or slow-cooking something. Venison? Salmon?

Her furies whisper: Human?

She wonders if she's trespassing. Cambry has always taken care never to steal from private property, lest she catch a bullet. Best to make your lifts in public spaces, difficult as it may be. She can't remember passing any sunken fences or signs, but she glances behind herself anyway to check. When she looks back ahead, she realizes the faraway man has stopped pacing. He's standing still now, like a scarecrow, halfway between his two nearest fires.

He's staring uphill. At her.

Cambry's blood turns to ice water. A tug in her stomach. She doesn't move, either, matching his stance. The distance between them is too far to shout. She could try to wave, maybe. But she doesn't.

The man keeps staring.

The wind changes direction, a low growl that shifts the trees, and the four smoke trails push leftward, drifting into the man's face. He doesn't seem to react.

In this surreal standoff, Cambry squints harder. This isn't her first time being stared at in the nine months she's lived like a refugee. She's been asked to leave more parking lots and campgrounds than she can count. She tries to discern more detail: The sleeveless outline of a wife-beater undershirt. Brown khaki pants. His hands move for something at his waist (Gun, gun, gun, her furies whisper, but it's not the right shape). He raises it with both hands to his face.

Time to go.

He studies her through his cupped hands. A pinprick of glinted light confirms—yes, he's viewing her through lenses.

Go, Cambry. Now.

But this surreal moment seems to stretch forever, the air clotting, and she strangely feels like she really should wave now. She almost does. She's self-conscious, spotlighted, feeling his distant eyes crawl up and down her body.

Her heartbeat rises. A frenzied rattle against her ribs.

Go-go-go-right-now . . .

And she turns and calmly retreats from the rise of grassy land, keeping her movements slow and casual in the gaze of this faraway stranger's binoculars.

The second she's out of his view, she breaks into a sprint.

Once her parked car is within eyeshot, she stops running and looks back.

To her muted terror, he now stands exactly where she'd been just moments ago. He doesn't see her yet. He's pacing on the grassy slope with his hands at his hips, moving loose rocks with his foot, searching the chalky soil for her footprints.

She drops to her knees behind the nearest tree, catching her breath.

At this closer distance, she can see him better. He's a towering guy. Bulging biceps. Buzz cut. Thirties or forties, with a distinct military look. He must have run, too, to catch up to her so quickly. He's searching the surrounding forest now, shielding his eyes from the sunset.

With a chill, she realizes she's being tracked.

She unslings her backpack and slinks lower, lower, until she's flat against the packed soil. The thin lodgepole pine barely covers her. Viewed from his angle, she's just an eye and a cheekbone peering from behind a trunk. His vision can't possibly be that good, right?

His binoculars probably are.

He's unarmed, at least. That makes Cambry feel better. She imagined he'd have a bolt-action slung over his back, or a hatchet in his hand. But he's empty-handed, save for those binoculars, and under the sleeveless wifebeater his flesh is lobster red. A nasty sunburn. His pants are formal-looking slacks. Was he changing his clothes, too? What was he doing?

He's still searching the trees for her. His scanning focus approaches Cambry's hiding spot, sweeping left to right—her stomach balls into a tight knot—as his attention passes her tree, studies it briefly, and keeps searching. Thank God.

Remaining stone-still and sunken into the yellow grass, she slides her right hand into her back pocket and feels for the reassuring lump of her KA-BAR, a three-inch folding blade. She wishes Blake hadn't stolen the pistol when he left. A gun—even that piddly little mouse gun—would be nice right now. She resents her backpack, too. It slows her down.

Only now, crouched behind a tree and catching her gulped breaths in the fading daylight, does Cambry grasp the severity of what just happened. This stranger ran a quarter mile uphill, into the trees, to reach her. Immediately. Without hesitation. He even left his four strange fires unattended. Now, more than ever, she wants to know what purpose they served.

She can feel it building. The electricity in her nerves. The whispers in her mind, urging her to pack it out and run, to tear off the page and restart. To be Cambry Nguyen, the cross-country demon with the six-minute mile, the girl who torched every bridge behind her, who barreled from friend to friend, city to city, lover to lover, the way a swarm of locusts devastates a crop and moves on. The woman who found flaws in every good thing and solved them by making them vanish in her rearview mirror, from the West Coast to the East and nearly back again.

Her mouth is dry. She hasn't had a cigarette since January, but she needs one now.

It's probably a misunderstanding, she tells herself. For once, she should try facing a problem instead of running. It's no big deal— property lines are blurry out here. On her route back from the camp- ground, she'd probably missed a rust-eaten sign somewhere and trespassed on some guy's private property, which gave him no choice but to follow her and ask her what she's—

The sunburned man's head snaps back. He sees her.

He doesn't wave. He doesn't raise his binoculars. He just launches into a silent, mechanical sprint toward her, resuming the chase.

Cambry runs like hell.

When she reaches her Corolla on the road's shoulder, her heart is slam- ming in her eardrums and her breaths are hoarse. She's in good shape— she ran a half-marathon last year—but her backpack jostles heavily on her shoulders and the straps rub her skin raw. She's not sure if the sun- burned man is still following her through the trees, or how close he is.

As she throws the door open, she doesn't even glance back to locate her pursuer—that would cost precious seconds. She dives inside, twists the key, stomps on the gas. The engine roars, the tires claw handfuls of grit, and she's off and racing under a billow of dust.

She catches her breath for a second time as she drives. Questions now, rising faster than she can think. Who was he? What was he do- ing? What would he have done, had he caught up to her? And more pressing: Shouldn't you call 911?

There's no signal out here, she knows. It's a dead zone.

When you get into town, though . . . shouldn't you call?

A gunshot pierces the air. She flinches hard.

A pothole. Just a pothole, slamming underneath the chassis. She rubs her arms, shivery with goose bumps. Even when she does get a 911 dispatcher on the line, she wonders what exactly she'll say: Hello, dis- patcher? I just saw a man tending to four small campfires.

Weird, yes. But illegal?

It all depends on what's in those fires, *an unhelpful voice tells her.*

It's a hell of a leap. She's miles into the sticks, and it could very well be his own property he chased her from. Another rut scrapes the Corolla's undercarriage. She lets off the gas a bit. The last thing she needs is another flat tire.

The sun is gone now. The magic hour, photographers call it, because the twilight is shadowless and dreamy, like a blue-tinged painting. And something else—Cambry always swore she could sense this, despite Lena's skepticism—she can feel electricity gathering in the air. The growing divide between positive and negative. Lightning is coming.

She passes familiar billboards for the Magma Springs Diner, then a pot shop—its slogan is "It's Surprisingly Easy Being Green"—and she feels better. She got away clean. As the road winds between raised humps of trees, she glimpses blinking red lights on the horizon. Radio towers. The refuge of civilization, not far away. Humans. Cars. Speed limits. Insurance. Rent. Dentists.

She exhales—she didn't realize she was holding her breath. She's coming up on Highway 200 now, tapping her brakes at the junction, when she hears the jarring bleat of a siren.

She checks her rearview mirror.

Oh, thank God.

A dust-caked police cruiser races up on her tail with a flashing light bar. She pulls over like an obedient citizen, and the cop parks smoothly behind her. Black and gold paint. Montana Highway Patrol. The siren cuts, but the lights stay up, strobing in her mirrors.

Cambry hates cops. And she hates how relieved she is to see one.

Even in the rush of the moment, she coolly prepares her story. She makes sure the hose and fuel can are zipped up and hidden in her backpack. It was a nature walk, she'll explain. Just a boondocking girl with a car full of psychological baggage, communing with the guardians of the afterlife, courting a nervous breakdown. Nothing more.

The state trooper steps out of his car and leaves his door ajar. As he approaches her Corolla, framed against the cool blue dusk, details sharpen. His tan-brown uniform is half-buttoned, untucked. He's sun-burned underneath. Binoculars swinging from a lanyard around his neck. Still red-faced, because he's sprinted all the way from their first encounter to wherever he'd parked his cruiser.

His uniform has a name stitched on the breast, visible now as he reaches her window.

CPL. RAYMOND R. RAYCEVIC.

CHAPTER 3

LENA

"YOU PULLED HER OVER."

He blinked. *Excuse me?*

"You pulled her over," she said again. "On the day she died. The day before you found her body. It was in the report."

A surprised beat—and then he nodded. "Did I not mention that?"

"No."

"I could've sworn I did—"

"You didn't."

"Oh." He frowned, and then glanced at the Shoebox recorder, quietly listening. "You told me to start with the night I found her body. June seventh."

"Why did you pull her over the day before?"

"Doesn't it say in the report?"

"I'm asking you."

"Speeding." He studied the smoke in the distance. "It was dusk, around eight o'clock—"

It was 8:09 P.M., Lena knew.

"And I saw that blue Toyota, right there, just tear ass past me. Going eighty, ninety."

She nodded, wondering if *tear ass* was part of the Montana law enforcement lexicon. But it fit. Cambry drove with a lead foot. Always running, like a tsunami was at her back.

"I stopped her." He spoke slowly, regretfully. "And . . . I spoke to her."

Despite herself, Lena leaned forward and hung on every word. A sour tug in her stomach. She was certain she already knew everything he was about to say, but it still felt momentous, like interviewing someone who'd witnessed Cambry's ghost. Everyone from her sister's life ended up on this pedestal. She'd even come to envy Cambry's boyfriends—the long line of terrible guys she had seemed to collect like bugs in a jar. A cocaine dealer (Terrible Guy #11), a woefully inept credit-card thief (Terrible Guy #6), and at least one narcissist (Terrible Guy #14, who carried a katana and wouldn't shut up about the novel he was writing). She'd been fascinated by awful people, it seemed, and used them for as long as they suited her.

And to Lena, it wasn't fair, because every last one of them— like Corporal Raycevic standing before her—was privy to things about her sister she could never know. All these awful people. She gripped a knot of her own hair and twisted, an eye-watering tug to the roots.

Raycevic continued: "I could tell immediately that she'd been living in the vehicle for some time. Battery, clothes, sleeping bag, backpack. Dirt under her nails. She looked tired. But people do, in that lifestyle. I've seen how it hardens you, not knowing where your next meal is coming from."

My sister knew how to take care of herself, Lena thought but didn't say.

She was living off the grid. Not helpless.

"Her eyes were red. She'd been crying. I asked her if she knew how fast she was going. She said it was an accident. She was apologetic, maybe a bit distant, like something was weighing on her mind—"

"She was apologetic?"

"Yeah. Why?"

Cambry was a social chameleon; many things, to many people, somehow all at once—but *deferential to authority figures* wasn't one of them. Back in seventh grade, she'd tied a dish sponge tightly with twine so it would dry as a compressed pellet, then removed the twine and flushed it down a school toilet. The building's pipes had to be excavated. Summer break had started ten days early.

Lena bit her tongue. "What did she say, exactly?"

"She . . . she told me her dirtbag boyfriend had ditched her in the middle of a cross-country trip. Left her broke and alone with just a few dollars, finding her way home—"

"That happened months before. In Florida."

"She *lied* to me. I believed it. I wish I'd known, Lena."

She studied his face behind his jet-black Oakleys, searching for cracks in his guilt. It wasn't professional, but it was authentic. He was every bit as wounded and sorely defensive as a real human being would and should be. He'd spoken to a desperately troubled young woman moments before her suicide, he'd had a chance to save her life, and what did he do?

"I gave her a warning."

"No ticket?"

"She was just trying to get home."

"That's all you have to say? I wish I'd tried that."

"No, you don't," Raycevic said. "You've never even been pulled over."

She scoffed. But he was right. Lena wasn't even sure she'd

ever broken the law in her life, unless you count a few underage beers and more than a few overdue library books. How would Raycevic know that, though? *Unless he researched me, too?*

"And then," he said quietly, "I let her go on her way."

"The day before you found her body under this bridge."

"Yes."

"The day she killed herself."

"Yes."

"Minutes before her estimated time of—"

"It's all in the report."

"That's all that happened?" For some reason, Lena relished asking this. Her mother used to pull this line on both twins alike, although far more frequently on Cambry: *That's all that happened, huh? Someone was just asking you to store it in your backpack?*

Corporal Raycevic broke away abruptly, leaned back over the guardrail, and stared down at the ravine floor below, like time had slipped back three months and he was once again discovering Cambry's crumpled body amid the granite boulders. The big man chewed his lower lip, as if he was about to divulge something major, before hurriedly changing his mind.

"Yes," he said. "That's all."

———————

The great thing about cops?

Everything has a paper trail.

After the medical examiner ruled the death a suicide, Howard County kindly provided me with a scan of the handwritten log that Corporal Raymond Raycevic had filled out, probably moments after he stopped Cambry for speeding on Highway 200. The PDF can be downloaded here, dear readers: HCEAS6919.pdf

Coincidence, right?

The same trooper who pulled my twin over for speeding would

discover her body under a remote bridge serving a closed road, just twenty-four hours later. Life can be so strange.

I'm trying to wrap my head around it.

Have you heard the one about the Japanese businessman? It's something of a party joke for awful people. In August of 1945, this guy was on a business trip to a factory in Hiroshima. When Little Boy dropped, he suffered thermal burns and temporary blindness. He was one of thousands treated for his wounds in the terrible aftermath, but he was one of the lucky ones, and just days later, he returned home to his grateful family, several hundred miles south.

In Nagasaki.

Just in time to catch the second one.

For some reason, that poor guy has been on my mind a lot lately. He's a reminder, I guess, of how random life can be. We live in a heaving sea of causes and effects. Coincidences happen every second. They don't necessarily mean anything.

Like Hairpin Bridge's ghostly whispers embedded in ten-megabyte widgets of crunchy static—sometimes white noise is just white noise.

Funnily enough, it was Cambry who told me that atom bomb story. We were eleven or twelve, I think, sitting on her bed. I remember she'd blared Blue Öyster Cult's "(Don't Fear) The Reaper" on repeat because she loved the part where Death tells the woman *We'll be able to fly*. Like dying is a superpower or something. Her room smelled like pumpkin because we'd just carved jack-o'-lanterns. Odd, how sounds and smells linger in the memory.

I even miss the bad things. I miss the way she used to call me Ratface (I have no idea why—our faces were exactly the same, according to science). I miss her nicotine breath. I miss the way she waited restless at every family event, like she was sitting on razor blades, lashed by the doubts and worries that her therapist called her *chorus of furies*. Even her flaws were operatic, like something from Greek myth.

We were identical twins. But not copies, like people guess.

I'd describe us more like a mirror's reflection—where her right is my left, and vice versa. I went to college. She went renegade. I can write a novel. She can clean a rabbit. I live in my mind. She lives in the moment.

I'm just me. She's the badass I want to be.

And now she's gone.

The word *dead* is so blunt. *Gone* is better. Or sometimes I try to tell myself that she's *set free*.

My sister always wanted freedom, right? Well, now she doesn't have to breathe. She doesn't have a body that needs to be maintained. She doesn't have to go to the dentist. She doesn't care about temperature or air pressure. She can go wherever she wants.

Forget Glass Beach or the Everglades. I like to imagine her on another planet, maybe a frozen moon, watching the rings of a colossal helium giant rise over bone-white glacier shelves. Or walking the yellow lava fields of Venus, leaving no footprints in sulfurous mud. Or studying the shimmering crystals inside Halley's Comet as it hurtles at thousands of miles per second through our sky and millions of others. My sister can go anywhere. I hope she finds what she's looking for. Wherever she is, I hope she still thinks about us from time to time. About me and Mom and Dad and the hole she left behind.

I wish I could stop thinking about solving the mystery of her death, turn off the busy clockwork inside my head and just *grieve*. But so many things nag at me, nipping at my thoughts. Maybe it's a curse, and now that she's gone, her furies have taken up residence in me. But I don't think it's paranoia. These are real loose ends that demand to be tugged. Like Corporal Raycevic pulling her over just an hour before her alleged suicide. Like how he described her—her, of all people—as *apologetic* for speeding. Or the most utterly damning evidence of all: the calls on her flip phone.

In my opinion, this should have been a bombshell.

Courtesy of Verizon's records, we know she dialed 911 sixteen times before her death. Every call failed, because there's no cell service between Magma Springs and Polk City. The first attempt, tellingly, is time-stamped at 8:22 P.M. Just thirteen minutes after Raycevic pulled her over.

There's an explanation for this.

I don't buy it.

I can't fathom why she would call for help sixteen times before ending up dead, and no one bats an eyelash.

There's only one explanation I can provide that feels plausible to me. Be warned, dear readers, it will sound like quite a reach when I first explain it. Maybe not quite as absurd as the same person catching a front-row seat for the only two military deployments of the A-bomb in human history, but hey, it's close. So bear with me, and I'll walk you gently through it.

But first, the funny part?

That Japanese man I mentioned—you assumed he died in Nagasaki, right? He survived the second blast, too. He lived a full life and died in 2010. God bless him. And I think about Cambry, twenty-four and full of wit and mystery, and the way our parents wept at her service when her sketches came up on the slide show. She always drew better than people can photograph.

Yes, life can be so strange.

"WHAT ABOUT CAMBRY'S 911 CALLS?"

Raycevic answered as if following a teleprompter. "She suffered from untreated schizoid personality disorder, and she was clearly in the midst of an emotional crisis. We urge anyone who's experiencing suicidal thoughts to call 911 immediately, and your sister tried to."

"You think she dialed 911 because she felt suicidal?"

He nodded.

"Sixteen times?"

"There's no signal out here, all the way from the campgrounds, to Magma Springs, to Polk City. I've been begging the county to let T-Mobile build their third tower—"

"Sixteen times, though?"

"Do you think I feel good about this?" His tone darkened. "On June sixth, I pulled over a troubled young woman, just an hour before she took her own life, and whatever the signs were, I missed them. That's my failure. Okay? I *failed*. Is that what you came all this way to hear me say?" He looked at the recorder. "On tape?"

"Sixteen times," Lena echoed.

"The county prosecutor covered everything. We have no evidence of anyone following her. No one spoke to her, aside from myself. Whatever was going on in her mind . . . her movements between my traffic stop and Hairpin Bridge were concluded to be a straight line. Nothing else is geographically possible. Your sister couldn't get an emergency operator on the phone, and she drove until she ran out of gas on this bridge, and took her life, and I'm *so sorry,* Lena."

I'm so sorry, Lena. Another familiar echo, as canned as a sound bite. Was it her boss who said it first? Her uncle? Her cousin? Did it even matter?

She didn't look at him. She couldn't let him see the tears building in her eyes. She stared out at the distant wall of smoke to the north, a furious volcanic churn rising and smearing into trails. It looked noticeably larger. Maybe it was coming closer after all.

Raycevic studied the smoke, too, and sighed.

"If you need someone to blame," he said, "blame me. I'm the one who let her out of my sight."

He took in a breath, and Lena bristled. She knew it was coming.

It's not your fau—

"It's not your fault, Lena."

There it was.

The classic. The original. It was only a matter of time before he stumbled across the blue-ribbon Thing People Tell You When Your Sister Commits Suicide. And here it was. Lena despised it because of what it suggested: If it isn't your fault or mine, it must be Cambry's, right? Let the living stay blameless. Blame the person who's not here anymore, who can't defend herself.

It made Lena so deeply sick. She clenched her fists.

Raycevic kept going: "Schizoid personality disorder is especially difficult. Someone described it to me once. It's not an affliction, like an illness with symptoms you can treat. It's how you're wired. It's what you *want.* You want the distance, to leave everyone a million miles behind you, to sever every human connection and just exist on your chosen terms in orbit around Saturn. And that solitude can make you happy for a while. Unless one day you discover you need help, and there's nobody to—"

"I'm so *sick* of hearing about her mental illness," Lena said.

He froze.

"People act like that solves the whole mystery: She jumped off a bridge because she was crazy. Because of a ten-year-old diagnosis from when she was a kid. Yes, my sister had problems. Yes, she was a loner. But I know her, and she was *not* suicidal—"

"Maybe you *didn't* know her." He tossed this out like an insult.

She was unprepared. It hurt.

He seemed to sense he'd overstepped, because he softened immediately and made sure the recorder heard: "Sorry, I . . . that came out wrong."

She said nothing. Nothing at all.

Maybe you didn't know her.

"Let me pose you a question, Lena. What are you doing?"

"Processing my grief."

"What are you *really* doing?"

Silence.

He came closer. "Why did you drive all the way from Seattle? Why not a phone call?"

She'd rehearsed an answer for this inevitable question, but it still hit her between the eyes. She was off balance now.

"I . . . I'm writing a book." She felt her cheeks flush with embarrassment, and she hated it. "About my sister. About her last moments on June sixth. There's so much I don't know about her, and I want to tell her story. With your help."

He considered this.

"When we were kids, she was the artist and I was the writer. Cambry always asked me to write a story about her. I never did. Now this is my atonement, I guess."

"I'm sorry if I sounded cold, Lena."

She half smiled. "I'm sorry I interrupted you, Ray."

Two fake apologies, spoken only for the Shoebox recorder. They stood ten paces apart. Like gunfighters in a Western.

From a distance and up close, Corporal Raymond Raycevic looked like two different men. He reminded Lena of a sports car one of Cambry's exes drove—fine-looking on the outside, gutted and cigarette-burned on the inside. His eyes were hollow and exhausted. His stomach gurgled with cancerous discomfort. But those biceps could probably punch a Clydesdale out cold.

"You look tired."

"I haven't slept since Thursday."

She waited for him to add a reason—*Insomnia? Graveyard shifts? My wife snores?*—but he said nothing more. Good enough, apparently.

From here, she could see inside his cruiser. The back seat was slashed and sun-cooked. There were patterns inked into the chestnut vinyl. One in particular, behind the driver's seat—she came closer to the window and recognized a hand-drawn dinosaur.

"You have some graffiti."

"What?"

She pointed. "Someone drew something on your—"

"Teenagers."

He walked back to her Corolla, his boots clicking dryly. She remained at the cruiser's back window for a moment longer, her gaze fixed inside on that curious cartoon dinosaur, etched in spidery blue ink. She couldn't look away. She'd seen it before.

No—she'd seen it many times.

CORPORAL RAYMOND RAYCEVIC DIDN'T LIKE HOW LONG THE girl lingered beside his car, peering through the tinted glass. His back seat was empty—so what was she staring at?

He caught himself staring, too. At her.

She looks exactly like her sister did.

There were superficial differences—Lena had long hair and bangs, while Cambry's had been self-cut and ponytailed. Lena was pale, Cambry bronze-skinned; Cambry's jeans had been frayed and browned with a dozen climates of sunbaked dust, while Lena's could have come off the rack yesterday. Underneath all of it was the same person, somehow. That they must have tried so hard to be different, to forge their own selves—maybe that made it all the more tragic that they couldn't escape each other.

Jesus Christ. He had to marvel.

It's like looking at Cambry's ghost.

Lena didn't notice. She was still squinting inside his car. It made Raycevic's insides clam up. He tried to remember—was there anything damning in his back seat? What could she be looking for, amid thirteen years' worth of slashes and stains?

No, sir. He didn't like this at all.

He needed to change the subject. "Okay," he said over a reluctant sigh. "I'm going to tell you the truth now."

"WHAT?"

"I lied to you, Lena."

She blinked, certain she'd misheard.

"And I'm sorry." He turned away again.

Lena's stomach fluttered with excitement at the trooper's words. *I lied to you . . .*

"Back at Magma Springs, I told you I couldn't imagine what it's like to lose a sibling, but the truth is, I can." He stopped at the guardrail and stared out into the smoke-shrouded hills. "I'm a twin."

She followed. But kept her distance.

"My brother's name was Rick, and he always wanted to be a cop. Ever since age five, when he'd arrest me with plastic handcuffs. And at eighteen, we both decided we'd take the same path with law enforcement. We both took the written, the psych panel, the fitness—but only I made academy selection. Rick washed out. It still surprises me, honestly, because I think he wanted it more than I did. Maybe he wanted it too much. And then I wonder if I only wanted it because I was following his lead. You know? Rick was the older twin, by two minutes."

Lena remembered her mother once telling her that she was Cambry's elder by a similar handful of hospital minutes. Not that it mattered. Cambry and her furies had always felt older, tougher, wiser.

He exhaled. "The night before I took my bus to Missoula, Rick put a twelve-gauge under his chin."

She felt like she should say something. She didn't.

"And you think I don't get what you're going through with Cambry's suicide, and it's true—I don't—because everyone's journey through grief and guilt is different. But I do have an idea of what you're going through." He looked back at her. "I have nothing but sympathy for you, Lena. And I'm urging you: Stop chasing her ghost. Look forward, not backward."

She looked forward. At him.

"And it was fifteen," he said. "She tried to call 911 fifteen times, according to the SIM card."

She said nothing. She was certain it had been sixteen.

Right?

"A clerk might have made a mistake when they were counting them for you over the phone," Raycevic said. "It was over the phone, right?"

Still, she said nothing.

The sun was high now. The shadows short. The sky a smoggy brown, thick with grit. The wind had ceased, creating a tense stillness. She was already thirsty, her lips cracking and her head beginning to ache. She wondered now if Raycevic was right about the call records. And if that was the case—what else could she be wrong about?

A metallic chirp interrupted her thoughts.

Raycevic recognized it. "Sorry. One sec."

She glanced back—it had come from his police cruiser. His radio, maybe. The Charger's front window was open a half inch, so the sound carried in the still air. Every sound seemed to carry. Every flexing grass blade, every footstep, every withheld breath.

No. She called 911 sixteen times.

I saw the records myself. I counted the lines.

The cop excused himself and jogged back to his patrol car

at a harmless-looking trot. She watched him squeeze inside and shut the door. She wouldn't dare let him out of her sight.

I'm not crazy.

She couldn't afford to doubt herself. Her mind swirled—the SIM card, the cartoon dinosaur in the Charger's back seat, the startling coldness in Raycevic's voice when he suggested she didn't know her own twin sister. Nothing fit. Nothing felt solid. Like a mouth full of loose teeth.

She tried to clear her mind and focus on the knowns. The facts, hard-edged and inarguable. Cambry's estimated time of death was 9:00 P.M.

This meant that, at the moment Raycevic pulled her over, she'd had less than an hour to live.

CHAPTER 4

CAMBRY'S STORY

The cop asks her name.

"Cambry Nguyen."

The cop asks how her day is going.

"Fine."

The cop asks where she's from.

"Seattle, originally."

The cop asks for her driver's license.

She fishes her wallet from her backpack on the seat beside her. Her hands are shaking, her fingers useless and numb.

"No need to be nervous," *the sunburned man says as he takes her license.* "You're not in trouble." *Then he turns and paces back to his black cruiser. He sits in the driver's seat with the door gently ajar. One foot resting on the packed dirt shoulder.*

He's checking you for warrants.

Cambry knows her record is fine—spotty, but nothing outstanding. Maybe she should have filed charges against Blake back in Florida, but the money was mostly his. The .25-caliber mouse gun was his, too, if he even bought it legally. Again, she wishes she had it now.

The situation doesn't feel real. Not yet.

Dusk has brought a chill to the air. The way a dream curdles into a nightmare. The sweat on her skin turns cold. She's already forgotten the cop's name, remembers only that it had two R's.

She watches him in her rearview mirror. He's not on his radio, which is strange. He's just sitting there, silent, staring back at her in the cooling blue twilight. Through the windshield, his face is a shadow. But he still has one foot on the ground, like he's ready to run. Ready to spring into motion. Ready for something.

Cambry places her right hand on the Toyota's shifter. The cop can't see this. Slowly, she closes her fingers around it, into a fist.

It would be easy to shift her car into drive right now. Her engine is still idling. Just a single metallic click downward. It wouldn't even be the first time she's run from the cops, technically. He'll realize immediately, of course, before she even accelerates, because her taillights will blink.

*But still—*You can drive away. Right now.

And he will chase her. Right? Of course he will—she'll be fleeing a traffic stop. That's a criminal offense. He'll flick his siren back on and she'll be the fleeing bad guy.

But . . .

At least if she drives long enough and fast enough, she'll encounter witnesses. Other cops, even, would be fine. She's almost okay with the thought of being dragged out of her car and handcuffed with a knee on her back and her face in the dirt, as long as it's one county over. As long as it isn't his knee on her back, here and now, with no witnesses.

She pulls the shifter downward. Slowly. The gears touch and rotate inside the framework, a tightening creak. The red line wavers between P and D. Park and drive.

Live or die. Do it.

She holds her breath.

Do it. Drive away.

She glances back up at her rearview mirror—the cop hasn't moved.

Still sitting in his seat, studying her, his face under a cowl of thick shadow.

Somehow, she knows he's not a real cop. Not at all. He's an impostor. A wannabe. Maybe he murdered some poor state trooper earlier today. Maybe he just rinsed the blood from a uniform that's not his, and sat down in a car that's not his, and I'm just the latest stop on his homicidal joyride.

She pulls the shifter farther down.

Farther. Farther still. The gears tighten and the lever touches the faintest invisible wall somewhere inside the mechanism. She can sense it, the knife edge. She's close. One last ounce of pressure, just a little more muscle in her wrist, and the Corolla will slip into drive.

If you don't drive away, right now, you will die.

This slips into her mind, a strange and distinct certainty. The same unwelcome feeling that made her petrified of Ouija boards, of asking if she was destined to die young. It was a strange phobia—not necessarily the fear of death, but the fear of being doomed. It was why that owl had bothered her today. How tragic, to journey all the way from Seattle to Fort Myers, and make it all the way back solo, only to die here in the homestretch, two states from home.

A chorus of urging voices: Cambry, do it. Do it.

He will murder you right now, if you don't shift into drive and—

The cop is coming back.

She hears gravel crunch under his approaching footsteps, brittle as eggshells. She lifts her hand from the Toyota's shifter guiltily, feeling the mechanism click back into park. Her cheeks burn with shame as his silhouette strides closer in her mirrors.

That's it, Cambry. That was your chance, gone.

Your fate is sealed.

He rests his elbow on the roof of her car this time, like it's his. He's looser now, more comfortable. He leans in and hands her back her driver's license, and as she takes it, she notices he's wearing black gloves. Had he been wearing those before? Or did he just now slip them on?

He says, "I need you to exit the vehicle, please."

"Say again?"

He leans in, one elbow still on the Corolla's roof. She can smell his chalky breath now. Strawberry-flavored antacids. "I need you to turn off the engine, exit the vehicle, and come with me."

"Why?"

"I'll explain. Come with me."

She keeps her fingers on the Toyota keys. Her knuckles tightening.

He smiles. "You're not in trouble."

"I know."

"It's just procedure."

Raymond Raycevic is his name, according to the black stitching on his uniform. She decides she should remember this and mouths it. In case that name belongs to someone's husband or father, facedown in a ditch somewhere. It's an eerie name, lyrical on her lips. Vaguely demonic.

"Look." His smile vanishes. "I already told you, you're not in trouble, Cambry."

Cambry.

Her name sounds alien coming from his mouth. It touches her like an ice cube between the shoulder blades. This makes it real, somehow. He's not a bodiless urge in her mind that she's been told to never fear. He's a human being, six-two, two hundred and fifty pounds, real skin and blood and bone standing in front of her, and he might be here to kill her.

He moves again. He paces around the Corolla's grille, studying the tires, looking the vehicle up and down like a car salesman, coming at the passenger window now—

"What are you doing?"

He doesn't answer. He reaches in through the passenger window—

"Hey!"—and lifts out her backpack by a strap. She grabs for it, too late.

"Hey, asshole. What are you doing—"

He unzips her backpack, dumping out her coat and fishing gear. He lifts out the red fuel can and sloshes it. He makes a disapproving face. She's seen this face before, on teachers and counselors. It's never fazed her like it does right now, because it's so clearly false.

"Someone's been siphoning fuel around Magma Springs," he says as he paces back to her window, gripping the rubber hose like a knot of pale guts. "A young transient woman living in a blue four-door. It's been the talk of the town."

"The talk of the town must be pretty fucking boring, then."

"This is serious, Cambry."

"Stealing gas?"

Raycevic frowns and drops the fuel jug to the asphalt with a thud. The rubber tubing, too. He gestures again, harder. "Get out."

"No."

"Get out, Cambry."

Cornered, she goes on offense. She can't help it. "What were you doing back there?"

He replies immediately, his voice alarmingly crisp, like a snake whipping back to bite the hand that grabbed its tail: "I'm sorry?"

"You were out there in the woods," she says. "Doing something with those fires. And then you saw me and chased me. All the way here." She looks at him directly. "Why?"

He says nothing.

"What was all that about? Huh?"

He sighs. Fussing with one of his gloves.

It occurs to her too late, after the words have left her lips—He has to kill me now. Because now he knows exactly what she witnessed. He knows she knows it's something of consequence. She's uttered her own death sentence, right off the cuff, like a dumbass.

I've given him no choice.

The pines whisper with friction. A breeze cuts through the open windows. It's going to be a chilly night. Cold for June.

"I'll explain it all," Raycevic says. "Okay? Is that what you wanted to hear? But one catch—I won't talk about it here. So let's go sit in my vehicle, and I'll give you a full rundown on what happened back there, and what you saw."

"How about you follow me into town?" she tries instead. "Whichever way the sheriff's station is, point me to it, and I'll drive there. You'll follow me there, and then we'll talk this whole thing through—"

He's shaking his head.

"Okay, but I'm not getting out of my car."

He shakes his head harder. She notices his other gloved hand has moved from the roof of her car. It now rests on the butt of his pistol. "I need you to cut the engine and exit the vehicle, ma'am."

"I need you to eat a dick—"

"Cambry." *He's still shaking his head in tight, clipped motions.* "You need to cooperate. It's more serious than you understand. I'm going to count to three."

"Then what?"

"You'll find out," he says, "if you don't exit the vehicle."

"You're not a cop."

He counts: "One."

Her gaze falls back to his palm, which rests on the black Glock holstered on his belt, and she softens. "Look. I'm just passing through here on my way home. I won't tell anyone what I saw—"

"Two."

"I don't even know what I saw." *She feels her voice break.* "Okay? Please—"

"Three." *He unbuttons his holster with two clicks and wraps his hand around the pistol.*

"Wait, wait," *she says, her hands darting up, palms out the window.* "I'm getting out. Okay? I'm getting out of my car and I'll go with you.

Can you just . . . take a step back, please?" She motions down, toward his feet. "So I can open my door?"

Silence. The moment cools.

Raycevic considers this and nods. He takes two steps back.

"Thanks."

Then Cambry Nguyen shifts into drive.

CHAPTER 5

LENA

LENA DIDN'T LIKE HOW LONG RAYCEVIC SAT IN HIS CAR.

He was still on his radio. He gripped the little black receiver to his mouth, glancing up at her periodically through the sun-tinted windshield. She saw his lips moving but couldn't hear his words. He'd rolled up his window for privacy.

She waved. He waved back with an apologetic smile. *I'm almost done.*

Lena glanced back out to the smoggy horizon and tried to stay focused. She'd been building momentum. This sudden wait had jolted her off her pace.

Who is he talking to?

She didn't like it. At all.

She held her iPhone in her right hand. No service out here, but in the wait she'd thumbed absently to her texts. To her sister's final message. The closest thing to a suicide note Cambry Nguyen had bothered to leave the world.

Lena normally slept through her phone's noises, but for some reason this message had thrashed her awake after midnight on June 8, as if charged with negative energy. She remembered snapping her eyes open to the chime, seeing the blue glow on her ceiling, rolling over and squinting to read her sister's last words:

Please forgive me. I couldn't live with it. Hopefully you can,
Officer Raycevic.

Lena had read it once.

Then she'd rolled over and gone back to sleep.

Suicide hadn't occurred to her. It happens to other people, other families. In her blurry mind, she'd assumed the text was intended for someone else. *Officer Raycevic* was a nickname for one of Cambry's deadbeat boyfriends, maybe, in Kansas or Florida or Sri Lanka or wherever the hell she'd floated to now. Just an out-of-context snapshot of her sister's nomadic world. Was it an apology? An inside joke? A subtle threat? With Cambry, it was probably all three.

Lena slept in until ten that morning. Her next phone call was from her mother, choking through tears. She'd been contacted by the Montana Highway Patrol.

Lena never told a soul that she'd ignored Cambry's text in the middle of the night. She claimed she'd found it only later.

And it didn't matter—at the moment Lena received it, Cambry had already been dead for over twenty-four hours. She'd typed the message minutes before her death and tried to send it from within Hairpin Bridge's cellular dead zone. The message sat in her phone's outbox until later, when paramedics transported her body. Inside her blood-caked pocket, against her cold thigh and fighting a dying battery, her shitty little Nokia flip phone pinged a tower at 1:48 A.M. and fired it off to her sister like a twenty-byte message from the grave.

To be ignored.

As humiliating as it was, she was still glad her estranged sister thought to text her. It came as a relief, somehow, that Lena still mattered enough to warrant a final message. Even one as bizarre and suspicious as this.

The last sentence, especially: *Hopefully you can, Officer Raycevic.*

What the hell?

What did that mean?

No one knew what to make of it. Why hijack a suicide note with a message to the random bystander who pulled you over an hour prior? Why not more for her shocked family, for the grieving blood relatives she left behind? Why not an explanation? Why not *anything*? At the service her parents had smiled stoically and done their best with it, but to Lena it felt like Cambry had texted her a personal insult. A middle finger from beyond the veil.

Forget the riddles. All she had to say, all Lena ever wished for, was *I love y*—

A metal clap jolted her thoughts.

A car door.

Raycevic was coming back. Finally. He was different now, wearing a toothy smile like a mask. "Sorry about the interruption."

"It's all right." She wiped her eye.

"That radio is like my wife," he said, forcing an abrasive laugh. "Squawking all day, all hours. Man, I would hear it in my sleep, if I ever slept anymore."

His lips pulled back into an anglerfish grin. Like the building tension of the last few minutes had fully evaporated, and he'd reverted back to the jovial, sympathetic (if mentally ragged) man she'd first met at Magma Springs Diner.

"Who were you talking to?"

———————

NINETEEN MILES AWAY, A MAN CLOAKED IN BLACK SHADOW held his radio receiver for a thoughtful moment before setting it back in its cradle with a click. Beside a handwritten note.

LENA NGUYEN. HAIRPIN BRDG

He paused, then added:

UNARMED

———————

"DISPATCH," RAYCEVIC SMOOTHLY ANSWERED. "FIRE ONE SAYS the wind changed. The Briggs-Daniels fire is pushing this way now, and everything south of I-90 needs to be evacuated. We should probably call it a day. Did you get your questions answered?"

"That's close enough."

He stopped six feet from her and raised both hands in an exaggerated shrug. His muscles coiled under tan sleeves. "Do you have something against cops, Lena?"

"Excuse me?"

"Cops. Me. The thin blue line." He patted his barrel chest, and it made a click, as if he were made of tungsten. His grin made her feel insects crawling on her skin. "I'm one of the good guys."

"I'm sure you are."

"Is this a Gen Z thing?"

"I respect cops, Ray."

"You're sure?"

"My uncle was a state trooper in Oregon." She looked him in

the eye. "He was the kindest, most decent person I've ever met. And I remember when he told me how often drivers flipped him off on the turnpike. They saw him as a storm trooper, not a human being. A lot of the public is like that. Pissed off. Distrustful. I really do believe law enforcement is the hardest job in the world."

He smiled, bashful. "Thank you—"

"It's *you* I have a problem with, Ray."

His smile vanished.

Something about this—the way he seemed to phase his expressions in and out—reminded Lena of Cambry's childhood Barbie collection. How, instead of playing with them, she'd used hydrogen peroxide to melt their faces into slurries of gray plastic, and then posed them on her shelves like faceless little department-store mannequins. It was eerie. Lena never knew why her sister did it.

Raycevic's smile had flickered back. He reverted to his teleprompter: "If you need to talk to someone else in my department, or if you distrust me, Lena, that's okay. That's your right. You've been through a terrible loss. Your sister was mentally ill." He put special emphasis on *mentally ill,* drawing out an extra syllable and studying her eyes for a reaction. "She was in incredible pain. Pain she never shared with anyone. And she made an unfortunate choice."

She refused to take his bait. *He's toying with me.*

Trying to rub salt in the wound.

She met Raycevic's gaze and stared into the robotic black shades, trying to find his eyes. "We didn't finish what we were talking about earlier. So, you pulled her over at eight o'clock?"

"Yes."

"But you didn't ask her to sit in your car?"

"No."

"She was never physically *inside* your car?"

That gentle smile answered her, all teeth. "That's correct."

Lena glanced back to her left and made sure the Shoebox was still recording. She didn't allow Raycevic out of her sight. She kept the armed man squarely in her foreground, her body turned ninety degrees against him for maximum mobility.

He was waiting.

She decided—yes, it was time to pull the trigger. The niceties were over. It had all been an act, anyway, from the instant she'd first met him outside the Magma Springs Diner today.

"My sister was an artist," Lena said. "She's brilliant. *Was* brilliant. She draws better than people can photograph, because any phone can copy an image, but Cambry catches the truth of it."

Raycevic's smile was evaporating again.

"There's this one thing she drew. Not a sketch. More of a calling card, a tag. It's a cartoon dinosaur, one of the smaller velociraptor-type ones, but friendly and expressive, you know? Like Garfield."

She gave him a moment to give an affirmative nod. He didn't.

"She's drawn it ever since elementary school, back when she wanted to be a cartoonist. She named it Bob the Dinosaur. And later, as a teenager, she scratched and inked it into everything. So now, traveling from ocean to ocean and back again, there's no question she must have drawn and carved Bob the Dinosaur into dozens of bar stools and tree trunks and restroom stalls all over the country."

She let the moment hang.

"So what's he doing carved into the back seat of your police car, Ray?"

CHAPTER 6
CAMBRY'S STORY

There's something eerie to how the state trooper watches her accelerate away. He's surprised by her deception, but he doesn't panic. He doesn't shout. He doesn't draw his weapon and pepper her back window with gunfire. He just watches her go under a billow of dust, a shrinking figure in her rearview mirror. And then he turns and calmly retreats to his cruiser.

He's going to follow you, Cambry.

This is a certainty. He will. The chase is just beginning. But right this moment, at 8:23 P.M., Cambry is alive, and her foot is clamped to the pedal, and the engine is throttling up, and she knows she's got a fighting chance. When her Corolla is halted in park, she's as vulnerable as a sitting bird, but when Cambry Nguyen is in motion? From Glass Beach to the Everglades, from white sand to white snow, the world races with possibilities, because motion is life.

And yes, motion is literally life, right now.

Holy shit.

She wants to punch her steering wheel. She's shivering, her nerves crackling with energy. Her skin erupts into goose bumps. Yes, yes, yes, that all really just happened.

What were those fires? Those four ritualistic fires that Raycevic had been tending to? *She's been thinking on them, turning it over in her brain, and she has a guess now. Like completing a jigsaw, it reveals a larger picture. The cop's binoculars, his sunburn, his panting desperation to catch her before she escapes back out into the world—*

He's following you.

Yes, of course, there he is. No surprise there. Corporal Raycevic's black Dodge Charger crowds up in her rearview mirror. He's caught up to her easily, and now pulls behind her in an aggressive pursuit. His car seems to bob on her tail, the snarling teeth of his impact grille closing to within twenty, ten feet. Close enough that, if she stomps her brakes at this very moment, she can almost guarantee she'll wreck them both. She considers this.

The road unrolls blacktop. Weaving through pines and prairie, crossing lazy foothills. Turn markers glint orange in her headlights, threatening a sharp turn ahead. She taps her brakes, letting Raycevic's headlights draw even closer.

I won't do myself any good if I crash, *she thinks. Raycevic would probably be delighted to watch her Corolla spin out and wrap itself around a tree. His work would be over. He could go home.*

Another sinking feeling.

He knows my name. *How much information is stored in police databases? Is it like the movies? Cambry's address was never up-to-date— she moved too much, too fast—but if her misdemeanors or her DUI are in there, then Corporal Raycevic knows her parents live in Olympia, Washington. If he fails to catch her tonight, he could pay them a visit and kill them instead. Or hold them hostage.*

She hasn't seen another motorist yet.

She checks her flip phone for signal—still nothing. This highway is empty, but maybe she can catch an access road to the interstate, which runs parallel. I-90 will certainly have other drivers. The thought of being near witnesses is reassuring. A psychotic cop wouldn't dare try anything in view of bystanders, right?

Unless he kills them, too.

Maybe he will.

A jarring pulse of red and blue behind her. He's flicked on his light bar. The wail of a pursuing siren. It doesn't sound like other sirens she's heard—it's too low-pitched, too heavy, like an underwater echo from a nightmare. Maybe it's the adrenaline clouding her thoughts.

She's also oddly offended. Do you think I'm an idiot?

She reaches out her window and flips Raycevic the bird. In answer, the siren cuts off abruptly.

At first this feels triumphant, like landing a good comeback. But it fades quickly. He was just acting out a ruse. Corporal Raycevic—if that's his real name—tried playing the role of highway cop one last time, to try to appeal to her sense of responsibility as a law-abiding citizen. Maybe it works with other people. Not Cambry. So, he discarded it.

His light bar remains on, though. The red-and-blue flash gives him more peripheral light to pursue her through the darkening country. The steady, relentless strobe of it needles into Cambry's thoughts, giving her a headache. She flips the rearview mirror down to reduce the glare.

For the next mile or two, they drive in silence.

She's going sixty—eighty in the straightaways, wherever possible. She wants to go faster, but the road is too dark and ropy, rising and dropping. The twists come hard and fast in the dying twilight. And Raycevic's Charger remains firmly planted on her ass, the same twenty feet behind her bumper. A beacon of vivid color, pulsing a silent heartbeat against glass.

Cambry isn't stopping. She won't. She's not stupid, and she understands the danger. She tries to think ahead. What will this cop try next, then? He'll need to force her to stop. He might try crashing into her, knocking her car into a spin. Or maybe he'll pull alongside her and shoot her through a window. Whatever he might do, he'll need to do it fast, because soon she'll be out of this cellular dead zone and able to call the police. The real police.

Time is on your side, Cambry. She realizes this with a funny twinge.

All you have to do is keep driving.

The next turn comes up fast—an ugly, banking ribbon—and she has to pump her brakes and cut her speed all the way down to forty-five. She hates doing it. The car pulls a bit, fighting her. A tire nudges the panic strip with a harsh buzz.

Keep moving, stay alive.

She tightens her grip on the wheel. Clearing the hard turn, she quickly accelerates, and so does the Charger behind her.

It's lunacy, but she's starting to feel good about the whole thing. Yes, time is absolutely on Cambry's side, and not his. All she has to do is keep driving like hell. It's a chase, but one she can win. Because eventually, one dark mile or the next, she'll come across another motorist, or the glimmering lights of the next town, or the magic threshold for the Verizon cell signal.

Then her gas light clicks on.

PART 2

THE PLASTIC MAN

CHAPTER 7

Cambry Nguyen knows from experience that without Blake's trailer, her Corolla can last roughly thirty miles on a low fuel light. That's the far-thest she's ever pushed her luck. From Fort Myers to Fargo, she's always been diligent to watch her maps, mind her location, and never stray far from a population center. Whether it's a few bucks at a gas station or a quick siphon from a parking lot, she's never been careless enough to let her tank run empty too far from civilization. But she wasn't counting on that asshole reaching through her window and grabbing her back-pack.

Thirty miles. That's the known limit.

Polk City is forty-two miles ahead, according to the next sign she sees. A twelve-mile difference. She wonders—what's the fuel reserve of a 2007 Toyota Corolla?

Thirty miles. Plus twelve more.

She stares at the dim orange fuel pump icon just below the E. Driving to Polk City is a major gamble, she knows. If she's wrong—even a mile short of forty-two—she'll coast to a halt in a dead car and he'll catch her defenseless on the road. A knife won't save her. He'll shoot her or strangle her or rape her. Whatever he was planning to do when he first asked her to step out, barely twenty minutes ago.

But maybe . . . maybe cell signal will resume sooner than forty-two miles? This is likely, since Polk City is a population center. There's bound to be some sprawl. But it won't solve her gasoline problem. Getting a successful 911 call out won't help her if he murders her on the spot.

"Shit." She punches her steering wheel.

The cop car still tails her. Plenty of gas in his tank.

Time is not on your side. *Her heart sinks.* Not at all.

The cop switches off his light bar behind her. Another act discarded.

Maybe it was interfering with his night vision? It's still something of a relief on Cambry's nerves. Now it's a clearer, simpler world of black night, headlights, and racing pavement.

She tries to collect her thoughts. It's already been a minute since she passed that green sign, so now it's forty-one miles to Polk City. She has one less mile in her tank. The engine itself is a ticking clock. Burning her finite supply of fuel, slurping away at a descending total every minute, every second—

Think, *she urges herself.* Just think.

This is a bad bet.

She can keep driving the remaining forty-odd miles to Polk City, and make it the entire way if she's lucky. She has no idea how much spare fuel she has. Her odds could be a coin flip. Or they could be significantly worse.

Magma Springs, *she remembers with a jolt. Twenty miles away. Maybe twenty-five, now? It's directly behind her. There won't be a cell signal—at least not until she's right in the middle of whatever their Main Street is—but she has enough gas to get there, for certain. The town itself is roughly the size of Polk City. Maybe larger. There should be a sheriff's department or a grocery store or a gas station or something with living, awake people inside it. People who can be eyewitnesses.*

"Okay," *she whispers.*

If you turn around . . .

"Okay, okay, okay . . ."

Another hard turn comes up—she holds her speed at seventy this time. The world banks like a racetrack. Loose change rattles in the console. She twists to avoid the panic strip and nearly overcorrects into the oncoming lane.

Coming out of the turn, the black Charger is still pinned on her tail. Headlights burn into her rear window. Just like the last turn. Raycevic is a trained pursuit driver; he knows exactly how these chases unfold and he's barely lost an inch on her.

She's already preparing for it, and she hasn't fully thought it through yet. But yes, she knows what she needs to do. Staying the course to Polk City is a mistake. She needs to turn around, to go back to Magma Springs, which is a safer bet and half the distance. She needs to slam on her brakes and turn around. Somehow, without getting caught. Or shot. Or rammed off the road.

She decides: She'll do it on the count of three. Just like Raycevic, standing outside her car with that wide smile, strawberry antacids caked on his teeth, his hand on his Glock.

"One." Her foot hovers on the brake pedal.

The speedometer needle hovers, too, at seventy-one. She can't slow down now, because that will be a tell. The cop will match her speed. And if she takes the turn too slowly, he'll seize his chance to ram her right off the road. She'll be vulnerable taking that turn, facing him broadside.

She imagines her car wrecking in the trees, tumbling and blossoming into a fireball—"Two"—and she grinds her molars. Her toothache is back.

You're going too fast.

No, she's going just fast enough.

And if he rear-ends you by mistake? And knocks you off the road?

A risk, but an acceptable one. Certainly better than running out of gas ten miles from the outskirts of Polk City, dead on the road with an armed psychopath on her tail. Better odds than anything else right now. That's an objective fact, she tells herself as his headlights scorch the edges of her vision.

Three?

She's afraid to say it. It's trapped in her throat like a cough. But she forces it through, forces her lips to part, to form the word:

"Three—"

She stomps the brakes.

The entire world seems to drop anchor. A brain-jarring impact without impact. The metal shriek of locking brake pads in her left and right eardrums. *The seat belt whips out of nowhere and clotheslines her, punching the air from her lungs.*

A flurry of shifting light—the Charger swerves hard to his left. His high beams flash as intensely as sunlight, and Cambry knows in the pit of her gut that he's not dodging her fast enough, that he's going to clip her tail and wreck them both. But the instant passes. He doesn't. He didn't. Her Corolla squirms right, skidding toward the road's shoulder with a scrape of gravel—she fights the wheel now—still sliding sideways on locked tires. Then another bracing impact-without-impact spills her against her seat, noisily tipping the cooler in the back seat, and then airy stillness. Her headlights stare at dark pines.

A complete stop.

No time to breathe. She thrashes forward in her seat, tasting the acrid odor of burnt rubber, heaving the steering wheel right and flooring the gas (the faraway scream of the Charger's brakes, too, slamming in enraged response), and she swerves into the eastbound lane, completing her turn.

A one-eighty, at seventy miles per hour.

"Holy shit."

Even her furies are impressed: *Not bad, girl.*

She brushes her hair from her eyes, accelerating. The road unfurls. Her path to Magma Springs, to civilization, to safety.

She flips her rearview mirror back into position—Raycevic is still fumbling his vehicle through a one-eighty turn of his own back behind her, shrinking into darkness. Fifty yards. A hundred. His reaction time was even slower than she'd dared hope. Maybe he'd been on his radio or something? She'd caught him off guard. She'd done the one thing he couldn't possibly anticipate in a life-or-death chase: she slammed on the brakes.

She feels like she's gained a full quarter-mile lead when she finally sees his headlights rejoin the pursuit behind her. Tiny faraway pinpricks of light.

"*Fuck you,*" she whispers.

It feels good. It's a minor victory, but it feels monumental. She's changed direction, toward a closer town. That's something. She takes the road's previous curve—now a hard left—and the Charger's headlights momentarily vanish behind the sloped land. She's gained considerable distance, and he's struggling now to close it. Hell, yes.

A sign races past, catching a fiery glint: MAGMA SPRINGS 22.

Even better than she expected! Twenty-two miles is doable, with eight to spare. The Corolla is certain to have that much gas in its tank. Better odds than making it forty-two to Polk City. Much better. But she'll still have to contend with an armed pursuer every mile of the way there, and when he gets desperate, he's liable to start shooting. She doesn't have a plan for that yet.

It's been a few seconds, and the cop's headlights haven't yet reappeared around the turn behind her. Something else occurs to her, just a whisper.

You can hide.

The cop is following her brake lights, which must be tiny red dots from his distance. The rest of the countryside is now pitch black. While visual contact is broken by the terrain, she could skid off the road, cut all of her lights, and let Raycevic barrel on past her to the next bend.

Do it, Cambry.

His headlights reappear. Still distant. Tugging closer.

Okay. The next turn.

She'll need there to be an access road, or at the very least a flat patch of earth, or else she'll just crash into a ditch. That would be bad. And she'll need to be cognizant of her dust trail. Anything that can give her location away in his passing headlights.

A clearing races by on her left, stalks of tall grass and saplings. Too fast to anticipate.

"Damn it." That would have worked, too. But the cop is still within eyeshot, and he would have just followed her off the road.

She promises herself: Next time. No excuses.

The next turn is coming up now. It's the same nasty bend she remembers from minutes ago. It had almost spilled her into the forest. A ribbonlike twist in the pavement, racing toward her in the night.

Her hair is in her eyes again. She sweeps it away. Her speedometer needle touches eighty, ninety. Inefficient fuel management, but necessary now. Her engine roars under the hood, breathlessly chugging its finite supply.

She knows, from a few minutes back, that she can attack this bitch of a turn at fifty and still stay on the road. This time, she'll try sixty. She'll need every second of her lead to get her car safely off the road and concealed in the darkness. Without leaving obvious tracks. And giving the dust trail a few critical seconds to settle.

Here it is.

At sixty, she's already chosen to cross into the oncoming lane to make for as broad a curve as possible. A head-on collision is the least of her fears. The road swerves away underneath her, a hard right, and she fights the wheel. The tires screaming again, the panic strip a furious buzz saw in her ears. She feels it vibrate her locked teeth. Again, the gnarled pine trunks whip past in her headlights, a strobing carousel of freeze-frames. Any one of them could turn her car into a fireball. They feel just feet, inches away. She keeps wrenching the wheel right, harder right, as the two-ton Corolla wrestles out of her grasp and the tight curve keeps going and going, more trees, more and more and more—

Then, abruptly, the road straightens.

She overcorrects, back into her lane. Hitting the panic strip again. Another buzz and a clatter of chewed gravel. But she's still moving forward, still racing, and she survived the hellish turn. It doesn't matter that she took the oncoming lane to do it—had another motorist been coming the other way, it would have been an instant murder-suicide—none of it matters, none of it at all, because it's just an alternative outcome that didn't happen. She's still alive.

In her rearview mirror, the Charger's headlights are gone again. The cop is probably just now cutting his speed to make the same turn. She tries to estimate how much time she has.

You have twenty seconds. Tops.

She searches all sides for a grassy meadow, a flat patch of earth, anything to skid off the highway onto and hide in the dark—and in her haste, she nearly misses something even better.

A gated-off road.

On a dusty little side shoulder, pitted with erosion tracks. A faded white sign—ROAD CLOSED—catches her lights over a locked metal gate. Coming fast, on her left.

She twists the wheel. Still going fifty.

Fifteen seconds now—

Her tires seize and squeal again. The gritty howl of rubber on pavement. She hopes the cop's windows aren't rolled down—otherwise he'll surely hear this, even from a quarter mile back around the bend, and he'll know she's stopping.

Ramming the gate is suicide, so she swerves around it, blowing through a six-foot sapling that cracks against her bumper like a gunshot and explodes into a cloud of frizzy leaves. Her vehicle jostles hard on the rough land, hurling coins from the console. Her seat belt yanks her collarbone again. Her mirrors are out of alignment now. Then she's back on pavement, completing her turn, leaving the locked barrier behind her, still racing—

Ten seconds.

Loose rocks clatter noisily against the undercarriage. Toothpick trees and low brush whip past on both sides. A dust trail obscures her rear window, lit blazing red by her taillights. A pothole bangs underneath her, another startling crash.

She keeps driving, hurtling forward. Putting more and more distance between herself and the main road. For this plan to work, she'll need to be far enough off the highway that the cop won't see her in his headlights. She also needs to cut her own lights, obviously, or he'll spot her in his dark periphery immediately. But when?

Five seconds.

It's a risk either way, she knows. If she stops too close to the road, he'll see her and swerve to follow her. If she keeps driving and waits too long to kill her lights, he'll see her, too. She twists her neck and looks back toward the highway through a shroud of dust. Watching for the Charger's headlights to reappear around the bend. Although, she reminds herself: if she sees him, it's already too late.

Zero. Time's up.

No. She's not far enough from the highway.

Stop the car.

She slams over another pothole, a trailing metal scrape. She can't stop yet. She's too close. The foliage is too low and sparse, the trees too thin. The sweep of Raycevic's headlights will reveal her Corolla hiding in the low prairie, as plain as daylight.

Stop the car, Cambry. Kill the lights.

She waits another second. And another—

Stop-stop-stop.

Finally, she stomps the brake and twists the key, cutting the engine dead. She swats off the lights and the world goes black. At that microsecond, on the sharp turn of Highway 200 behind her, the pinprick headlights of the cop's pursuing Charger streak into view, like twin shooting stars.

She holds her breath.

She waits, submerged in darkness. Her dust trail catches up to her and floats past, peppering her roof with grit. She watches the cop car's faraway headlights complete the turn. His high beams scan the grassland, casting racing shadows among the brush, and their predatory light touches her vehicle's blue paint, revealing its form in merciless detail.

Cambry's stomach twists into a knot as the car's interior lights up around her. For a moment, her dashboard, her steering wheel, her clenched knuckles—all as excruciatingly bright as afternoon sunlight.

Then darkness again.

He's straightening with the highway. She can hear the distant thrum of his engine. He's driving fast, making up his lost time.

Her lungs burn. She's afraid to move.

A new color: arterial red. The Charger's taillights suddenly light up the road behind it. He's slowing as he approaches the junction. He recognizes the sign and the gate. He must be familiar with the area. She swallows panic, gripping her key in the ignition. He's already seen her.

Now, every second she waits is lost time. If she turns on her engine and resumes running, she can still preserve some of her lead. If her cover is already blown, why wait? Why let her time burn away like a lit fuse? She watches the cop car slow further at the junction as a voice in her mind races: He saw you. He's going to turn left. He's going to turn left and follow you.

The Charger glides to a complete stop.

Silence.

Well, that's unexpected.

Her fingers are clenched around the Toyota key now, just a single twist from awakening the engine. Tight enough to imprint a pattern into her palm. Her knuckles ache with pins and needles. She relaxes her fingers, just a little.

He's parked now, right in the center of Highway 200, about a hundred yards from her. Just a few paces from the gate. His engine idles, a low growl. Lights on.

She watches through her rear window. Still afraid to move. Her lungs bloat inside her chest like hot balloons. She's getting dizzy, her thoughts starting to swim, but she won't allow herself to breathe. She can't. It's nightmare logic: if she breathes, he'll see her.

For another torturous moment, nothing happens.

Then the Charger's door swings open, silent but startling in its swiftness, and Cambry coughs her breath out. She gasps, as if surfacing from deep water.

The cop steps out. He's a black silhouette against his headlights. Even from a distance, she can discern the same details she remembers:

The brim of his hat. His ram shoulders. His barrel chest. He's a big guy, almost a bodybuilder, and he looks even bigger in profile. It chills her blood, to be chased by a man with the proportions of the Incredible Hulk.

She's hidden, she reassures herself. He can't possibly see her in the dark without night vision.

Does he have night vision? Infrared?

The cop leaves his door ajar and strides to the back of his vehicle. He's in a hurry. He pops the trunk and leans inside. His dark form ducks into the red glow of his taillights, as red as a demon, before he disappears from view again.

He doesn't see her. He can't.

Right? The flatlands are lumpen darkness. Sporadic trees and spotty foliage. She wishes she could sink into it. Just melt downward, car and all, like slipping under dark mud.

The cop reappears. Again passing through the red glare of his brake lights, again looking like a muscle-bound devil. He carries a weapon now. Cambry is no expert on firearms. This year, she shot Blake's pocket pistol a few times, just enough to be believably threatening if they were ever mugged at a campsite. But she's certain, even across a great distance, that what Raycevic is carrying is an assault rifle.

He carries it lightly, like a broomstick. He stops by his ajar door. He looks left, then ahead. Left, then ahead. He's staring at the locked gate—maybe he sees the sapling she took out—and supposing which direction she fled. His movements are clipped, twitchy. Nervous.

He's not sure.

Cambry remains frozen in her car. Her Toyota key still tight in her fingers. One twist is all it will take, and then her driving lights will snap on and she'll light up like a Vegas billboard. She can't open her door and escape on foot, either—the dome light will go off. She's trapped inside her car.

The adrenaline of hiding, of being hunted, stirs in her stomach. It's not an entirely bad sensation. She remembers being the little girl who dominated at hide-and-seek. Even indoors. She'd slip off her shoes and tread silently in her socks. She'd evade Lena and the other kids for what felt like hours at a time, changing positions, sliding out of closets, creeping from room to room of her cousins' house like a wraith. There's something exhilarating to not being found.

Meanwhile, the cop scans the distance for her. Too dark for binoculars. He holds that sinister rifle to his shoulder as he searches, ready to fire. Thank God he doesn't have night vision.

He has to decide, she realizes. One or the other.

Stay on the highway or take a left onto the closed road? He has a fifty-fifty chance of choosing correctly. Cambry has a fifty-fifty chance of breaking contact and escaping. It all comes down to a coin flip, under an anxious black sky. The air builds with electric charge. She can feel it in her teeth.

The Toyota keys rattle in her fingers. Her hand shakes. The apprehension of it is killing her nerves, and it must be killing Raycevic's, too. He's losing time. He knows it. She knows it. It all comes down to his choice.

Please choose wrong. *She hopes.*

Please stay on the highway.

The realization comes to her now. Now, of all times. It comes in on tiny crawling legs, like an insect under a door. She understands now. This cop, Raymond Raycevic, was destroying a body out on that remote property. The four campfires, caged in pyramids of stone, were designed to hold heat. Like little furnaces. To bake human bone into powder. He was cremating a body, one chopped piece at a time.

Cambry's stomach writhes. Acid in her throat.

This cop, Corporal Raymond Raycevic, is a killer. And she stumbled across his evidence disposal site. She witnessed him in the act. So now he desperately needs to eliminate her before she tells someone else and blows his secret. That's it. That's the only realistic explanation for what's happening.

He sets his rifle on the seat and climbs back inside his Charger. He slams the door with clear anger. The sound reaches her a fraction of a second later, a dry clap delayed by distance. The patrol car's driving lights change as he shifts into gear. This is it. The moment of truth.

Please stay on the road.

The vehicle lurches forward toward the junction, and Cambry wants to cover her eyes, wants desperately to look away.

Please-please-please—

And Raycevic continues straight down Highway 200. Past the white sign, past the road, past the smashed sapling and the locked gate. Past Cambry's hiding spot. She doesn't believe it at first. She can't.

Yes. He's leaving.

Watching him go, she cries out, half a scream and half a gasp. So much tension, let out as suddenly as a punctured balloon. A rush of blood to her skin. A seizure of joy in her throat. Yes, it was a coin flip, all right, and she called tails, and he called heads, and thank God, she just won—

Lightning crosses the sky.

A jagged bolt leaps east to west, fracturing the sky into cracks of silent fire. For a microsecond, every inch of the prairie lights up, as if every rock and every tree is X-rayed in a double flash. Even the interior of Cambry's Corolla ignites as bright as daylight for a single horrible instant.

On the highway, the cop slams on his brakes. His tires squeal.

As he skids back around to turn at the gate and rejoin the chase, it takes a full, disbelieving second for Cambry Nguyen to comprehend what happened. What just happened, against all odds. She twists her key, starting the engine again.

"You've got to be fucking kidding."

CHAPTER 8

LENA

"YOU'RE HIDING SOMETHING," SHE TOLD THE COP.

"Excuse me?"

"You heard me, Ray."

He just stared. Caught flat-footed.

"And you know what? It's okay. Because I haven't been entirely honest with you, either." Lena glanced at her sister's car.
The Shoebox recorder on the hood, its white cassette spokes
turning. She felt the temperature change, the sun dimming behind a wall of dirty smoke, and chose her words carefully, because they couldn't be taken back: "Something doesn't sit well
with me. It hasn't. For three months. That's . . . part of the reason
I tracked you down, Ray. And arranged this meeting."

"The investigation—"

"Doesn't add up," she said quietly.

For a long breath, Corporal Raycevic didn't speak. He re-
garded her in the unforgiving daylight, but distantly, like he was
running through a checklist in his mind. Finally, with a squint,
he spoke. "Walk me through it, Lena. I'm not a detective, but
outline everything that's bothering you."

"You first. You haven't explained Bob the Dinosaur."

"I already did. Not everyone I detain is cuffed. Kids, they draw things in the vinyl—"

"How did *Cambry's* dinosaur get there?"

"You're making me say this?" He pulled off his black Oakleys and rubbed his eyes with his fingertips. "I don't want to say this, because I'm going to sound like a jerk on your tape—"

"Little late for that, Ray."

"I'll be as delicate as possible. Have you heard of an old Nickelodeon show called *Rocko's Modern Life*? There's a green chameleon character. I forget his name. But that's exactly what it looks like. Some fourteen-year-old shoplifter in Polk City scratched a supporting character from a Nickelodeon show into my seat five years ago, and if it looks like Bob the Dinosaur to you, that just means your sister's character wasn't original. *Sorry.*"

"You have a pretty good memory."

"I was making an example."

Don't give him room to breathe.

She pointed to her sister's Corolla. "See the big dent on Cambry's bumper? Like she rammed it through a small tree or something?"

"Yeah?"

"That wasn't on it when I last saw her."

"Yeah?" he said. "When was that, Lena?"

This landed like a dagger between her ribs. She didn't answer—because the answer was *over a year ago*. Thirteen months. At a family barbecue. They'd barely spoken. Cambry had been sullenly drunk, and Blake (Terrible Guy #17, or maybe #18) had been embarrassingly grabby. Moreover, cars get damaged all the time. A dent proved nothing.

Raycevic studied her. He knew he'd drawn blood.

Twins are supposed to be close, right? Inseparable, sharing DNA, like little mirror images. But Lena and Cambry had been trapped birds inside that tiny thousand-square-foot house, and when age eighteen hit, they'd exploded out into the world in wildly different directions.

"There's no conspiracy," Raycevic continued with a strut. "The investigation ran its course. It was a weekend, so the M.E. was late ruling it a suicide, and Homicide was already hard at work going through my laundry, dusting every square inch of her vehicle—and mine—for suspicious fingerprints, signs of a struggle, foreign hairs or fibers, *anything at all*—"

"The brake pads were worn."

"She drove it to Florida—"

"The brakes were mentioned on the report. Remember?"

"Look, Lena." He looked pained. "This is getting above my pay grade. I don't have the report in front of me. And as much as I wish I was, I'm not a detective—"

"*Recent wear on vehicle's brake pads,*" Lena said. "Quote, unquote. As if she'd slammed on her brakes, because she was being chased and evading someone—"

"Or she saw a coyote."

"I think I know why you're not a detective," she said.

No wind or ambient sounds filled the uncomfortable silence. So Lena pressed on and filled it herself, with something she'd been aching to say all day: "I don't believe my sister killed herself."

"You need to accept that she did."

"She wouldn't." She fought a tremor in her voice. She hated it. It made her sound childlike, on the verge of tears. "I know Cambry. I know my sister. On a cellular level."

He was close enough now to touch her arm. "Lena, she—"

"*Stop* calling me Lena. You don't know me."

He froze. As if bitten.

She caught her breath. She hadn't meant to snap—raising her voice had always felt like an admission of weakness. Strength is quiet, insecurity is loud, and her voice had echoed crisply over the valley. But she couldn't stop now. She was just getting started.

"Another thing. Only one of Cambry's notebooks was found in her car. She was on the road for nine months, from Seattle to Fort Myers and almost back again. So there should have been hundreds of sketches—in ink, pencil, everything."

"Maybe her boyfriend took them."

"They separated in Fort Myers. The missing drawings are after Florida—"

"You studied every page?"

"You're *goddamn* right I did." She looked at Raycevic head on. "They were California, Texas, Louisiana. The Santa Monica Pier, Mitten Buttes, oil derricks, alligator heads—"

"She stopped drawing after Florida. Or she tossed the notebooks—"

"She would never do that."

"You're sure?"

"Yes."

"Positive?"

"She would never toss her drawings, Ray."

"Okay." He sucked on his lower lip. "Because she did toss *herself.*"

Silence.

She studied him, paying special attention to his eyes—waiting for another flash of horror, regret, apology. Jokes can misfire. This wasn't a joke. He was *smiling.* It was designed to hurt. It did.

That's how it's going to be, she thought. *Fine.*

She forced a smile, too, hard as granite. "You know what clinches it, Ray? What seals it in my mind, that you know more than you're telling me?"

He waited.

"This bridge is haunted. According to the internet. Some-

times called the Suicide Bridge. It's famous for four or five jump-
ers, back in the eighties—"

"You told me this."

"I did. Thirty minutes ago. And you told me you'd never
heard of it. But in your written report, you named it as the Suicide Bridge. Your exact words. You added some bullshit little
flourish about the bridge's tragic history, and how you sincerely
hope it's the last life ended here."

His expression didn't change.

"Good performance," she said. "But you overdid it."

He didn't blink.

"You lied to me. Again—"

"I haven't lied to you *once* today," he hissed. A shocking snarl
to his voice, like a wounded animal, and Lena edged back a half
step. "Am I . . . am I supposed to remember every single local
legend? There's a portal to hell in the Magma Springs Cemetery.
Johnny Cash allegedly took a shit in our mini-mart restroom
once. I forgot about a bridge that I have a passing familiarity
with, over a quarter of a year ago—"

"You pulled her over," Lena whispered. "An hour before her
time of death."

"Do you have something to say?"

"And then the next day, you *found her body*—"

"Do you have *something to say,* Lena?" He bristled, blocking
the sun. "Because if so, you'd better say it outright. I don't have
the patience for this mysterious chickenshit."

She looked back at him. The words were there, on the tip of
her tongue. But uttering them would change everything. There'd
be no coming back from it. The entire situation could unravel.
She'd rehearsed this moment for weeks. Months. She'd practiced
in front of mirrors, in the shower, on the road, and now here she
was, tongue-tied and blank-eyed.

He was closer now. "Say it."

She could smell his breath. Strawberry antacids. And a sweet, goatish odor, like bacteria on his gums. She could see the tartar on his teeth.

"Say it, Lena." Even closer. His tone had changed, bullying now. Still, the words stuck in Lena's throat.

"Say it—"

———————

He killed her.

I am sure of this. Beyond sure. I have never been more certain of anything in my entire life, dear readers.

Corporal Raymond Raycevic, a highly decorated seventeen-year veteran of the Montana Highway Patrol, murdered my sister Cambry Nguyen on June 6 of this year. He threw her body off Hairpin Bridge to make it appear to be another in its curious line of suicides decades ago. He couldn't conceal the coincidences—like the fact that he pulled her over shortly before her death—but he managed everything else. Her soft tissue was pulverized on impact with granite at free-fall velocity. There was no forensic evidence recovered in her car, nothing incriminating in her barely used flip phone, and no signs of foul play. Just another runaway, low on gas in the middle of nowhere, ending her life on a tragic impulse. The cover story worked on everyone—except me.

He. Killed. Her.

Yes, dear readers. That's what this entire post is about. It was never about *Lights and Sounds,* or me, or my grief, or the whispering ghosts of the Suicide Bridge.

It's about Cambry's murder.

My sister did not kill herself on the last leg of her cross-country trek, in a random leap off a semifamous bridge. Her alleged mental illness is neither a motivation nor an excuse, as it so often is when troubled people are the victims of crime.

As for her suicide text message? Fake, I believe.

Yes. Fake.

Here's a screencap—<u>1384755.jpg</u>. Received at 12:48 A.M. on June 8. Mom and Dad and everyone struggled to find sense in it, and no one questioned the authenticity of her last words. But as the fog of grief thinned, I started to think about it more critically.

Please forgive me, she texted me. I couldn't live with it. Hopefully you can, Officer Raycevic.

Excuse me, but what the fuck?

There's a lot of weirdness to unpack here. I don't even know where to start.

1. It's not Cambry's voice. It's not even a decent imitation of Cambry's voice. I know my sister. This was written by someone else. Someone pretending to be a twenty-four-year-old woman—and failing hard.
2. It's cliché. Take it from a voracious reader and hopeful (someday) author. The first two sentences are the blandest, least imaginative swing at a suicide note ever attempted. All it needs is a *So long, cruel world*.
3. It's specially designed to let "Officer Raycevic" off the hook.

Yeah.

Let me explain that last part.

If you allegedly found a woman's body under a bridge, but you were also on record as the last person to see her alive at a traffic stop, you'd be suspect #1. What better way to cloud that suspicion than to reframe the narrative and have the victim personally name you as trying (and failing) to help? *Sorry, Officer Raycevic, you didn't realize I was about to kill myself, but you tried!*

Then you're no longer a suspicious party—you've recast yourself as a tormented hero now cursed to live with guilt. You missed your chance, Ray. You could have helped save the life of a suicidal woman on that remote highway if only . . . IF ONLY . . . you'd been more perceptive to the signs. Eh?

As cover-ups go, I can't decide if it's brilliant or idiotic. Maybe a little of both. It worked, after all. On everyone else.

Yes, dear readers: that means Corporal Raymond Raycevic himself typed the suicide note on Cambry's flip phone. He fabricated that little Robert Frost masterpiece, found my number in her address book, hit send, and let it sit there in her outbox for later.

Bottom line?

She.

Did.

Not.

Kill.

Herself.

People who commit suicide go to hell, I remember our mom telling us once after one particularly brutal marathon of Sunday school. I don't know if she still believes it—that her daughter is burning in a lake of fire right now. But it gives my mission a powerful and crystalline urgency: I'm going to rescue Cambry from hell.

I will catch her killer tomorrow.

I know what I'm up against, and I know the severity of making this charge. By all accounts, Corporal Raymond R. Raycevic has a valorous record. Last year he rescued two children from a burning trailer. He heroically shot a fugitive in a gunfight on I-90, where he's credited with saving a deputy's life. Back in 2007 he jumped into the Sun River and pulled an elderly woman out of a wrecked truck. On paper, he's basically Officer Jesus (if Jesus shot one guy). And I have to admit, when I called him, Raycevic sounded like a decent guy over the phone. Genuine, even. If he's a walking, talking insect, he's got the human act down pat. I imagine he's quite lovely until he peels off his skin.

Why should he fret, anyway? The case is closed, history is written, Cambry's body is cremated, and he's still working his beat (or highway, or whatever state troopers patrol). Tomorrow I'll see him in the flesh, and

I'll ask him the questions that have been burning inside me for months. He doesn't know I know. He has no clue he'll be walking into my trap tomorrow. He's in for a surprise, dear readers.

I'll make him confess to Cambry's murder on that bridge.

I have a plan.

SOMETHING OCCURRED TO HIM. "YOU'RE RECORDING ME."

"No shit, Ray."

He blinked. A surprised flutter, like he was processing new information. He must have forgotten about the Shoebox recorder studiously logging every word, every breath, every pause. Had he incriminated himself yet? Hard to say. But he'd sure come across as a bullying asshole.

Because she did toss herself.

That was a career ender. It could go viral all by itself, but Lena was after bigger revelations. And it delighted her to see the big man off balance. He'd underestimated her, all right, and now he was paying dearly for it. She stepped back, giving herself more room. She didn't like allowing him so close to her, his fetid strawberry breath in her face. Close enough to grab her throat.

Her calf bumped something—the bumper of her Corolla.

No. *Cambry's* Corolla, always and forever.

She maneuvered around it and lifted the Shoebox recorder. She held it protectively to her chest.

"You're recording me," Raycevic said, "because you believe I had something to do with your sister's death. Is that right?"

She nodded. "That's correct."

Somehow this felt like an anticlimax. For months she'd daydreamed of accusing him powerfully, articulately, like a prosecutor leveling a scathing charge before an enthralled courtroom. She'd wanted the microphone to hear the conviction in her voice. But she'd lost her nerve somewhere in the moment, and he'd taken control of the conversation. He'd been so *close* to her. So big.

He still was. He slurped his tongue over his teeth, as if he were chewing tobacco. He glanced at her—she tried to look stoic, like the heroine in an action movie—and then down at the recorder. "Turn it off," he said finally. "Then we'll talk."

"No."

"Turn it off."

"Still no."

"Turn it off, *please.*"

"Did you really think saying *please* would help?"

"I'm making you an offer," he said. "I will tell you what you want to know, if you turn that thing off. What I'm about to tell you has to be off the record."

"Non-negotiable," Lena said. "The mic stays on."

The cop held out a calloused palm. "Can I at least . . . look at what you're taping me with?"

"You must think I'm stupid."

"If you want the truth—"

"*Hey.* That's close enough." He'd been creeping closer again. He halted midstep, like they were playing freeze tag. His eyes glowered.

They stood six feet apart. To an uninvolved party, they'd look like a state trooper pulling a civilian over for a traffic violation, and perhaps exchanging a few testy words. Lena repositioned and moved around her car. Giving herself a few more paces of distance. And an open escape route, if he attacked and she needed to suddenly backpedal.

He watched her move.

It was all in the open now. Her intentions, his. She caught her breath. The recorder listened against her chest, its spokes quietly turning. She already wished she'd worded it better, made it more of an accusation. More of a spectacle. Not a simple admission to his question: *That's correct.* It was her big moment, Cambry's big moment, recorded forever for court and history, and she'd succumbed to stage fright and ceded control to him. Like a scared little girl.

Chickenshit, he'd called her. That was public record now.

Nothing happens like you plan it.

Last night in her Seattle apartment, she'd dreamed about Cambry. A real dream, not a nightmare. No guts, no gore, no horror—just a face-to-face moment. To Lena it felt desperately important. There was so much to ask. So much to say. This was her chance to tell her sister she loved her, that she'd always loved her and admired her across all the distance between them, and that she was sorry for everything she'd done—

But in her dream, Cambry sat on her hands and refused to even look at her. She turned away, blinking away tears. Sullen, heartbroken, cold. As if embarrassed.

Lena, go.

When Lena tried to touch her arm, she flinched away. No eye contact.

Go, she hissed. *Go, please.*

Lena didn't understand.

Just go.

It made no sense to her. Why *go?* Why now? They were finally reunited for a blurry moment, but somehow Cambry and her furies didn't want to be there. Her sister was always restless. Even in death, she would rather be somewhere else.

You have to go now. Her voice hardening. *Go.*

No love. No warmth. Just cold urgency.

You're running out of time—

Then it ended.

The dream evaporated.

Lena awoke alone in the darkness before sunrise in frustrating dismay. Leaden heartache. She felt rejected. Like this was the spiritual equivalent of *Sorry, I dialed the wrong number,* and Cambry didn't really want to talk to her. Even now. Even as a ghost.

Even in Lena's imagination.

Before she'd left, she'd typed the dream into her blog, and then swallowed it like a pill. On the drive to Montana, she'd sculpted the dreamy nonsense into a narrative. Cambry wasn't being cold; she was just ashamed of something. Guilty, maybe, for leaving her family without closure? Ultimately, it didn't matter. Lena assured herself the dream was her sister's troubled spirit urging her forward (*Lena, go*), out the door to Hairpin Bridge (*You're running out of time*) to confront her killer and avenge her.

And now here she was.

Here he was. He still watched her across their uneasy stand-off. Something darted between them, gray and flecked. Like a windswept snowflake.

It was ash.

He looked at the recorder in her arms and sighed. "It's true."

"What's true?"

"I followed your sister. On June sixth."

Her stomach twisted.

Corporal Raymond Raycevic licked his dry lips and spoke slowly, making every syllable distinctly clear for the recorder. "I stopped her, Lena. But not for speeding."

He paused, letting it sink in.

She loathed him. She loathed his power over her. She loathed herself for submitting to it.

"Cambry saw something she shouldn't have seen," he said. "When I stopped her vehicle, I asked her to come with me so I could protect her. But she didn't trust me. I was trying to calm her down. I didn't want to use force to restrain her, but I was getting ready to. I told her I'd count to three, and then she agreed to come with me and get in my vehicle."

She didn't, Lena knew. She wouldn't have.

"She looked me in the eye and said yes, that she would get out, if I took a step back to give her room to open her car door. I did." His lip curled with annoyance. "She floored it and sped off."

Now that's the Cambry I know. For a moment it was like her twin sister was alive again, revealing new surprises, and Lena's heart clenched into a painful fist.

"I chased your sister, but I'm not the bad guy, Lena." Raycevic softened and looked almost hurt now. "You never really considered that, did you?"

More flakes of ash drifted between them, like dead pollen.

"You admit you chased her?" she asked.

"Yes. Trying to *save her.*"

CHAPTER 9

CAMBRY'S STORY

Cambry estimates her low-fuel light has been on for five minutes. It's difficult to judge time with an adrenaline high, during a careening chase down treacherous hilly roads, but according to the Corolla's digital clock, it's 8:35 now, and approximating a mile of fuel consumption per minute, she reasons she has twenty-five minutes of gas left. Maybe a few more, if she's lucky. If the timing of that lightning flash was any indication, she sure as hell isn't.

Nine o'clock.

That's when I die tonight.

Another bolt crosses the sky like a blink of daylight.

She expects thunder, but it never comes. The anticipation of it sets her nerves on edge. Her mouth is dry. Her eyelids feel like paper. The night air rushes through her open windows, a chilly blast.

The clock changes to 8:36. Twenty-four minutes left.

This road had better lead to the interstate.

She's just wagered her life on it.

She's committed to this direction. If she turns around, she's dead. He'll lift that black rifle from his passenger seat and rake her with bullets. Even if she manages to pull another dizzying one-eighty, she can't possibly slip by him fast enough. She'd die with holes in her face.

This road must lead to the interstate, right? She's studied the local maps at Dog's Head and knows I-90 runs parallel to Highway 200, separated by ten miles of granite foothills and low prairie. *What are the odds of the road being a dead end?*

Better than your chances of getting past him. And that rifle.

She tightens her grip on the wheel and stays the course. *This isn't Plan A or B or even C, but with a calculated roll of the dice, this will take her to I-90, and the interstate will have constant traffic. Even out here, in Howard County. Traffic means witnesses. Witnesses mean this cop on her tail can't gun her down without cooking up one hell of a cover story.*

Still . . .

He probably is, right now.

He's almost certainly got a spare gun. Isn't that Dirty PoliceWork 101? If he's the type to burn evidence, he would almost certainly keep a papers-free handgun rattling around in his trunk to be planted near her bullet-riddled body. Or even an airsoft gun, as long as it looked authentic enough to justify a split-second response. Whatever he is— whatever he wants to do to her—the worst thing she can possibly do is underestimate him. His broad, false smile lingers in her memory. Candy-coated venom.

And he's gaining on her. Those piercing headlights, intensifying in her mirror.

She hopes to God she made the right decision. By her geographical knowledge, the chances of this closed road being a dead end are decently low. But another obstacle? Much higher. The road could be washed out or blocked by a rock slide. Or it could lead to a busted bridge. Any of these scenarios will force her to stop, and stopping is instant death.

It's closed for a reason, Cambry.

She runs the numbers in her mind. If the road is clear (a gamble), it can't be more than ten miles to the interstate. It's ten more from the interstate to downtown Magma Springs, her original destination. Even assuming she doesn't encounter another motorist (unlikely), and the cell signal doesn't return until she's downtown (also unlikely), she'll still be okay. With five extra miles in her tank, even.

You'll be okay. As long as you drive straight, and don't deviate again.

And as long as the road isn't blocked ahead.

That, too.

Trying to hide at the turnoff back there had cost her a few extra minutes and miles—not to mention it had diverted her onto a new course. And it gave Raycevic time to grab his rifle from his trunk. So all in all, a poor outcome. But it was worth the risk. Who can predict lightning, of all things?

Maybe he can. Whoever he really is.

She remembers a Halloween story that used to fascinate her as a teenager. She's told it to Lena numerous times, and she has added different flourishes in each telling, but here's the gist of it: A young guy is living it up at Mardi Gras with his friends and breaks away from his fellow groomsmen to take a leak in an alley—where, to his terror, he bumps shoulders with the gaunt figure of the Grim Reaper. Oh, shit, right? The man flees the alley in panic, drives to the New Orleans airport, flies to a random continent, then rents a car there and drives hundreds of miles farther, farther, farther, until the car dies, and after seven days of hiking into the snowy tundra, he takes refuge in the deepest, darkest, most hidden cave he can find.

The Grim Reaper is there, waiting to take his soul.

He has to ask: "How did you find me?"

And oddly, the Reaper seems equally puzzled: "I was told you'd be here. What were you doing at Mardi Gras?"

No one can outrun fate.

Not even you, Cambry.

The Charger's headlights crowd up behind her. The muscular roar of his engine intensifies, morphing into something raw, primal, flesh-eating. It gives her a shiver. She's imagining him as more than a man, and that's a mistake. He's not a supernatural being. He doesn't haunt these highways like a roving demon. He's just a man, a man she witnessed doing something illegal, and now he's after her to cover up his secret. A man can be outsmarted. A man can be eluded. And a man can even be bargained with. Although she's not about to try.

She thinks about her parents. About Lena. She tries to picture their faces. It's been over a year.

Her car strikes another pothole—a bracing metal shriek. She's still over five hundred miles from home, technically, if there's even a place she can call home *in Washington—but she's closer than she's been since November. Closer than ever, in a way.*

The Charger pulls closer and its high beams project a long shadow of her car against the racing pavement. For a moment, she glimpses the silhouette of her own spotlighted head, the shadow sweeping right as Raycevic pulls up on her left.

She twists her neck to look at him. Fighting the eye-watering brightness, she glimpses his dark form inside the car, as black as construction paper. His window is open. His left elbow rests on his door. In his hand, hanging loosely out the window, is a small shape she can't quite discern in the hurtling light, which is fine, because she already knows exactly what it is.

He's pulling alongside you. To shoot you.

She's minutes from the interstate now, so he has to make his move. Even if it's as sloppy and violent as a drive-by shooting. He needs to stop her from reaching civilization at any cost.

She pushes the gas harder. The engine roars.

The black shadow inside the Charger accelerates, too. Right behind her, his own eight-cylinder roaring in furious reply, reeking of burnt oil and carbon monoxide. Swinging up on her left side, like he's trying to pass her. She knows it's a losing game.

She ducks against the steering wheel. It doesn't matter, because if she slouches low enough to be shielded from gunfire by her door, she's too low to see the oncoming road. And who's to say bullets won't just pierce the door anyway? This isn't a movie. It's real life, where death comes abruptly and unfairly. Like it almost certainly did for whoever Raycevic was feeding, piece by piece, into those four small fires.

It's 8:41 now. Nineteen minutes to live.

She's afraid to look back again, but she does.

Oh, God, he's so close now. *He shouts something at her, muffled by the air whipping between them. She can't hear it, and even if she did, she knows it's a lie. It's just words. She can't trust anything he says, because the Glock is in his hand.*

Aimed at her.

"Leave me alone," she screams into the wind.

Maybe he heard. Maybe he didn't. He shouts something else to her, removing his other hand from the wheel to cup to his mouth, his voice barely breaking through the roar of twin engines, the howling slash of air. It's something simple, just a few syllables. Pull over, probably.

"Leave me alone," she screams back. Louder. "Please."

She gives it another pump of gas, but it doesn't matter. His Charger is effortlessly faster. He's pulling closer, almost parallel to her now. Maybe he's trying to box her in? She can see the pistol more clearly now, aimed at her through the windshield in his hand. She wonders why he hasn't fired a shot at her yet, or put a bullet into her tire and sent her tumbling in a bruising wipeout. There are no witnesses out here. No cars, no homes. Just silent, uncaring forest.

He shouts again, a single word, and this close, she can almost hear it. Just barely.

It sounds like: Please.

For a heart-fluttering moment, she wonders—what if he's not trying to kill her after all? What if that's why he hasn't shot her yet? Maybe there's something else in play, some extra dimension, and he's just a local guy trying to save her from a situation she can't yet comprehend.

He shouts again. This time she hears: Don't want to hurt you.

Now Cambry's foot hovers over the pedals—gas or brake? Raycevic is catching up, just three feet behind her. Another few seconds and their cars will be exactly side by side, and they'll be able to turn their heads and make eye contact through the windows. No glass between them.

He's lying.

She gets it, in another wild flash of lightning: He needs to shoot her from a specific angle. He can't just blow a hole through his windshield, because he's still a cop with a day job, driving a state-issued vehicle, and that would be tough to explain to his sergeant. No, he needs to shoot her exactly sideways, through his open passenger window. That's why it's open. That's why he's pulling in close—for a clean, unimpeded shot.

He's almost perfectly parallel now. Raising his pistol, aimed at her.

She begs into the rushing air: "Please, please—"

Both vehicles pass another hump in the road. A moment of stomach-fluttering weightlessness, and then a hurtling downward crunch throws Cambry against her seat. She bites her tongue and almost loses her glasses. The time is 8:43 now. But she saw something.

Holy shit.

Dead ahead—yes, she knows she saw it—a pair of red taillights over the rise. Maybe a half mile out. She's not certain of the distance in the dark. She just knows she glimpsed the back of another vehicle, on this very same road. Traveling the same direction. Not far ahead.

Oh, God, there it is.

There's your witness.

CHAPTER 10

LENA

"SAVE HER FROM WHO?"

"Turn off the recorder." Raycevic nodded down at it, as if he knew he was being watched. "Turn it off, and I'll tell you."

"No deal."

His voice bristled. "*Turn it off.*"

"You're lying—"

"I'm not the bad guy, Lena." He clasped his hands together in a prayer-like gesture. The huge man was almost groveling. "Yes, I chased your sister on June sixth. Yes, I lied about it in my report—but for a good reason. She was driving like a bat out of hell, almost ninety, running scared. We were barreling down this winding road. I couldn't stop her. And she didn't trust me anymore—"

Lies. Every word of it could be lies.

"I wouldn't trust you, either, Ray."

"I couldn't make her stop. So . . ." He cleared his throat. "I pulled my gun on her. Not to shoot her. Just to try and force her to stop."

Yeah, no shit, she didn't trust you, Lena wanted to say. But she couldn't form the words. It was staggering, being in the presence of someone privy to Cambry's last moments alive. Lies or not. She caught herself leaning in, hanging on his words—because in a soul-sick way, yes, she wanted to believe Raycevic was telling her the truth. "You chased her. You pulled a gun on her. But how'd she die?"

"She killed herself."

"Bullshit." Back to this.

"She jumped off this bridge, right in front of me—"

"Yeah? Did she write that suicide text, too? *Hopefully you can live with it, Officer Raycevic?*"

"She did."

"That wasn't my sister's voice."

"It was, Lena. You just didn't know her."

"You're lying. You've already incriminated yourself." She remembered to breathe. She was firing questions faster than he could answer. Her sinuses ached—the start of a migraine. "Fine. Who were you trying to protect her from?"

Raycevic turned away.

He stared off Hairpin Bridge, refusing to look her in the eye. She almost grabbed his thick shoulder and tugged him back to face her. Just like Cambry in her dream (*Go, Lena*), everyone held all the answers but refused to talk. It was exasperating, being so close to the truth.

"I don't think you understand," he said. "I'm giving you one last chance. I'm not threatening you. You can still walk away, right now. Just go."

Just go, Cambry's ghost whispered in Lena's ear. *Lena, go.*

Please go—

"Leave Hairpin Bridge. Move forward, live your life, put your sister in the past, and honor her memory. There's nothing good for you here. The truth will wreck you." He licked his lips.

"We can go our separate ways, you and I, and we can let this situation be. Think long and hard."

She didn't have to. "I'm not leaving."

"You have to."

"I *can't.*"

"Walk away," he said again. "I'm begging you."

He was *begging* her.

His choice of words thrilled Lena, to be in such a position of power over this man in uniform, and she replied with something she immediately regretted, something that landed like a curse:

"Over my dead body."

THAT'S THE PLAN, LENA.

Corporal Raymond R. Raycevic pulled a long breath through his nose and looked away from her, off Hairpin Bridge's western overlook. On a clear blue day, a viewer could see past Magma Springs all the way into Watson County, and trace Silver Creek's hairline path all the way to Lake Saint Byron.

Today was not a clear day. Brown smoke clung to the hills like acrid rain clouds, gritty and poisonous. Visibility was less than a mile. The air tasted like charcoal. The Briggs-Daniels wildfire was indeed coming their way—he hadn't been lying about that—but at this point, Lena didn't believe anything he said. So be it. He'd tried, hadn't he? He'd warned her. He'd given her every opportunity to leave, to give up her search, to go home.

She was too determined.

He wished Cambry had never sent that goddamn suicide text before she died. It had unleashed dozens of chain reactions, tipping hundreds of dominoes, some of which were still quietly toppling three months later. All from one text message. One error.

And now it had brought nosy Lena to his doorstep. To be dealt with.

Over your dead body, indeed.

He should have smelled this trap from the very first email. No therapist on earth would endorse tracking down the cop who discovered your sister's corpse, driving to the very site of her suicide, and marinating in the hideous details. Asking about the blood and guts. From minute one, Lena had been too alert, too poised, to not have an agenda. Hell, even the email's subject line had been suspicious—*RE my sister's death on 6.6*—as eerily formal and detached as a party invite.

He stared out into the hazy horizon. He couldn't look at her. Eye contact was too much. How clever she must have felt. So pleased with herself. What arrogance, to expect to lure him out here and capture his admission on tape without incident.

You have no idea, he thought, with a twinge of sympathy. *You poor, grieving girl.*

Worse, he'd proven her right. He'd allowed himself to be drawn all the way out here into her snare on Hairpin Bridge. He'd been distracted this week after what happened on Thursday. He wasn't sleeping and his guard was down. That was on him. But cockiness is a killer—Ray knew this all too well—and Lena was getting there herself.

Because she'd already stepped into a snare, too.

These foothills of Howard County were a trap all their own—the nearest cell towers were split between Polk City and Magma Springs, and they were early generation. There was no signal anywhere on this road. Certainly none on Hairpin Bridge. If you mean to hunt a wolf, you pick an area that's advantageous to you. You don't crawl face-first into its dark, dripping den and challenge it to a debate. That was Cambry's first error—

Lena, he corrected himself. Lena's error. He had to stop doing that.

Hell, who brought more weapons to Hairpin Bridge today? His duty pistol was a Glock 19 with three spare mags. He had a Taser. Pepper spray. A .38 Special concealed on his ankle. And his big-boy gun, an AR-15 in the trunk. Even if you stripped all of the toys away, Ray was a big man, half protein shakes, built like a fridge. He could lift this tiny Asian girl in a one-handed suplex and smash her skull against the pavement. It wasn't even a contest.

What did Lena have? *A tape recorder.* How scary.

Because it was a well-documented fact that Hairpin Bridge received no cell service, Ray knew it was impossible for Lena to be recording him on an internet-connected gadget. It was only that clunky-looking analog recorder he had to worry about, and it was only here. Six feet away.

A recorder can be smashed.

So really, he could confess to anything on it. He didn't need to be so cautious. As long as he destroyed the recorder—alongside Lena's body—he'd be fine.

The problem was Lena.

Not the little bitch herself, but the trail she'd leave. Even with all the fuss over the Briggs-Daniels fire, there were witnesses at Magma Springs who could pin her to him. Lena was clearly a bit of a loner, like Cambry before her, but she wasn't stupid. She'd certainly told other people in her life—friends, roommates, family—what she'd planned. Where she was going. Who she was meeting. And perhaps why.

A disappearance wouldn't play well at all. He'd be suspect one. Again. How humiliating it was, to be on seven days of paid leave while some dick from Missoula rummages through your life. Not that his life was great now. His wife, Liza, refused to speak to him, which was honestly how he liked it. He hated looking at her. Every time he saw her, he swore he saw five new pounds of blubber jiggling on her upper arms or under her chin. So, best not to look at her.

He considered turning back around and surprising Lena right now, grabbing her by her shoulders and pitching her over the bridge's railing. He might be able to sell that. A tormented young woman decides to join her twin sister in death by committing suicide at the exact same site, stunning the hapless cop who brought her there. Gen Z and their avocado toast, huh? He liked the sound of it, but that was the problem. It was too neat. It wouldn't withstand the scrutiny—

"*Ray?*" she asked behind him. "Can we continue?"

He didn't look back. He couldn't. Christ, he hated this girl. He hated the smug deadpan of her voice. He hated the way she was forcing his hand.

He took another breath and decided: There would be no body. And he would craft an alibi later. Lena Nguyen would become one of the disappeared ones. As cutely poetic as it might be to hurl her smug ass off Hairpin Bridge and testify that she'd planned a suicide all along, it was simply too much. He had to be practical. Bodies make the news. Missing people don't.

Yes, he'd shoot her.

Here and now. As Rodney Atkins says: If you're going through hell, keep going.

"Ray? *Today,* please?"

He rested his palm on the checkered heel of his duty weapon. He breathed in again. Studied the smoky horizon. Feeling better now.

He'd turn around and do her quickly. No explanation. He owed Lena that much. She may have ruined Ray's day, she might've been the turd slapping into his cereal bowl to cap off a truly awful week, but it wasn't her fault. She was *reacting,* just like him. She was a lost soul sent spinning by grief, and she'd landed in something she couldn't possibly understand.

And he had to marvel: *The balls on her, to confront the wolf in its den.*

"You're something," he said. "You know that?"

Behind him, Lena said nothing.

"But you made a mistake," he said, quietly popping the holster's button with his thumb. "If it's all true, and I'm really a murderer, and I killed Cambry in cold blood, then you're a complete idiot for driving all the way out here with me, alone. And confronting me *without a gun*—"

He was interrupted by a metallic snick.

LENA NGUYEN HELD HER 9-MILLIMETER BERETTA PX4 STORM in both knuckled hands, aimed squarely at Corporal Raycevic's forehead. "That's why I didn't," she said.

He stared.

His eyes goggled. His lips agape. Dumb, oafish surprise, like he'd just discovered his car had been towed. In his shattered world, this gun must have materialized impossibly out of thin air, instead of from Lena's concealed waistband holster, where it had been all day.

Loose-fitting clothes, *for the win.*

For the past two hours, the pistol had been clamped to her lower back like an itchy tumor, clammy with sweat, and now it was finally in her hands, aimed at Raycevic.

The cop's palm was still frozen on his sidearm. Resting flat. The holster's button unclasped by his thumb. This was dangerous.

"Hands up," she hissed.

Still, he only stared back at her. Not defiant; just dumb. Pants-down disbelief. Maybe he'd forgotten he had his hand on a perfectly functional firearm. Or maybe he was just waiting for his chance.

"*Now,* Ray."

Finally, he lifted both hands. Palms out.

His department-issued Glock was Lena's primary concern. With the holster unbuttoned, he could grab it and fire in under a second. She considered stepping in close and grabbing the pistol herself, but she'd be within his reach. Vulnerable to a counter-attack. Raycevic had over a hundred pounds on her, and real combat in his muscle memory. Cops are trained to fight.

She decided she'd make him do it, instead. "Clasp your hands together. Behind your head."

Grudgingly, he did.

"Now turn around."

He did, his fingers interlocking behind his buzz cut. The dumbfounded stare had melted away into embarrassment. He was probably wishing he'd frisked her. How deeply humiliating it must be, being held at gunpoint by a twenty-four-year-old civilian.

She considered—again—reaching for his Glock and grabbing while he was facing away from her. But it was still too risky. His biceps looked like fat pythons. For a big guy, he could move fast.

Raycevic was too dangerous.

"Get down," she said. "On your knees."

"Are you going to shoot me?"

"Not if you get down."

He wavered for a moment, looking out at the smoky brown horizon, as if drawing strength from it, and then he lowered to the concrete. With his hands still clasped together behind his head, he hit his kneecaps on the roadway painfully. Left, then right.

Lena followed him down with the Beretta's sights. Her index finger on the trigger. This, she knew, would be the most dangerous part.

"Now, Ray," she said in a monotone, "when I instruct, you will slowly lower your right hand toward your gun. You won't turn around. You won't look back at me. You will slowly lift your gun out between two pinched fingers, holding it like it's a shitty diaper. And you'll toss it off the bridge." She crouched as she spoke, ten feet behind him in a careful marksman's stance.

Still kneeling, Raycevic seemed puzzled. "You're not going to . . ."

"What?"

"You're not going to take my gun?"

"It's a Glock."

"So?"

"I hate Glocks."

"*Seriously?*"

Lena fought a satisfied smirk. He'd made a lot of assumptions about her today, no doubt—and he sure as hell hadn't figured her for a gun nut.

The huge man sighed. He looked dizzy, nauseated. The tables had just turned on him so suddenly and violently. He was still disoriented by the power shift.

Lena was ready. She placed the Beretta's squared front sight center-mass, right on Raycevic's spine. She locked her elbows in an isosceles shooting stance. The pad of her index finger gently touching the trigger. She squeezed the pistol tightly enough to imprint the weapon's grip into her palms. *A good, tight grip makes for a good, tight shot,* as one of the instructional posters at Sharp Shooters said.

A drop of sweat hit the pavement.

She took a breath. Let it half out. "Now," she said. "Slowly."

The kneeling cop's right hand moved down toward his waist.

He flipped the holster's leather guard—already unbuttoned—in a smooth, instinctive motion—

"Hey. *Hey.* Slower—"

And he lifted the pistol by its heel, pinched between his index finger and thumb, exactly as ordered. It came up into view—a black, blocky thing, all right angles. Lena really did hate Glocks.

"Now throw it."

Still facing away, he raised it and flicked his wrist. The pistol twirled over Hairpin Bridge's guardrail and, after a few airy moments, lightly thumped two hundred feet below.

Three seconds, Lena thought. She'd been counting.

If Cambry was still conscious when Raycevic threw her off this bridge, she would have been alive for three full seconds of terrifying free fall.

"Can I stand now?" he asked.

"Nope." She studied his belt. "Throw your Taser, too. And your pepper spray. And that baton-looking thing right there."

"For Christ's sake—"

"And your keys. Definitely your keys."

One item at a time, Corporal Raycevic's state-issued gear vanished over the blistered guardrail and thumped down in the arroyo below. There was now only one firearm in play, and Lena controlled it—unless, of course, there was another in Raycevic's patrol car. She hadn't seen a rifle or shotgun mounted between the front seats, but there was the trunk to consider. This was why she'd asked him for his keys. They flew over the railing last of all, with a light jingle.

"That was a big key ring." Lena whistled. "Was one of those your house key?"

"It was. Are you done yet?"

"No. I'd like you to sing a song for me."

"Fuck you."

"Do you know any Katy Perry?"

"What you've just done is a felony," the cop said. "I'm turning around."

"Fine." Lena adjusted her grip on the Beretta. "But keep your hands up there, behind your head. And if you take a single step toward me, Ray, I swear to God, I will kill you."

"Doesn't matter. You've already assaulted an officer." He turned to face her with a dry squint. "You'll get ass-rammed in court. Nobody is going to care about your dead schizoid sister. You're looking at a class C with a firearm. You know what that means, right? Hope you didn't make plans for the next fifteen years. Hope you didn't want to *vote* afterward. What now?"

"You sing Katy Perry's 'Firework.'"

He spat onto the concrete between them. It landed heavily, a jellied glob.

"I'm not going to prison," she said. "You are."

He huffed again, red-faced in the sunlight. "Really, Lena? This is your plan? Hold me at gunpoint so I tell you a story? I *didn't kill your sister—*"

"You keep saying that."

"She killed herself."

"You *murdered* her, Ray. At nine P.M. on June sixth."

"I didn't. I'm starting to wish I had, though."

"Are you trying to get shot?"

He punched his chest. "Go ahead."

She'd expected the truth to come pouring out by now. On the drive here, she'd imagined Cambry's killer would try to barter with her, or even beg. But he was still defiant. Pissed off.

A question flickered through her mind: What if Ray was telling the truth? *What if he didn't actually kill her?*

Someone did.

She thought about Ray's twin brother, Rick. The convenience of that little sob story. Maybe he didn't really shoot himself at age eighteen. A twelve-gauge under the chin will obliterate a human head, right down to the dental records, after all. Maybe Rick was still alive and Ray was *protecting* him. If he'd always wanted to be a cop and he was rejected by the academy—hell, maybe he stole Ray's car and uniform one night and joyrode? And he took his fantasy too far and murdered Cambry, and now poor good-guy Ray Raycevic was struggling to keep a lid on it?

Unlikely? Yes. But no more unlikely than the official cover story. Or that poor Japanese man catching two A-bombs to the face in one week.

Worse, it meant Cambry's real killer was still out there.

She'd researched Raycevic's internet presence extensively in the weeks building up to this—she knew about his extended family in Arkansas, his test scores, his petty gun-forum arguments about what grain of .17 HMR is best for killing varmints—but his brother never, ever came up. It was as if he'd buried Rick himself. Just like Cambry.

And now Lena was here to dig.

"You know . . ." Corporal Raycevic ran his tongue over his lip. He studied the gun in her hands, and then the bridge's cracked roadway between them. Then his eyes lit up, as if struck by an idea. "How far apart would you say we're standing?"

She realized Raycevic was standing.

He'd been kneeling, just moments ago. *How did he do that?*

"I'm guessing . . . ten feet, maybe?" He played dumb. "Would you say we're standing about ten feet apart, give or take?"

"Get to your point."

"We train for what's called the *ten-foot doctrine*. Let's say a suspect is armed with a knife. And I have a firearm. If he's within ten feet of me, he's an imminent danger to my life."

"Because you're a crappy shot?"

"I took the regional centerfire bronze with my AR-15 last

year," he said coldly. "No, Lena. Because guns don't have the stopping power you see in movies. You know that, right? You've shot that Beretta before, I hope? You didn't just steal it from Dad's closet. You know how to load and unload it? Clear jams? Where the safety is?"

She said nothing.

He squinted. "You do have the safety off, right?"

Still, she said nothing.

"See, getting shot doesn't send the victim flying backward into a wall, like in the movies. Newton's first law: the force is only equal to the weapon's recoil in the operator's hand. So, if a suspect with a knife has decided he wants to stab me, I can fatally shoot him several times as he crosses the ten-foot distance between us, and he can still cut my throat before he succumbs to his wounds."

He studied the ten feet between them, his lips moving. He was making a show of counting the paces it would take.

Then he glared back up at her, his voice slowing, hardening to a menacing whisper. "I don't have my Taser anymore. But I'm a strong guy. I can bench three-ten. And I'd wager, Lena, that I can probably break your neck with just my hands. Even if you shoot me three times on my way to you, I'll still snap your spine between my fingers before I bleed out. Unless you can shoot my heart or my brain. Think about it, Lena. Can you hit a moving target, that fast?"

"They're both pretty small targets," Lena said.

He lost it. "Jesus *fucking* Christ—"

"I bet a groin shot would work, too."

"You're playing with fire, girl."

"I mean to," she said, taking aim and closing her right eye.

She put the Beretta's front sight into sharp focus and allowed the two rear sights to blur. So did Raycevic. The key, she knew, was that front sight. That dark little block. A strange truth of marksmanship, and maybe life—that to hit your target, you must allow it out of focus.

"You're bluffing. You need me alive, Lena." He stared down the barrel. "Because you need to know what I know. You can't shoot me. You'd like to, but you can't and you won't. The gun you're pointing at my head is just an empty threat."

She watched his smirk grow.

"You desperately need the information up here." He tapped his temple. "That still puts me at an advantage, because I know that no matter what, you won't dare pull the tri—"

She pulled the trigger.

IT HIT RAY AS A DEAFENING EXPLOSION OF PRESSURIZED AIR. A blast of heat and scorched grit on his cheeks, rattling his teeth, warping his eardrums.

This is it, he thought—this girl had just killed him. She'd just blown his brains out over Hairpin Bridge to dry under the scorching summer sun. It was all over, instant oblivion, *Do Not Pass Go, Do Not Collect Two Hundred Dollars,* and no one would help his father remember his Sunday meds or explain to his wife what had happened, or cover up all of his secrets, like the dead kid rotting at the bottom of his well, as the neurons in his brain fired a final salvo and a random memory flashed: *A child's shoe.* Red and white, with two Velcro straps—

No. He pushed it away.

I'm a good guy.

Then he hit a kneecap on the concrete and caught himself with an outstretched palm, his ears ringing a warbling bird cry. And following the concussive boom of Lena's gunshot, a strange and metallic sound reached his ears. Like a . . . *slap?* He didn't know how else to describe it.

He looked up through watery eyes, blinking away scorched gunpowder, and saw Lena still standing in a rigid shooting stance, aiming over and past him. Then she fired again, two more ear-splitting blasts, as rapid as a double-clicked mouse.

Ray flinched again.

He realized Lena wasn't aiming at him—she hadn't been aiming at him on the first shot, either—as he heard two more distinct metallic slaps. The same sounds he couldn't place.

They came from behind him.

Still on a knee, he turned around as the echoes faded, in time to see that three-by-three-foot UNINSPECTED BRIDGE sign still wobbling on its post, as if disturbed by wind. It stood at the bridge's entrance, just above the structure's famous Marbleworks twist, a full fifty yards back. Too far to discern the small-caliber bullet holes that were most certainly punched through it.

She'd shot the sign.

From fifty yards.

Three times, in rapid succession: slap, slap, slap.

He looked up at her—again—as she lowered her aim back to him. His right eardrum still rang furiously. Her first shot, before he'd reflexively hit the deck, had been close. The bullet might've passed within inches of his right earlobe. He could be facing permanent hearing damage in that ear.

None of this was on Ray's mind. He was still stuck on what he'd just witnessed, paralyzed by it, and he couldn't fathom how this small-boned, doll-like Vietnamese girl could drill a target three times, half a football field away like that. At *twice* a hand-gun's effective range.

"Yeah," she said. "I know where the safety is, asshole."

His mind raced: *Where . . .*

"Next one goes through your balls, Ray. How's that for an *empty threat?*"

He hated himself for flinching, for undermining his own

ten-foot doctrine and wavering in the face of her sudden gun-fire, in spite of all of his training. But still he had to marvel at her, openmouthed.

Where in the hell did she learn to shoot like that?

———————

Surprise: I took up a new hobby.

I should clarify, dear readers, that I've always had an entry-level familiarity with firearms—our father had insisted, to our mother's chagrin, that both of his twin girls know how to shoot and clean a Ruger 10/22—but after Cambry's bizarre suicide and my ensuing emotional tailspin, I found myself desperately needing a refuge.

Some people find Jesus.

I found shooting.

I immersed myself in it. I sold my TV and spent $900 on a pistol—a Beretta Px4 Storm in 9-millimeter. I memorized the manual. I watched YouTube instructional videos. I bought a membership at a local indoor range where women shoot for free on weekdays. Boy, did I hold them to it.

In just over two months, I estimate I put ten thousand rounds downrange. Probably more.

At the front counter you can buy poster-size paper targets for fifty cents each: shambling zombies, cartel thugs holding big-breasted hostages, the always-deserving Jar Jar Binks. My favorite, though, is "The Deck of Fifty-Two." It's exactly what it sounds like: a pack of life-size playing cards arranged on a grid. I tape it up and send it to twenty-five feet, thumb fifteen rounds into the seventeen-round mag, and then slowly and systematically fire five-shot groups into every card, one at a time. Left to right. Three cards per reload. Two hundred and sixty rounds a day.

Every weekday, a new deck of fifty-two.

My first week or so, I struggled to keep my hits on the intended cards. But I persisted. I recognized my bad habits and corrected them. I kept punching paper Monday through Friday in a rote routine, left to right, five per card, three per mag. By week three, I was proud to see my shot groups shrinking to the size of a grapefruit. Now at week nine, my bullet holes almost always touch, like ragged little clovers of scorched paper.

And that's just the live ammo. Double that—maybe triple it—in dry-fires. I practiced trigger control by firing plastic dummy cartridges (snap caps) many more times a day inside my apartment with the blinds drawn, until the pads of my fingers were raw and blistered.

The key to marksmanship is squeezing the trigger without allowing your body to anticipate the blast. The gunshot should surprise even you, the shooter. Otherwise your muscles tense in anticipation and your flinch contaminates the shot. It's like shooting hoops or honing your golf swing—all about good habits. I dry-fire every morning after waking up, take the bus to work, hit the range to live-fire into a deck of fifty-two on the way home, research Cambry's death for a few hours in the evening, dry-fire another couple hundred times, and collapse into bed weary, soul-sick, on an empty stomach. Monday through Friday. Repeat.

I dry-fired into my chin once.

For research, dear readers! I promise.

I admit, I was curious what it would feel like. What might have gone through Cambry's mind if she really did contemplate suicide at the edge of Hairpin Bridge, hanging by her fingertips at the knife edge of oblivion. (Turns out it felt exactly like any other trigger pull. The human body knows when it's being fooled, I guess.)

I called it a hobby earlier, but I'll be honest: there's no joy in it. I don't give a shit about the craft or the sport. I sample-fired a few—a Glock, which I hated, and a SIG Sauer, which I liked but couldn't afford—before choosing the perfectly adequate Beretta. To me, shooting is a rote action, as grim as facing the aisles at work. Whether I'm pushing papers at two or punching holes in them at six, it all feels about the same.

I had bad nights.

Bad weeks.

If I'm honest, all three months have been pretty awful.

But every minute of it, I grew increasingly certain that this stranger who phoned my family, this Corporal Raymond Raycevic, was involved in Cambry's death. It was in her suicide text. It was in his *voice*. Somehow I knew it. This conviction built in me, every day. It was the reason I got out of bed in the morning, drank a thermos of black coffee, and dry-fired beside my bathroom mirror, so I could pretend Cambry was watching in my reflection, urging me to keep practicing, to keep pulling that trigger. It was my lifeline in the darkness: my sister didn't kill herself, because someone *killed* her. And with every 9-millimeter hole I ripped through a playing card, and every click of a firing pin striking a snap cap, I was hardening myself to take the bastard down.

For Cambry.

I can't emphasize enough how valuable it is to be doing *something*. Even if it's this. If I didn't have this crusade, I don't know what I would have done. Ghost hunting, maybe? Painting?

And even still, on the bad nights when the trains are loud and the bedsheets cling with sweat and I can't sleep, the worst thing I can fathom is driving all the way out to Montana . . . only to discover I have it wrong. That poor old Raymond, perhaps out there writing a speeding ticket right now, is just a normal God-fearing guy and not the secret monster I've convinced myself he is. That Cambry really did drive out to that remote bridge, leave her car idling on an empty tank, and leap over the guardrail to her death, her atoms rejoining a pointless universe of dead stars.

That terrifies me some nights. Keeps me awake.

Yes, I might be wrong.

I have my deep, diamond-hard conviction, but the truth is: I won't truly know until tomorrow. When I'm face-to-face with him. Standing on the very bridge Cambry allegedly jumped from.

And I'm not walking into this rendezvous unarmed. He'll underestimate me—especially at first, when I show up carrying a laughably outdated Shoebox recorder—but I sure as hell won't underestimate him. If I'm right, he's a man with the competence of a cop and the savagery of a criminal. I'll be grateful for my Beretta and every minute of bloody-fingered practice with it.

All of this gun talk isn't to brag. I'm a respectable shot now, but I have no formal training. I've never been in a gunfight. I don't know jujitsu or anything. Charlize Theron in *Atomic Blonde* would still thoroughly kick my ass. But grief leaves you reeling, empty-handed, searching for a devil to rage against. I guess I'm fortunate, then, that I found mine, and he turned out to be very real.

Cambry: However tomorrow unfolds, I promise I will get him. I'll trap him. I'll make him confess to the entire world what he did to you on June 6, and what he truly is.

I do know this: he's not a cop.

He's a man-size insect that crawled into a uniform. Whatever his formal decorations may say, he's hiding a monstrous act in his closet, and he's a disgrace to every brave man and woman with a badge. He's a wrong that needs to be righted.

I'll get him, sis.

SHE'S GOT ME.

Ray knew he was in a decidedly tight spot here. Held at gunpoint under a hammering afternoon sun. His words recorded. His Glock, his Taser, his keys, all at the bottom of the ravine. He couldn't reach the radio in his vehicle, or the AR-15 in his trunk. But he still had one final hope: a holdout weapon on his ankle. A snub-nosed five-shooter in .38 Special gripped in a tight holster against his sock, clammy with sweat.

Lena didn't know about it.

She'd backed up to twenty feet away, keeping the pistol trained on him. Her posture was relaxing a bit, he noticed. Her elbows bending. She was coming down from the adrenaline kick. You can't live dialed up to ten, after all. Your body won't allow it. Sooner or later, you'll have to settle back down to a seven or eight, and so, too, would Cambry's revenant.

She's nothing special, Ray decided as his stomach growled. *She's not like her sister. She's not a survivor. She's not a killer.*

She's just a mixed-up girl with a gun.

For all her posturing, her tough talk, and even her trick shooting, Lena was still in hopelessly over her head here. She had no idea who Cambry was. No idea what she'd stumbled into. And no—she *definitely* didn't know about the revolver on his ankle.

Otherwise it would be at the bottom of the ravine, with his other equipment.

Ray just needed to hike up his trouser leg and grab it. That was, maybe, a one-second motion. Another second, he estimated, to crouch, take aim, and fire. Lena was a formidable markswoman, clearly, but all he had to do was shoot first.

I just need an opening. He watched her.

She took another step back. She was looking anxious, seasick. A pallor in her cheeks. A growing tremor in her hands. Coming down from the high does that. She'd probably murdered scores of paper targets—but what about the real thing? The real thing shoots back.

"What's wrong?" he asked her.

She didn't answer.

"Huh?" He couldn't resist. "You didn't plan this far ahead?"

Instead of speaking, the young woman did something unexpected. She switched her grip on the weapon in her right hand, now unsupported (Ray considered making a move for his .38

Special now, but didn't), and she drew her left hand back to her loose hair. She curled a lock around her index finger and, in a wincingly sharp motion, twisted it.

Just like he'd seen Cambry do, in that same vehicle, three months ago.

They really are twins, he thought.

He knew this shouldn't get under his skin—hair-twisting is a common nervous tic, like nail-biting—but it still felt, in some strange way, like he was outnumbered. Like the dead girl from June and the living girl here were the *same person,* somehow, united against him. Two versus one. Here to punish him for his sins. He thought about the dead kid in his well and swallowed with a dry throat.

Lena was back to holding the Beretta with two hands.

Ray's .38 was growing heavy on his ankle now. Life or death would come down to a few flinching seconds. He rehearsed it mentally: dropping to a knee, tugging up his right pant leg (*one one-thousand*), grabbing the revolver's checkered grip and twisting it free (*two one-thousand*), aiming it up at her, finding a sight picture on her chest, squeezing the trigger (*three one-thousand*), and . . . well, that's it. Either he'd hit her or he'd miss.

His odds were decent enough. If you stacked him and Lena together on a shooting range, she might shoot the tighter groups on paper. But real life isn't a shooting range. There's confusion, fatigue, adrenaline, fear. Sweat on your fingers. Sunlight in your eyes. The *pucker factor,* his father called it.

He could see it now—a tremor to the weapon's barrel. Lena's forearms were getting tired. She wasn't exactly built for this. The longer this skinny little thing held her stance, the more her accuracy would degrade. She was vulnerable.

He pushed a little harder. "You have a blog, right?"

She looked vaguely surprised.

"*Lights and Sounds*. Nerd shit. You review text-based video games, sci-fi novels about spaceships, weird-ass horror movies. Confessions of a retail worker. That's you, right?"

She blinked.

I hit a nerve, he thought. *Good.*

"Don't be surprised." He smirked. "You researched me. I had to research you, too."

He was waiting for her to twist her hair again. Then he would draw while her guard was down. It would take her precious moments to reform her shooting stance and accurately return fire. Nervous tics are nice. They make you predictable.

"You don't have many friends, do you?" He kept pushing. "Or a boyfriend?"

She said nothing.

"Or leave your apartment much?"

Nothing.

"Social anxiety, maybe?" He rolled his shoulders in a faux stretch, loosening up to draw. "You're twenty-four. College-educated. English major. You work at an electronics store on the verge of Chapter Eleven, making minimum wage and spending your evenings alone on your computer, laboring away on a blog that nobody reads. And your sister was out experiencing things, seeing white desert and Mount Rushmore and the Everglades and glass beaches. You were jealous, huh?" He studied her face, imagining the bloody crater his .38 Special would make. "You have no idea who Cambry really was, by the way."

He dropped that like trash and waited for her reaction.

She didn't react at all.

Fine. He continued: "You know what? When we first got here, I thought you were just a sad-sack introvert who'd never gotten laid. I felt sorry for you. I genuinely wanted to help you achieve some sort of peace here with your grief. Before I knew you brought a gun and an agenda. But you mentioned . . . hey, you wanted gory details, right?"

He gave her time to answer. She didn't.

"Yeah, you did. You wanted to know what Cambry's body looked like down there on the rocks. And back then, I didn't share details, because it would've been inappropriate. But we're past that now. Far past it." He stared down the gun. "Your sister looked like she *melted*, Lena."

Her jaw quivered. Just a faint twitch of her lip—but he noticed.

"At free fall, she'd been traveling over a hundred feet per second. To decelerate from that velocity to zero, against solid granite, basically makes every organ in your body weigh ten thousand times more than normal. So even though she was still human-shaped . . . well, it's like being ripped apart on a cellular level. Total annihilation. Her organs burst and leaking. Her brain liquefied. Her bones full of cracks. Big brown water balloons of blood pooling under her skin."

Tears glimmered in Lena's eyes. She reached for her hair—and then she changed her mind, restoring her two-handed grip on the weapon.

Ray's heart heaved. *Do it.*

He was ready to draw. His thumb and fingers kneaded the air with anticipation. He pushed again: "Cambry's forehead was crushed in, like a stomped grapefruit. She had bugs in her mouth. Her eyeballs were soggy, blown out on strings, leaking tears of blood. Flies burrowing in, laying eggs."

Lena took this all in, like a stone. Saying nothing. Giving nothing.

And she looked exactly like you, he almost added.

He knew he was getting to her. Every word left an imprint. Some left dents. All adding up. She was about to break, to cave in and twist her hair again. He was ready.

You have no idea who you've tangled with, he thought as he studied her. *You poor, dumb girl. You think you're the wolf here, just because you can shoot.*

The .38 was a tumorous lump on his ankle, begging to be let free. Lena adjusted her shooting stance again, and Ray's hand nearly went for it. Almost. She was trying to fight her tic— trying—but she couldn't resist her own nature. She needed to twist her hair again. It was her sensory comfort, her weakness, and today it would get her killed.

I'll blow your smug face off.

As long as I have my hands—

"Wait. You still have handcuffs, right?" Lena looked at his belt. "Cuff yourself, asshole."

SHE WAS SURPRISED—THE COP LOOKED SUDDENLY CREST-fallen. He stared down at his slacks, and then back up at her. A strange, furious disbelief.

Good. She would feel better with the big ape handcuffed. He was too dangerous, even at gunpoint. She drew the Beretta's sights to his face, trying to hide the tremor in her arms. "I said *cuff yourself.* Slowly."

His glare intensified. Fear stirred in her gut.

In answer, she curled her index finger into the trigger guard. He saw.

Then his right hand moved—"Hey. *Slowly.*"—toward his belt, and he unlatched two metal rings. They jingled faintly, making that cliché sound they do on television.

"Cuff your hands behind your back," she clarified. "Not in front."

"I need to kneel," he said, gesturing down toward his ankle. "To get them around my back, it'll be easier if I crouch and—"

"Nope. Do it standing."

He glared at her again.

"Go on." She pointed with the Beretta.

For a long breath, Raycevic held the silver cuffs in one hand, like he was trying desperately to think of something else to say. To stall. Then, grudgingly, he fastened them around one wrist and tucked his arm behind his back. His other wrist engaged unseen with a scissor-like snick.

"There. Happy?"

"No," she said. "Turn around."

"Excuse me?"

"Turn around. So I can see both hands are cuffed."

He rolled his eyes. Then, reluctantly, he turned to show her both wrists behind his back. As she expected, only his right was secured. His left hand held the cuff inside his palm.

"You really thought that would work?"

He grinned wolfishly. "It was worth a try."

"Try harder."

"Say that again."

"*Try harder?*"

"You sounded exactly like her. The way you said it."

"You can cuff your other hand now, Ray."

He turned sideways so she could watch him slip the cuff around his left wrist. Then he fumbled. "I . . . I can't do it from behind my back. I'll need you to help close the cuff with your—"

"Seriously, Ray?"

After another pause, the faux surprise vanished from his eyes. Another act tried and discarded.

That's right. Keep underestimating me.

"Worth a try," he repeated, without the grin this time. With his right thumb he closed the cuff around his left wrist. Then he spread his bulging arms, ratcheting the metal jaws tight. "Happy?"

"Getting there," Lena said, easing her grip on the pistol, letting her muscles rest. Pins and needles in her fingers. "And by the way—all that stuff about the state of Cambry's body? Awful as it was, with the liquefied guts and the blown-out eyes, my nightmares were still worse. So thank you, Ray. For shining a light on the monster for me."

He smiled. "Careful what you ask for."

More ashes drifted between them on silent winds, gray and darting. Like the half-glimpsed spots that float in your eyes. Lena blinked on reflex.

He didn't. He stared at her coldly, cinders collecting on his shoulders like apocalyptic snow. "If you shoot me, you'll never know what happened to her."

"I already know."

"Do you?"

"You confirmed it. When you lied to me."

"Yeah? So far, the only person who's drawn a gun is you, Lena." He squinted into the smoky distance. "And if anyone were to drive by and see us here, this situation would look an awful lot like a trooper under attack."

"Good thing you locked the gate."

His eyes narrowed. "Good thing."

For both of us, she knew he meant.

It didn't matter that they were speaking right now. It was only air and noise. If she let her guard down for a split second, Raycevic would seize his chance and headbutt her, kick the gun from her hands, and crunch her skull under his size 14 boot. Even handcuffed, he could kill her. Mercilessly. The way he killed Cambry. She imagined her sister's face dented, concave— *like a stomped grapefruit.*

It was real. All of it. It really happened.

She would never admit this to Raycevic, but for the past

weeks she'd nurtured a secret and childish hope: that when she arrived here at Hairpin Bridge, the internet myths would turn out to be real. She'd witness a spectral ghost or hear a whisper. The veil between past and present would be thin here, and her sister wouldn't be gone. Not really. Maybe Cambry was reliving her final hours at this very second, her story unfolding parallel to Lena's like a reflection.

Hope is poison. Lena knew this.

She exhaled and tried to clear her mind. No ghosts. No echoes from the past or messages from the grave. Just a guilty man, staring back at her.

He wrinkled his nose. "You're not really writing a book about her. Are you?"

"I am."

"Why?"

She knew she didn't have to answer. But she did anyway, and this time she didn't have the energy to lie: "It bothers me when other people tell Cambry's story. When she died, it's like she stopped being a person and became public property. She became this troubled loner who got sad and jumped off a bridge. If anyone can or *should* tell her story . . . it's me."

She almost left it there. But he was still waiting.

So she spoke the hard part: "My mom is a strict Catholic. And she's heartbroken, because she believes Cambry is in hell. Because she committed . . . you know."

"I see."

"That's it." She felt her cheeks flush. "That's all of it, I think. I . . . I guess I just wanted to prove to my mom that her daughter isn't in hell."

"So here you are."

"Here I am."

Silence.

She didn't like opening up to him. She knew she was only handing him blades to cut her with. But she got the strange sense he was mourning, too. Like they shared Cambry, somehow.

She hadn't told him the full truth, anyway.

After the service, she'd visited her parents' house in Olympia to bring them dinner and noticed the pictures of Cambry were all gone. Some walls and shelves were still freshly bare, with lines etched in dust. At first Lena assumed the photos were being displayed elsewhere or reframed, but in the following weeks they never reappeared. Her sister had left them all with something deeper than the normal grief of having, loving, and losing. They never *had* her to begin with. She was always a runner, always looking out over the next hill, and now she was infinitely farther away than Texas or Florida. And worse, it's a pretty shitty faith dilemma to have. If their God exists, their daughter is burning in hell. If He doesn't, she's gone entirely on a cellular level. Which is worse?

That night her mother drank too much wine and gripped Lena's wrist tightly enough to leave bruised finger marks. She said through shimmering eyes: *You're my daughter, Lena, and I love you.*

You're my one daughter.

It's sickening, becoming an only child in an instant.

This was the moment Lena decided she wouldn't just capture her sister's killer. She would tell Cambry's story, too. It was too important to be told by anyone else. She would give her mother and father a version of their daughter they could remember and love. A version that didn't steal from their wallets, that didn't get arrested for shoplifting, that didn't reek of weed and cigarettes and barrel out the door at age eighteen to never call them back, and that didn't leave them now for real, just as cruelly and abruptly.

The true Cambry was out there somewhere. Lena would find her. At any cost.

Raycevic studied her. She regretted giving him this.

"Trust me." He smirked. "If hell exists, Cambry is there."

"Keep talking and I'll send you there myself."

"Scary line. Did you hear that in a movie?"

"I know what you are, Ray."

"No, you don't. You came into this with your mind made up already. That's your fatal flaw, Lena. See, I'm not a bad person. Even if I was—let's say I really did take your sister's life—I've saved lives, too. Multiple people are breathing today, right now, because of my actions. You've researched me. So you know my record. You've read about the woman I rescued from the river."

She had.

"My commendation for saving a deputy under fire."

Yes, she had.

"The kids I pulled out of the burning trailer."

Yes, yes, *yes*. The governor had even presented him with a medal. Somewhere in Billings was a park bench named in honor of the valorous Saint Raycevic, who charged heroically into a meth-lab fire. She wished the damn kids had burned up in there, just so he couldn't gloat about it.

"You may hate me, but I'm still one of the good guys, Lena." He stood straighter, seeming to swell and grow before her eyes. "Okay? You can't argue that four isn't a bigger number than one. That's still a total gain of three people. *Three* human beings who should be worm food right now, but aren't, because of me. Because of what I do. I work my ass off at it. I'm born to do this. I protect the public. More accurately, I *save* people. I have saved people. God willing, I will keep saving people. Why would all of those lives, past, present, and future, add up to less than your sister's?"

A line of spittle hung off his chin. He licked it back up, lizard-like.

Now we're getting somewhere, Lena thought. "Are you confessing?"

"No," he said. "I'm defending myself from a personal attack."

"Do you believe in hell?"

"I believe in balancing the scales."

Balancing the scales. Like being a good person boiled down to math.

"Okay, well, here comes another personal attack: You murdered my *fucking* sister, Ray. And you had to cover it up. So you threw her body off the bridge, to stage it like another suicide—"

"Nope. Try again."

"You beat her to death first—"

"That leaves bruising."

"Or you strangled her."

"That leaves ligature marks—"

"Not always. Not if you had her head in a plastic bag."

"She died on impact. The M.E. ruled it."

"Okay. You picked her up and threw her off the bridge, then, while she was still alive." Lena struggled to keep her voice level, controlled. "*Why?*"

"You're still wrong."

"Then enlighten me, Ray."

"Why would I do that?" He chewed his lip, the daylight vanishing from his eyes. "You want something, Lena. That makes you controllable. Because for as long as what you want is inside my head, you won't dare put a hole in it."

She realized she had nothing to say to this. It enraged her. For a moment she considered making good on her threat and shooting him in the balls.

Am I ready to do that?

She wasn't sure. Her hands stank with gunpowder from the

three shots fired already. There was something unsettling to firing a gun outside of the structured confines of the range. It was real now. It made her oddly self-conscious. Like driving barefoot.

He smirked. "You assumed I'd just cooperate?"

He'd read her. It was his job to read people, and he'd already identified Lena as a rule follower. Face-to-face conflict made her cheeks burn. She was naturally passive—making plans only when others suggested, speaking only when spoken to, taking action only when absolutely necessary. And now here she was on Hairpin Bridge, holding the gun, making the demands.

"Now what, Lena?"

It should be Cambry here, she knew. *Not me.*

I should be the dead one.

Back when Lena and Cambry were twelve, they used to spend summers at their uncle's farmhouse in east Oregon. The farm itself was perfectly boring for a kid—the cable was pixelated and the alpacas were prissy assholes. But a mile down the road, the neighbor kids had a rope swing over a creek, and occasionally their father blew up tree stumps with Tannerite. One walk back under a darkening evening sky, the Nguyen twins came across a brown shape on the road.

It was a whitetail doe, struck by a logging truck and dragged under the tires. Her eyes found them drowsily. Lena remembered watching the animal try to stand with a severed spine, her hind legs flat and limp. When she tried to brace her front leg, the knee bent backward like a broken stick. She cried a strange throaty whisper, like a cat's purr. In her twelve years, Lena had never felt so powerless before. She couldn't touch the suffering animal. She couldn't walk away. She couldn't do anything at all, and she hated herself for it. She just stood and stared and cried until her throat was raw.

At this time, twelve-year-old Cambry quietly slid off her backpack (even back then, she preferred to carry a pack) and knelt with one palm on the doe's ribs to feel the gentle rise and fall of her breaths.

With her other, she cut the animal's throat.

It should be her here. Lena wiped her eyes. *Out on this bridge, facing a duplicitous killer cloaked in a badge and a uniform.*

Not me.

"Don't you . . ." Raycevic eyed the Shoebox recorder. "Don't you need to change out VCR tapes on that piece of shit?"

She'd forgotten about it. The cassettes recorded ninety minutes. She tried to remember—how many minutes had it been now? Seventy? Eighty? There couldn't be much time left. And she'd be vulnerable when she flipped the tape over. She would make Raycevic lie down for that part.

"You're something." He studied her. "You work at an electronics store, and that's the best you could do? Digital mics are, like, forty bucks—"

"Practice ammo is expensive."

"You should have stayed home, Lena. In my line of work, you learn to pick out the wolves from the sheep, and you're one hundred percent sheep." He looked her up and down. "Is there a spiritual angle to this? You think Cambry's ghost sent you here to get me? Did you dream about her or something?"

Lena, go. She pushed her sister's voice out of her mind.

Please, go—

"Are you trying to prove you're as tough as she was?"

"No. Cambry was always the tough one, and I accept that." She was aware that Raycevic was steering the conversation, dominating her even while at gunpoint. She bit her lip, and it came out like a slashed vein, despite herself: "Sometimes I used to think that my sister and I were the same person, just cut in half. Like that's what twin siblings are, on a cellular level. Our shapes are jagged, incomplete. I got the book smarts. She got the street smarts—"

He snorted derisively.

She looked him in the eye. "Rick got the morals, didn't he?"

"Cambry sure didn't."

"What?"

"You heard me."

"What does *that* mean?"

"You know. After what she did to her boyfriend in Florida." She stopped.

"You . . . you knew about that, right?"

She shook her head.

"Really?" He rolled his eyes. "Your sister drove off after they got the windshield repaired. Just left poor Blake at a gas station out by Fort Myers with a few dollars in his pocket. She stole *everything*. Their shared supplies, the money in the lockbox, his trailer—"

No, she wanted to say.

No, that's backward. Blake ditched her. He left her. He was Terrible Guy #17.

"She stole his pistol, too," Raycevic said. "A little .25-caliber Baby Browning—"

"They interviewed Blake?"

"They did, yeah."

"He lied, then. He stole from her—"

"I'm curious how you'll explain this part, Lena. If your sister had Blake's gun with her on June sixth, why didn't she defend herself with it? When I chased her?"

She didn't have it. That's why.

There was no record of a .25-caliber Baby Browning, whatever that was, recovered in her car. Ditto for her KA-BAR knife.

She was robbed in Florida. That was how it happened.

Lena had planned for this. Corporal Raycevic had everything to lose. Of course he would lie. She'd expected to disregard or challenge most of what he said today. This conversation was already a mistake. She shouldn't have let her walls down, even an inch. He would do anything to get under her skin, to tip her off balance, to dull her reflexes—

He glanced sharply left. He saw something.

Lena followed his gaze—backing up a step in case it was another trick, to keep him in her sight—and scanned the hills off Hairpin Bridge, but saw nothing. Just gauzy, toxic smoke. Much thicker now. Pines turned to prickly shadows in the mist.

Looking away from him made her nervous. She glanced back at him.

He nodded. "See it?"

"See *what?*"

"There."

She squinted again. Just acres of gritty smoke.

He's toying with me.

"Take my cuffs off," he said. "I'll point it out for you."

"You're a funny guy."

"Your sister thought so." He grinned, all crusty teeth.

Again, she almost shot him where he stood. Her finger found the Beretta's trigger, her guts squirming like a ball of centipedes. She saw red, the warm spurt staining Cambry's hands like brake fluid as she sliced the doe's throat, and she wanted to scream in his face: *What do you see out there, Ray? Cut the mysterious crap. What the hell do you see?*

That smug, creeping smile. "It's getting closer."

She looked again, searched for the road's hairline path among the trees, and now she saw it along the valley of Silver Creek. Maybe a half mile out. A dark smudge in the dirty air. Inching into clarity.

An approaching vehicle.

CHAPTER 11

"THIS IS A CLOSED ROAD," SHE WHISPERED.

He shrugged theatrically.

"I *saw* you lock the gate—"

Another shrug. "The combination gets out."

"Did you call someone?" She looked him up and down, searching his brown uniform for a shoulder radio, a microphone, anything she could've missed. "Is that your backup coming?"

"I told you. Truckers use this road to make a shortcut to the north, to hit I-90 without passing through Magma Springs. It's illegal, but it saves about an hour—"

"Did you call someone?"

"I didn't call anyone."

"When you were in your car earlier, on your radio—"

"If I'd called someone," he said icily, "you'd hear sirens."

She repositioned left, so she could watch both Raycevic and the incoming vehicle. She kept the Beretta trained on the big man, but her arms were still shaky. Her body was fatiguing. If she were back at Sharp Shooters, firing at her usual deck of fifty-two, her five-shot groups would be inexorably drifting off the cards. She wasn't even sure if she could hit that sign now.

Raycevic laughed, as if he'd peeked into her mind and liked what he saw. It was a harsh chainsaw sound that originated deep in his belly. She had never heard this man laugh before and found it profoundly ugly. "This guy . . . he's going to drive right past us. He'll see everything—"

"Shut up."

"Who looks like the bad guy here?"

She couldn't let herself appear nervous because that would only delight him. But this was a serious problem, approaching fast. Raycevic was exactly right: to an uninvolved party, she'd certainly look like the aggressor, holding a uniformed cop at gunpoint.

Shit. She hadn't anticipated this. This road was supposed to be locked and closed. Isolation was the plan, the assumption, and why she didn't just meet this murderer for coffee in a Starbucks—

"He'll see your gun," he whispered.

"So?" She forced a confident shrug. "He'll call the police. Your buddies will show up. We'll all go to the station and I'll tell them everything. That helps me."

"Does it?"

"The truth will come out."

"You're sure?" he said. "You're recording me this whole time, yeah, but what have you really learned? Go ahead. Listen to the whole thing. You're holding a cop at gunpoint, so step one is you getting arrested. Do you think you have enough evidence right now to prove that I killed your sister?"

"You admitted to following her. On tape."

"Tapes can disappear."

"You're *literally* saying that on tape."

She wondered how deep his professional connections were. In the fuss of her own arrest, could he really make the recording disappear? Could his career really withstand all of the added scrutiny at this point? It seemed impossible. Unbelievable. The world doesn't work like that.

"What if my buddies shoot you?" Raycevic supposed. "You are holding a gun."

"We'll sort it out." She watched the vehicle draw closer. It was a red eighteen-wheeler, she could now tell. It charged uphill through the hazy air. Sunlight glinted fiercely off the windshield.

A minute away. Maybe less.

"Yeah?" He licked his lips, glancing between her and the oncoming truck. "I don't think you really want interference, Lena. Any more than I do. Because you're here to solve a mystery that's been tormenting you at night. And you haven't solved it yet."

"And you haven't killed me yet."

He smiled.

We both have unfinished business, don't we?

"Here's the deal," Raycevic said. "I'll tell you exactly what happened to Cambry. How she died. What I saw happen. If you just hide your gun, please, so that dickweed thinks I'm just pulling you over for a traffic violation and keeps driving."

Lena said nothing. Thirty seconds now.

"My handcuffs are a giveaway. I have a backup key in my vehicle, if you'll help me take them off," he said. "And I'll stand here and pretend to be writing you a citation—"

"Try harder, Ray."

"Got a better plan?"

She didn't.

She glanced at the Shoebox recorder, still listening, and wondered what she'd really captured so far. How much of Raycevic's description of Cambry's last moments was true or even reliable. He'd pulled her over. She'd bolted. He'd chased her. She'd eluded him, first with a daring one-eighty, and then with a clever detour into a side road. Spoiled only by an unlucky lightning flash.

Why was she running? Why was he chasing her? And what *happened next*?

All questions. All burning in her mind.

Hairpin Bridge was Lena's controlled experiment. She wasn't sure if she was ready to let the variables of the outside world in yet. Even if Raycevic's career went down in flames, he could hold his tongue. Tapes could disappear. The truth could remain lost.

And she was so close. *I have to know.*

I have to know exactly what happened to you, Cambry.

"Ticktock. Make a choice, Lena."

"I'm thinking."

"Think faster. He's about to see your gun."

The truck reached Hairpin Bridge's opposite ramp, belching a cloud of black exhaust. A hundred yards out now—just seconds from witnessing the standoff. And that wasn't even the worst possibility.

This guy could be Raycevic's backup, she knew. Here to kill her.

She couldn't get that thought out of her mind. The convenience of this new development bothered her, that a bystander would bumble through an abandoned road on a closed bridge, at right this very instant. Perfectly foiling her trap. As the seconds ticked down, Raycevic's voice melted into poison in her ear, a rotten whisper: "Did you get what you came for, Lena? Can Cambry's ghost rest?"

He's saying this only because he wants me to lower my gun.

So when his twin brother in the truck starts shooting, I'm an easier target. She imagined a mirror-image Raycevic—big brother Rick, alive and well—driving toward them now in the truck's dark cab. Same flinty cop eyes. Same bulging action-figure arms and buzz cut. With a rifle on a gun rack, waiting to be lifted and fired at her. In the rock-paper-scissors of gunfighting, rifle beats pistol. Every time.

Somehow that clinched it. It clinched everything.

She moved again, nodding sharply. "Stand here. Don't move."

"What are you doing?"

"I said *don't move*, Ray."

She circled behind him and aimed the Beretta to the back of

his neck. Her finger tense on the trigger. Her heart thudding in her neck. She positioned Raycevic between herself and this new arrival.

A handcuffed human shield.

She leaned left around the cop's bulky shoulder and watched the truck approach the bridge's final stretch, exposing as little of her face as possible. If this guy was an ally of Raycevic's and he took a shot at Lena from his cab, he'd need to shoot through Raycevic first. As long as he wasn't a gold-medalist sniper, he'd have serious trouble.

Right?

"Smart girl," Raycevic whispered.

"Shut up."

"Believe me, Lena, I *wish* he was my backup."

The truck slowed, idling now at a walking pace. The windshield was tinted dark. No view of the driver inside. But he certainly saw them. Lena tried to visualize this stranger squinting through the glass at them with undetermined motives as the air brakes whined a final cry and the truck stopped.

Just thirty feet away. On the bridge's opposite lane.

The world hung on a knife edge. Just the low breath of ashy wind, and the diesel growl of the truck's engine. Like a caged animal.

She held her Beretta to the tanned skin on the back of Ray's neck, careful not to expose herself. Like a villain taking a hostage in a movie, shortly before the good guy blows their brains out with a single sure shot. *Now I really do look like the bad guy,* she realized.

"Nice, Lena. I think he's spooked—"

"Stop talking."

"Or what? You'll execute me? In front of him?"

She wiped sweat from her forehead. What next?

It was hard to think. Smoke and sunlight burned her eyes.

Her mouth was dry. She repositioned again, exposing even less of herself, with her trigger finger curled tight—now maybe a quarter ounce of pressure away from killing Raycevic. She held her breath, studying the big truck, waiting for the rattle of gunshots to shatter the silence. For something, for *anything* to happen, to relieve this suspended moment.

Another breath of smoky wind. The bridge seemed to wobble underfoot.

The rig sat in silence. Another chuff of exhaust.

"Idiot," Raycevic muttered.

"What'd you say?"

"I said he's a clown-fart fucking *idiot*. For stopping a ten-ton rig on an unsound bridge." He sighed, annoyed. "We're all going to end up at the bottom of the valley."

Sure, Lena thought. *What else can go wrong today?*

Hairpin Bridge was built in the thirties. Closed in 1988. Rust-eaten, paint cracked away like dry skin, lashed by bitter winters and a merciless sun. She hadn't considered until now how dangerous it might be to park multiple cars on it, suspended two hundred feet in the air.

Everything, suspended.

The heavy silence dragged on and on. She read the stenciled print on the trailer: SIDEWINDER. The word was somehow familiar. It flitted through her mind, stirring a memory. Another time, another place, a past life refracted through the prism of Hairpin Bridge, perhaps.

Sidewinder—

A sharp, glassy squeal.

She jolted, nearly yanking the Beretta's trigger and blowing Raycevic's throat out. It was the truck's window rolling down, inching to halfway. From the shaded darkness, a face peered over the glass at them. At thirty feet, she could tell only that the driver was an old man—not Raycevic's twin, at least. Scruffy gray hair. Flushed red cheeks. And strangely—a black eyepatch.

"Are you all right?" he shouted. Another surprise: he spoke in a thick Irish accent.

Raycevic shouted, "I'm under attack—"

"Shut up." She jabbed the barrel into his neck.

The one-eyed truck driver froze in fear. He'd already glimpsed the gun in Lena's hand. He got it. He was now comprehending the gravity of what he'd stumbled across: a hostage situation, *with a cop*—

"Get out of your truck," Lena commanded.

The truck's door creaked open and the old man obeyed, sliding down the footrail and landing clumsily on his feet. He was fat, dwarfish, wearing a T-shirt and cargo shorts. Pale Q-tip legs. At this distance, she was confident she could shoot him centermass. If she needed to.

His Irish accent spooked her, though. Like a jutting split fingernail. It was the last thing she expected to hear from the driver of a semitruck in rural America.

She focused. *First things first.*

"Hands up," Lena shouted. "Pull up your shirt."

He obeyed. His shirt hiking up, revealing flabby white flesh.

"Now turn around."

He did. No guns on his back, either.

"Do you have a gun in your cab?"

He shook his head. Blankly. His hat fell.

Raycevic grumbled, "I stop these guys all the time. I guarantee he's got a shotgun in his cab—"

Lena ignored him. "What are you doing here?"

"The fire is—" The trucker pointed back, his voice muffled by another stir of wind.

"What?"

"I said, *the fire is jumping I-90*. If so, this road will become an evacuation route. They sent me to unlock the second gate, to clear a path to Highway 200."

The gate we passed.

The damn wildfire. Still, Lena had no way to verify this. No reason to trust his word on any of this. But the horizon had darkened noticeably since they'd arrived, smoke banding the sky like oily brown paint. The air tasted like cinders.

At least this fat little man was unarmed. That made her feel better.

She squinted up into the shaded cab. "You . . . have a radio in your truck, right?"

He nodded.

"Call the emergency frequency, then." She tried to explain, but the words were thick as peanut butter in her mouth: "This cop—he's dangerous. He murdered my sister on June sixth and he staged her death to look like a suicide. I need you to call the authorities and get every cop in Montana out here right now, because I can prove it."

"Can you?" Raycevic whispered.

The old man with the eyepatch still stared at Lena, paralyzed and useless. His hands still raised halfway. His belly still exposed. She wished he'd tuck his shirt in.

"Call the cops," she repeated. "*Now.*"

That did it. He nodded, turned, scrambled up the truck's footrail, and slipped inside the cluttered interior. The red door swung behind on him on a dry hinge.

She heard his faint voice as he lifted the handheld receiver: "Emergency-one, emergency-one. I've got, uh, an officer held at gunpoint—"

Officer held at gunpoint. There really was no nice way to phrase it.

The door gently clicked shut, muffling the rest.

Corporal Raycevic cursed under his breath and his big shoulders slumped. It must have been finally sinking in, that he'd soon be explaining this whole mess to his superiors. But first, Lena knew, she'd be arrested. The authorities would take her gun, which was fine, and her Shoebox, which was also fine. Like Raycevic said, items can disappear—and she had a plan for that, too. She wasn't naive.

But still, she worried.

Do I have enough evidence? Do I know enough—

A metal click made her jump. Fear bloomed in her chest.

She glanced back to the cars. On her Corolla's hood, the Shoebox recorder had reached the end of its cassette. The tape needed to be replaced.

Too far away to reach.

Raycevic knew this, too. "Okay, Lena."

In a startling motion, he turned around to face her. She knew she should step back to protect herself from a headbutt or a counterattack—but showing weakness was even worse. She stood her ground, keeping the Beretta's barrel trained right on his forehead. Inches away.

"I'll tell you the truth," he said, glancing at the Shoebox. "Now that we're off the record."

Don't back up, Lena. Don't give him an inch.

She didn't.

"What I'm about to tell you . . . you can repeat it to everyone at the station in Magma Springs, but they won't believe you." He smiled. "You can scream it. Write all about it on your nerd blog. Doesn't matter. They'll think you're lying. Or you're crazy, just like your schizoid sister—"

"Say it, Ray."

He licked his lips. He was enjoying this too much. Nothing ever seemed to rattle Raycevic for long. She wanted to jab the Beretta's barrel into his eye socket and twist, to scream at him to stop toying with her, to please stop gloating and just *tell her,* and again her mind returned to last night's dream, to the frustrating nonsense of Cambry's words, to the way she urged through teary eyes: *Go. Lena, go*—

Not *I love you, sis.*

Not *I'll always be with you.*

Basically? Her message from the grave boiled down to: *Leave me alone.*

It sickened her. Made her heart squeeze in her chest. And the situation on Hairpin Bridge had changed again, twisting, complicating into something darker and deeper as she held the trigger on Corporal Raycevic and waited for his next words.

Last night, she'd woken up before she could respond to Cambry—and she hadn't known what she'd say to her twin's ghost anyway, real or imagined—but now she did.

What the hell did you pull me into, sis?

CHAPTER 12

CAMBRY'S STORY

Don't stop, Cambry.

Whatever you do, don't stop.

Her speedometer grazes ninety and the Corolla's suspension jostles over cracked pavement. Trees whip past on her right and left. A ticking clock in her fuel tank. She dreads checking the digital clock in the dashboard but does anyway. The time is 8:44.

Sixteen minutes to live.

Ahead, the red taillights have disappeared again, but she knows they're out there. Somewhere up ahead is a witness. She just needs to catch up. Before she runs out of gas.

The cop is already on her. His Charger pulls parallel to her, unshakable. She can see the dark man's form clearly through the windows. The Glock is still in his knuckled hand, resting on his steering wheel. He has a clear shot on her now, less than ten feet between them. But he hasn't taken it. Why?

He saw the taillights, too, *she reasons.*

An innocent bystander is a game changer. He's considering the likelihood of this faraway witness hearing his gunshot. In another second or two, he'll probably decide that at a quarter mile, gunshots could just as easily be rolling thunder, and he'll shoot her anyway.

So?

So.

Make a choice, Cambry.

She decides she's done waiting. She twists her steering wheel hard left, swinging directly into Raycevic's side. He sees her swerve coming—barely—and cuts his speed with a panicked stomp and a squeal of locked brakes. Still, she nearly clips the Charger's front panel.

She half wishes she'd hit his car and wrecked them both. It's suicide, but ruining this asshole's night holds a certain appeal.

Now she's got the oncoming lane, racing at eighty, and she's forced him back. Holding the opposite lane denies Raycevic an angle on her from the left and forces him to attack her from the right side, firing left-handed. It'll make his shot inconvenient, at least. As tactics go, it sucks.

Another rise in the road—another shrieking touchdown of chassis kissing pavement—and she glimpses those red taillights again. They're slightly larger now, slightly closer. Not close enough.

"Come on," she whispers, stomping the gas. "Come on."

Raycevic must be changing his strategy, too, as he swerves around behind her. The gun isn't in his hand anymore. He's got both hands on the wheel, driving with his full attention. His high beams swing up on her right side now, crossing the road's center line, and it occurs to her how recklessly they're both driving. How cataclysmically deadly a crash would be. The world has changed so dramatically in the past hour, ever since she first spotted those four strange fires.

Those four ceremonial pyramids of stone, cracks glowing with caged flame.

The strange dreamlike moment that started it all.

As the Charger closes in like a predator, she can't stop her racing anxieties. Terrible thoughts, as heavy as cannonballs in her stomach. She imagines the patrolman out there earlier today in his wifebeater, getting scorched by an afternoon sun, tediously sawing a human body into sections to feed into each small furnace. A foot in one. A forearm in another. Does he drain the body of blood first? He must, to get the temperature high enough to crack bone. Maybe he strings the corpses upside down with a slashed jugular, drip-drip-dripping into a tin bucket—

Headlights scald her eyes. The Charger nuzzling up close on her right. Closer.

Focus, Cambry. He's on you.

She can't. Her thoughts are a furious churn. Now she sees Corporal Raycevic grunting with exertion as he cranks a hacksaw through a throat. Pausing to wipe sweat from his brow. Or maybe he prefers to chop instead? The thunderous crack of an axe splitting a femur—

Focus-focus-focus.

Hand-feeding those bloodless little body parts, cubed sections of drained flesh and knuckled bone, into those stone furnaces until nothing remains—

Cambry.

She swallows hard.

You will die here if you don't focus.

The cop car holds parallel to her. A distant flash of lightning silhouettes the man inside. His hat, his ears, his bull shoulders. The barrel of the semiautomatic rifle resting on the seat like a passenger. But incredibly, he's still got his big knuckles clasped to the wheel. He's focused on driving. This is his chance to pull his pistol and take a kill shot. Why hasn't he?

It's 8:46. Fourteen minutes.

Ahead, the car's taillights appear again. A brief flash of distant red hope. Then they tug away as the road flexes into another bend.

Her heart flutters. She's closed some of the distance. The car is closer now. Maybe two hundred yards between them? On the next straightaway, she'll know for sure. She's catching up.

Which means Raycevic can't shoot her. Not without risk. On a cool summer night like this, the unsuspecting man, woman, or family up *ahead could be driving with their windows down. This close, the rattle of gunfire might not blend so seamlessly into thunder. This psycho cop can't allow one homicide to spill over and become two, three, or more. He's forced to hold his fire. This delights Cambry—it feels like a victory. Yes, Raycevic is getting desperate, his arsenal of guns useless, as she nears the taillights of her anonymous savior.*

Which means he has one option left—

No.

She doesn't want to think about this. She shoves it to the back of her mind. Refuses to look at it. She wants to enjoy this moment, this delirious reversal as Raycevic realizes he can't shoot her. That in a way, she's already escaped him. She's already within earshot of civilization.

But he has one more likely attack.

No, no, no.

And she knows it. She can't ignore it. Her stomach twists into ropes, greasy heartburn in her chest, and she finally, finally accepts it: Cambry, he's going to ram you off the road.

Right now.

It's his only remaining option.

Inside the cruiser, she sees the cop's posture change. His left elbow rises in a hard twist and that's Raycevic's tell, a tenth of a second before his cruiser swings at her, a two-ton right hook.

Cambry stomps her brakes. All reflex.

Her world rockets backward. The seat belt whips into her shoulder again, and the Charger swerves in front of her, tires screaming with gritty friction. The vehicles do a strange smoky dance, a whirling do-si-do at seventy. For a blinking split second, his side doors light up in her high beams and she can read HIGHWAY PATROL *stenciled in white, as crisp as daylight. Then Raycevic keeps spinning, his rear bumper swinging achingly close to her front panel, and Cambry's stomach clenches into a ball—but the vehicles pass without impact. Inches between them.*

Raycevic keeps skidding left. Left. Too far—

She realizes that he was counting on her vehicle being there. Her Corolla was supposed to take a hit to the rear panel and absorb the kinetic energy into a fishtail spin. Instead, she'd slammed on her brakes. While he kept skidding leftward, unable to correct his swerve—

She cranes her neck to follow him. Yes, you asshole!

He keeps twisting, a dizzying one-eighty, and grinds up against the gravel shoulder. His headlights strobe at her again, only this time pointed backward. Off the road now, his suspension bucking violently on the uneven land. A firecracker-flash of orange sparks as his bumper scrapes rock. A storm of dust and rubber smoke, cut by headlights.

Cambry feels her car lurch. She's at a complete stop now.

So is the stunned Charger, thirty feet ahead, spilled off the road. Facing her.

She can't hold it. She laughs, hard spasms on a raw throat. Her window is still rolled down, and so is Raycevic's, and she knows he can hear her laughter. That makes it even better.

She recovers fast and accelerates. Slammed back into her seat by a fresh surge of forward motion, she ducks behind her door as she drives past the stalled cop car. She braces for gunshots as she passes. Aching silence. Her car punches through his dust cloud, and she flinches under the staccato rattle of small rocks peppering her windshield.

No gunfire. Nothing.

She risks a backward glance at him, exposing her head. The Charger is still skidded off the road into the weeds, pointing in reverse. This time there's no lightning to illuminate the dark interior. Maybe his airbag has exploded in there. Maybe he's hurt. This gives Cambry another dark thrill—she hopes he's got a gash on his forehead or a concussion. Maybe he's bitten his tongue clean off.

In another instant, she's far past him. Racing on into the night.

She shouts out her window again, into the leaf-blower rush of cold air. It starts as another fuck you, but midbreath she tries to throw in cocksucker, and it comes out a confused jumble of obscenities. It is what it is: A wild, joyous hymn to surviving another second. To eluding the Reaper. To being alive.

Another bolt of lightning crosses the sky, a violet flash of exposed clouds, stunning in its power and closeness. Like concert floodlights, the most stunning storm she's ever witnessed, turning the trees green and the rocks white and the ground alive with racing shadows. She's never felt so present. She can feel the electricity in her teeth, building for the next flash. We're all stardust, right?

The spun-out cop car disappears in her rearview mirror. Going, going, gone. She leans into the road's next turn and drives faster, her nerves on edge, bracing for the inevitable artillery crash of thunder. But like the gunshots, it never comes. Only the roar of the motor and the howl of the wind in her ears. Just the storm's silent fury.

And ahead—those red taillights again.

"Thank God," she whispers. "Oh, thank you, Lord, thank you, Jesus."

She's gaining fast on the faraway car. With every twist of the serpentine road, she tugs closer in the darkness. Homing in on it.

"Thank you, Holy Ghost."

She's running out of divine entities to thank. She's not religious, at least not in any way she can admit. But there's something exhilarating to this wild drive under silent lightning, pursued by a dark man in a black Dodge Charger. With salvation ahead.

She mashes the horn with her fist.

The car ahead is still too far away to hear. She lost some distance when she baited Raycevic into his spin. She checks her rearview mirror.

The cop's headlights pinprick behind her. Back in this merry chase.

"Shit." But she knows she should have expected this. Like a pursuing figure from a nightmare, Raycevic is down but never out. She looks back ahead at the faraway taillights and bleats the horn again, again, punching it with her knuckles. The Corolla's horn has always been weak. She tries flipping her high beams off, then back on.

No response.

She's still too far behind. So she tries something she hoped she wouldn't have to: cutting her headlights entirely. Off, then on. Off, then on. The oncoming road pulses pitch black before her, vanishing in totality between frightening heartbeats.

Off. On. Off. On. She smacks the lever harder, dropping in and out of racing darkness, aware of Raycevic's headlights rapidly gaining on her tail.

Ahead, the brake lights pulse. A response.

They see it.

"Yes," she hisses.

The taillights grow brighter. Like twin red lanterns gliding in blackness. The driver is pulling off to the right, grinding up on the road's shoulder.

"Yes, yes, yes—"

She finds herself instinctively tapping her own brakes as well, slowing down to pull over alongside this stranger. But Raycevic is just a minute behind her, closing in fast on them both.

Ahead, the vehicle's brakes whine. A complete stop now.

Cambry knows she can't waste a second. She'll need to convince this bystander to let her into his vehicle, to drive them both away. Before Raycevic's headlights catch up. Before he can start shooting. Otherwise all she's accomplishing is dragging a second victim into a murderer's cross hairs. Third, technically? Another collection of body parts to be parceled out into those little fires.

She stomps her brakes. Stopping, too, behind him.

She unbuckles her seat belt. Throws the door open. As she scrambles outside into the skin-prickling quiet, the cracked roadway feels strange underfoot. Like stepping out of a swimming pool after hours of weightless floating. In the blackness behind her, Raycevic's light bar switches back on in an eruption of blue and red—Of course, he's acting the part of cop again. His lights are joined by a wailing scream. A moaning, ghostlike siren.

It dawns on her now, as she lowers her shoulders and breaks into a gasping sprint toward the semi's cab, that Corporal Raycevic, fewer than thirty seconds behind them both, enjoys a profound advantage in this situation, too. After all . . .

If you see someone fleeing a cop car, who do you assume is the bad guy?

Who do you help?

By now, the driver sees Raycevic's lights. He's wondering right now if he's being rushed by a fleeing criminal. He's probably already got his hand on the stick, about to throttle up and leave.

She runs faster. Pumps her arms. Almost there. She tries to shout, but her lungs are empty.

Cambry, you look like the bad guy.

"Help!" she manages to scream.

Her voice is lost under his siren. She can't believe it, any of it. The hateful ludicrous insanity of it all. Like the spectacularly ill-timed lightning, this dark man possesses some unknown power, and no matter the choices she makes, Cambry Nguyen is destined to die tonight. Within minutes now. She's already drawn the skull card. Nothing can change her fate.

This is why tarot cards, Ouija boards, and psychic readings have always terrified her. For as long as I can remember, my sister has always deeply feared learning that she's fated to die. Not the death itself, just the knowledge of when it happens—and this makes sense. She's lived her entire life on the move. Why shouldn't she be terrified of the one thing she can't outrun?

———————

At this point I should warn you, dear readers: the known record of Cambry's movements becomes incomplete after she exits her car at 8:48 P.M. The testimony I recorded on Hairpin Bridge becomes unreliable. Up until now, Corporal Raycevic's account of the events of June 6 has been verified down to the minute. You'll just have to go with me on what happens next.

Trust me, please.

––––––––––

As my sister reaches the semitruck's cab, squinting up to find the driver's black form inside, Raycevic's intensifying light envelops the world at her back, tracing her running shadow on the concrete, glinting off the trailer's sides, which are pocked with rivets and stenciled with the now-revealed print:

SIDEWINDER.

CHAPTER 13

LENA

"WHAT HAPPENED NEXT, RAY?"

"I was still catching up behind her. I didn't see it happen."

"You didn't see *what* happen?"

He licked his lips. "We need to go back to the beginning. To what happened before June sixth. You wanted the truth? Congratulations. Here it is."

She kept an eye on the semitruck still parked on Hairpin Bridge's opposite lane, the driver still inside on his radio with emergency services, as Raycevic took a shaky breath and whispered, "Cambry was my girlfriend."

"Excuse me?"

He repeated: "She was my girlfriend."

"Uh, wow. No."

"Yes."

"Try harder."

"I was having an affair with her." He forced an ill smile. "My wife got fat, you know?"

"You're lying."

"I *was* lying. Until now. I misdirected the investigation into her death. I kept my romantic involvement with Cambry under wraps, because I have a marriage and a career to protect."

Romantic involvement. The words went straight for Lena's gut, as heavy as a roiling mass of maggots. Squirming, shivery revulsion.

"Think about it. Just please, hear me out, and think about what I'm telling you. Think about all the lost time in Cambry's path, between when she robbed Blake in Florida and June, when she died on this bridge. That's four months unaccounted for. She lived nomadically, stealing, using, paying with cash, and giving her name to no one. What does someone do with all that time?"

"She drew. She read. She smoked. She enjoyed the solitude."

"For four months?"

"She was traveling."

"No, Lena, she was traveling *until* March. But I promise you: April, May, June, she lingered in the greater Howard County area. Black Lake. Rattlesnake Canyon. Magma Springs. The investigation didn't conclude this, because I scrubbed the evidence."

I scrubbed the evidence. Uttered so casually.

She couldn't believe it. He had to be lying. She felt herself getting flustered, her tongue thick in her mouth. Her thoughts refusing to fire.

"Why would I lie about this, Lena?"

None of these new pieces fit together. Cambry's Corolla had been minimalist and sparse, yes, but so was her sterile bedroom all throughout Lena's childhood. Her stuffed animals were ignored. Her Barbies were turned faceless. Cambry didn't collect objects. She collected sights and sounds.

She forced herself to speak. "You . . . you admit, right there, that you destroyed evidence."

He nodded. "Anything that connected her to me, and to this

region. Receipts. Her knife. Her stolen gun. My number in her flip phone. Her—" He stopped himself.

Her drawings. Her heart squeezed with rage.

Still, it didn't make sense. A big question: "How did she die, then?"

"I told you. She jumped—"

"*Bullshit,* Ray. My sister would never talk to you. She sure as hell wasn't your girlfriend."

"I'll prove it, Lena."

"Yeah? This'll be good."

"I can." Twisting his cuffed wrists, he slipped his fingers into his back pocket. "Right now. I'll show you a photo I have of Cambry and me fishing on Black Lake, taken the day before she—"

"I'm supposed to believe you keep a photo of a *dead woman* in your wallet?"

"It's all I have left."

His voice wavered with something that sounded like heartbreak. It was the best acting she'd seen from him all day. It halted her. What if he was telling the truth? Was he really one of Cambry's trademark Terrible Guys, to be used up and discarded?

Unthinkable. She couldn't reconcile it.

The handcuffed cop was still struggling to produce his photo from his pocket. His fingers fumbled behind his back and then a wallet dropped to the concrete with a dry clap.

He looked back up at her. Almost apologetic. "I loved her."

I loved her.

Her stomach swirled. Nausea now.

"Our grief isn't the same, Lena, but please know I lost her, too." Raycevic swallowed. "And I'm sorry I lied to you about my involvement with her before her suicide—"

I loved her. His words looped in her mind, awful echoes: *Why would I lie about this?*

The wallet rested on the pavement at his feet. It was right there. Right *there*. Reach for it? She urged herself not to, reminded herself that it was almost certainly another evil trick. That he'd seize on her moment of distraction, knock the Beretta from her fingers, stomp her skull in with his boot—

"Two steps back," she ordered. "Give me space."

He did.

Keeping the Beretta trained on the cop and her finger on the trigger, she quickly knelt and picked up the wallet. The moment passed; he didn't attack. She opened the billfold one-handed. A taco-stand punch card fluttered out. A few loose receipts.

He watched. "In the back. The very last photo."

But now another problem: She couldn't swipe through the tightly packed cards one-handed. She had to keep the Beretta in her dominant hand, aimed at Raycevic. This was non-negotiable. She couldn't let her guard down.

She wouldn't.

That echo again: *Why would I lie about this?*

Then two things occurred to Lena Nguyen, like twin thunderclaps inside her skull. The first: their positioning had changed gradually over the past thirty seconds. Raycevic now stood five paces to her left. He'd been edging gingerly away ever since he first dropped his billfold on the pavement. This hadn't been a fumble. It had been deliberate, as careful as a chess move. He was edging away from her, as if anticipating a lightning strike.

The second: an answer, finally, to Raycevic's question. It chilled her spine.

He's trying to distract me.

She had her back to the parked SIDEWINDER truck now. This had been necessary, because Raycevic's subtle repositioning had guided her away from it—*He's distracting me*—and she couldn't see the semi's darkened cab and didn't dare turn around, because that would blow perhaps the only advantage she had left—*He's distracting me*—and reveal she knew his girlfriend story was all a ruse and recognized the hidden gunsights tingling on the back of her neck at this very instant.

He's fucking *distracting me.*

She held a swollen breath in her chest, looking at Raycevic. His wallet in her left hand, the Beretta in her right. Afraid to exhale. Afraid to move.

He's distracting me so his buddy in the truck can shoot me.

CHAPTER 14

CAMBRY'S STORY

"Help!"

Cambry doesn't know if the stranger inside the truck heard her. She's almost at the cab now, her heart thudding in her throat.

Behind her, Raycevic slams his brakes.

Here, now, the scream of tires on gritty road as the pursuing Charger slides to a rocky halt. The siren still wailing. The red-and-blue light bar still throwing wild shadows. She knows the cop has that wicked rifle resting in his passenger seat, ready to lift and aim at her back.

She reaches the cab.

With a running leap, she hits the footrail and catches the silver handlebar under a sky-splitting flash of lightning. She pulls herself up on aching biceps, reaching the driver's side window and squinting inside. The interior is pitch black. She can't see the driver. She slaps the dirty glass.

"Help. I need help." Just an urgent slap. Trying not to look threatening.

A sharp metal clap behind her. It's Raycevic, opening his door and climbing out. His boots click to the road in rapid sequence.

To hell with it. She pounds the glass with her fist.

"Cambry," the cop shouts. "Stop—"

Despite being outside his car, his voice sounds oddly muffled, but she knows why—He's leaning back inside to grab that rifle.

Out of time, she tries the handle. Unlocked! She wrenches the door open, nearly losing her balance on the rounded footrail.

Inside, perfect darkness. Still no driver.

"Hello?"

No answer. Worse, her night vision is fried by the police lights. But she knows she can't stay here, hanging on the side of the cab, or Raycevic will pick her off with the semiautomatic rifle he's almost certainly lifting from his car and aiming at her, right this second.

She lunges inside.

Inside is a heated, stuffy atmosphere. She catches herself with her palms on a leather seat cover, clammy with moisture. A dense locker-room odor. Like stale sweat and socks. And something else, something both sweet and putrid, which she can't identify. It's organic, heavy, animal. She blinks, rubbing her eyes, catching her frenzied breaths.

Yes, the cab is empty. No driver. Too dark to see anything else.

Where did the driver go?

She knows this is impossible. Where the hell did he go? He didn't just disappear. The truck wasn't just driving itself. Her mind darts back to Death waiting patiently in that Siberian cave.

I was told you'd be here.

Outside, Corporal Raycevic's siren cuts. The sudden silence is overpowering. She can hear her racing heartbeat. Her eardrums full of blood.

Frantic now, she gropes for the ignition—no dangling keys. The truck's driving lights are on. The dashboard display is lit up, a wan orange glow behind a contoured steering wheel. Again, this is impossible. A man was just in here, his body occupying this still-warm seat, driving and breathing and sweating, just moments ago. Where did he go, if not thin air?

What were you doing at Mardi Gras?

The driver door bangs shut behind her, startling her. Just the wind.

She wishes for another strobe of lightning to light up the cab. In the dark, she feels defenseless. And that odor hangs in the air, dank and musty, like a dog blanket.

The radio, she remembers. Truckers have CB radios, don't they? Yes, they do.

The seats are covered with crunchy paper. Newspaper? Magazines? It's still too dark to see, but as her retinas adjust, she finds a lumpen mass on the truck's dashboard. To the right of the steering wheel, a few feet away. A black shape with no lights or visible details. A radio?

She reaches for it.

Her outstretched fingers touch a cool surface. It's studded with tiny bumps. It feels like soft leather—much softer than the cab's damp and crusty upholstery. And there's something wrong about the shape, too. There seem to be no defined edges or corners. Instead, her fingers trace smooth slopes. Curves. Almost what she'd describe as coils.

Raycevic's voice outside. Muffled by the door.

Cambry keeps exploring with cautious fingertips, searching for dials or knobs or a receiver on a spiral cord, for anything recognizable, and finds only more smooth curvatures. She'd sell her soul for a flash of lightning now. Her index finger stops at the uppermost ridge of one and follows the raised edge. She feels a sequence of tiny bumps. Like bones under hairless skin. Vertebrae.

Too small, and too numerous, to be a hairless cat or a dog.

Outside, Raycevic shouts again, louder, still muffled—

And now Cambry hears a low wheezing sound inside the cab with her. It originates just inches from her face. She feels it on her cheeks. The breeze lifts her hair. Like a stream of air escaping a punctured tire. She wouldn't describe it as a hiss. Not at first.

It's a snake.

She freezes, her fingertips flat against cool scales.

You're touching a giant fucking snake.

It strikes at her from the dashboard, a violent whipcrack. She feels the sting of displaced air on her face and screams, recoiling backward into the leather seats. Spilling some unknown beverage in the console, scooting away, away, away, all animal terror, her nerves ablaze with adrenaline, until her back slams against the truck's driver's side door. Toward Raycevic.

In a single frantic moment, the cop outside and his black rifle are completely forgotten. Her entire world is this snake, this goddamn nonsensical snake that was just inches from her face in the darkness, and the sickly nightmare logic that brought it here, into the cab of this derelict semitruck. It's like a hallucination, all of it. Bad shrooms.

She screams again. Swears at it. Is it venomous? Was she bitten? She doesn't think so. She touches her cheek. No blood.

But yes, it's a giant impossible snake coiled up on this trucker's dashboard, still hissing at her. It must live here. She hears the dry friction of its scales as it repositions. It must be ten or twelve feet long, a python or a boa or an anaconda, coiled up in a black heap on this trucker's dashboard like an ornament. She almost laughs at the silly terror of it. Seconds ago she'd been blindly feeling it up, rubbing her hands all over its scales. Molesting it.

Incoming footsteps on the road. Raycevic, coming fast. He shouts again, something desperate.

Cambry Nguyen is desperate, too, because she's inside a truck with no keys and a goddamn python. This is not an improvement over her previous situation. She needs to move. The driver's side door leads back to Raycevic and instant death. So she crawls toward the passenger door, over the knobbed stick shift, over crunchy papers.

The hissing intensifies. The snake strikes at her again from the left.

She hits the passenger door. Gropes for the handle, twists it open. The door swings outward, giving way to free fall. She spills outside into the cold night, reaching for the handrail in midair, missing it, and hitting her hands and knees on the packed-dirt shoulder.

The footsteps change. Raycevic is running now. On the truck's other side.

Go, go, go!

She scrambles upright and backs away. The semitrailer is a tall black rectangle against the police lights. The forest is snarled and thick with junipers here at the road's edge. The pines are tangled forms, some man-size, some towering. She can ditch her Corolla and flee now, and she has a decent head start to vanish into the low foliage with her life.

She hears a metal creak—it's Raycevic opening the cab's driver's side door. He doesn't know she's already outside. That'll cost him precious seconds. Even more, if the snake bites him in there. Yes, she has the lead on him.

Too slow, asshole.

Whirling away from the truck, she launches into a sprint—

And slips.

There's an alien plastic surface underneath her feet. As slick as pond ice. Greasy, squealing. She hobbles and twists an ankle, confused and off balance.

Finally, the pulse of lightning she's wished for.

A seizure of light reveals a slippery sheet has been laid out on the ground here on the road's shoulder. She's walked right out onto it. Creased gray tarp, unfolded to the size of a room. And, six feet away, to her immediate left—one of the short trees isn't a tree at all.

It's a man.

He's turning to face her with equal surprise. In a blurred flash of brightness, he looks like an astronaut. Only after darkness has fallen again and the image is seared into her retinas do the details emerge, and she comprehends what she just saw.

The stranger was cloaked head to toe in plastic. Like a raincoat, but shiny and colorless. It clung to him in wrinkly folds. Blue surgical gloves on his hands. Little plastic booties on his feet. Only his face was exposed—and only because he'd been affixing a respirator mask the instant the lightning struck.

Operating scrubs, *she manages to think.* Like a surgeon.

And now, again swimming in blind darkness, she can't see him. But she can hear him. He's coming for her, less than six feet away and lurching closer, the squeaky, squelching sounds of plastic flexing and hugging skin as he moves—

The Plastic Man.

She screams in a hoarse voice. Suddenly all of tonight's horrors, the pursuing cop, the four pyramids of ritual fire, even the python in the truck, melt away. Her stomach has turned to water, the world spinning as she staggers backward in a dizzy rush. She should run—she should pick a direction and run now, but her hiking boots lose traction on the slick plastic and her knees turn to mush.

And those creaking, wrinkling sounds draw closer in the blackness, quick but unhurried, as the Plastic Man comes for her.

CHAPTER 15

LENA

Every night, Cambry, you die in my dreams.

Each time, a little different. Sometimes you're strangled by some variety of taut plastic. Sometimes you're executed by gunshot. Sometimes you're gagged and raped and hurled off the bridge like garbage. Sometimes, more exotic—you're decapitated by a swift stomp of a shovel, or eviscerated, your guts unrolling from your belly like glistening black snakes.

I know most of these deaths are impossible—the churn of an overactive mind. But I'm trapped in them. I sink into them. If nothing else, I hope whatever I learn from Corporal Raycevic tomorrow will replace imagined horrors with real ones.

Stop thinking about it, people tell me. Just stop, Lena.

As if I could *turn it off*?

Don't remember the bad, they say. Remember the good instead. Don't dwell on the nightmares of your own making, the glistening intestines and trapped screams, or the possibility of a rape going unnoticed by the medical examiner. Focus on the happy memories you have with your twin, before she became a pancake. But I'm always tugged to the bad, and an even worse truth: I don't have that many memories of Cambry at all.

Good memories? Bad memories? There's just not much there. I have another confession to make here, dear readers, and this one hurts: I was never close to my twin.

That's awful, right?

Twins are supposed to be inseparable.

I know it's awful. But we weren't much alike. Or maybe we were too much alike—like the negative ends of a magnet—and we repelled each other all through our eighteen years of living under the same roof in Olympia. And socially, we ran in different circles—mine played Magic: The Gathering in game club, while hers tipped porta potties and pissed in the fuel tanks of construction vehicles.

Forget the bad, Lena. Remember the good.

And I just have to smile back at them like a stranger behind the windows of a locked house because no one understands that there *isn't* any good. Or there is, but whatever's there is a precious resource as scarce as fucking unobtanium. My sister was a stranger to me, a stranger I desperately wish I knew. Now I never will.

Isn't that pathetic? I'm the grieving twin, and I'm driving all the way to Montana to risk my life and solve her murder, and all the while no one realizes that I barely even *knew* her. Aside from sporadic text messages, we hadn't spoken in well over a year.

If her ghost could see me now, she'd probably wrinkle her nose. *Why do you care so much, Ratface?*

I'm gone. Just let me go.

I'm afraid to, I guess. It's hard to let go of someone you only half know. She's an accumulation of traits and observations, like used carbon paper in my brain. She loved classic rock. Her favorite holiday was Halloween. She always tried to put cilantro on everything. She hated being indoors. As a girl she'd run away into the woods behind our house—sometimes all afternoon, to our parents' exasperation—and come back dirty, mosquito-bitten, with a jar full of slugs, centipedes, and garter snakes.

And I remember how she used to dominate at hide-and-seek.

Even indoors, she'd somehow remain undiscovered for ages while we searched for her, creeping from room to room like a shadow. When she finally got bored and came to us, she explained it so matter-of-factly: *I took off my shoes and walked in my socks so you wouldn't hear my footsteps.*

Duh, right?

It's ironic, though, that the most vivid memory I have of my sister would involve her leaping off a bridge.

This was summer, years back. Senior year. Ellensburg, the morning after a concert at the Gorge. This was one of the few times we ever joined socially. She was with her friends, including her current boyfriend—Terrible Guy #10 or #11, I think. I can't remember his name. Only that he was twenty-eight and we were eighteen. Growling voice, shaved head. You've probably seen him on an episode of *COPS*.

"You have to clench your butt cheeks," he says.

There's a black railroad trestle that spans the Yakima River down by Holmes. The jigsaw wood frame stands thirty feet up, barely a fraction of Hairpin. The river below is deep enough to dive.

"Clench them," he repeats. "It's science."

My sister is perched on the bridge's edge like a tanned rock climber, her hands clasped, her calves taut, her unpainted toenails over blue water far below. "Why?" she asks.

"It's something I learned from Boy Scouts. See, you hit the water feetfirst from this high, and it's like landing directly on a fire hose, which is why you have to clench your butt cheeks."

"I don't understand."

"It's simple."

"Can you please elaborate?"

"It's science, Cambry." He's annoyed now. "I got a merit badge in this, okay? You gotta clench your butt cheeks so all those gallons of pressurized water won't explode inside your asshole and just fuckin' *obliterate* everything up there—"

"I see."

She's getting bored with him, so she looks over the truss frame at me instead.

I'm hot and uncomfortable. Chasing a weak buzz with PBR and cheap weed that burned my throat. I'm perched up there on the oily railroad ties with her, Terrible Guy #11, and a few others. I'm not jumping with her. No way. This was Cambry's idea. For a moment, I'm afraid she'll make fun of me again. I don't fit in with her friends. Never have. Never will.

But she smiles at me. "Think I'll die?"

"What?"

"Think I'll die, sis?"

"Not if you clench your butt cheeks," her boyfriend says.

But she's asked me, and now she's waiting for my answer, and I'm not sure what to say. The black railroad tie is between us like a countertop, bleeding sticky tar, and she's leaning away to grip the edge by her fingertips and hunched toes. Even in my memory—she's a living, breathing mystery.

On the black wood between us, a few different variations of Bob the Dinosaur are marked in chalk between squashed PBR cans.

She leans back farther. Away from me, over the void.

As her question lingers in the air: *Think I'll die, sis?*

I decide I can't answer her. I won't. *I don't know,* I want to say. *You're the one who has to jump off a perfectly good bridge into a mosquito-filled river.* We're all hungover, dehydrated. No one else wants to take a death dive into the water. No one else has a change of clothes, anyway. I don't even think she does.

But it's there, so she needs to jump off it. And not just that, but she's decided she wants to try to catch a particular trestle beam that juts a few inches out from the framework. Ten feet below us, twenty above the water. Like a trapeze artist. Just because she can, or she's curious if she can. I remember thinking: *I hate her. I hate her impulses. Her reckless curiosities.*

Do you think I'll die, Lena?

No. I won't answer her.

She rolls her shoulders back. Hanging off the wooden tie by one hand now, by her chewed fingernails. Her other arm free and dangling. She asks me a different question, no less obtuse: "Do you think there's an afterlife?"

"Like heaven and hell?"

"Anything."

"Like ghosts?"

"*Anything.*"

I think before answering. "I do."

She nods thoughtfully as she hangs over the blue water. Like something down there is calling her. She looks back at me, flicking her bangs from her face to reveal a melancholy smile. "I don't."

It startles me. I've seen my sister frown and cry, but I've never seen that face before.

Then she lets go.

She slides right off the bridge's edge, her hand swishing away, her body and voice and all her mysteries disappearing in an instant, and I crane my neck down to follow her through the framework of trestle beams as she plunges—

"Clench your butt cheeks—"

It feels like she's airborne for a full second, but I know it's not possible at thirty feet. Midair, I see her reach for the jutting beam, and her outstretched fingers miss it.

I hadn't exactly been rooting for her.

But her wrist whacks painfully off the wood on her way down. I can still hear the sound it made, almost a tick, like the pendulum of a grandfather clock.

And then she's gone. She breaks the river's surface with a violent clap and a geyser of green-white spray hits the bridge's underside. The speckle of landing droplets. I barely glimpse the spreading ripples through the structure's wooden bones, only enough to know that she hit the river feetfirst as Terrible Guy #11 instructed, although I would never ask about the status of her butt cheeks.

As we wait for her head to appear in the water below, I feel truly alone. Her friends have nothing to say to me. I have nothing to say to them. I'm a less-fun copy of Cambry and we're joined here because the show tickets were a Groupon. I just trace my fingers over Cambry's chalk drawing of Bob the Dinosaur, accidentally smearing the character's eyes with my thumb.

Someone drops a PBR can. It pings off the beam she tried to catch and splashes down.

Cambry's ripples are gone now, taken by the current.

Her boyfriend crawls past me, squinting, bumping aside another beer can. Everyone is crowding closer to the edge now. He's the first to voice it, but it's been building in everyone.

"She's . . ."

I reposition, too, slippery fear rising in my chest as I watch the water for movement. For the flow of her dark hair. For an arm, a leg, any sign of life . . .

"She's gone."

―――――――――

MAKE HER GONE, THE HANDWRITTEN NOTE READ.

Marked with spidery blue pen, the college-ruled paper was taped to a deluxe Quadratec CB radio encased in the truck's dashboard in a custom and costly retrofit. The radio reached ninety-six channels, six of them emergency frequencies, two law enforcement only.

A second note, taped higher:

LENA NGUYEN. HAIRPIN BRDG. UNARMED

Above the radio, atop the dash, a female Colombian red-tailed boa rested in a lake of bright sunlight. She was coiled into a clump the size of a soccer ball, but stretched to her full length, she would measure eleven feet. Her scales ran a vivid fade from pale earth to dried blood, glossed with silver. Her eyes were lidless, unblinking.

The dashboard was crusted with downward streaks of brown and chalky white, where fast-food napkins had failed to wipe away boa feces. Below the glove compartments, a floor of crumpled burger wrappers and fry cups climbed two feet deep around skyscraper stacks of vintage *Playboys* and *Hustlers*.

Down in the center console, a Golden Rule bottle—*Sweet Tea with Real Sugar, None of That Artificial Stuff!*—rested in the cup holder, half-drunk, its glass neck alight with sunlight. A smeared print of a man's lower lip on the bottle's rim.

Inches farther, a twenty-count box of Remington Express .30-30 caliber Winchester cartridges—*Proven Stopping Power for Medium Game*—rested on the driver's seat by the seat-belt buckle. The box's cardboard flaps were open, exposing golden primers in a plastic cradle. Seven were absent.

Within arm's reach of this box, in a pocket of shadow, crouched the truck's single occupant. The man who nested here in this roost of crunchy porn and reptile shit hunched on his knees in the floor space by the truck's pedals, his right elbow resting on the steering wheel for a firm firing stance. The rifle he held was a Winchester lever-action cowboy carbine, with a blued-steel barrel and a polished walnut stock engraved with the signatures of the entire cast and above-the-line crew of the 1969 John Wayne film *True Grit*. The firearm was nestled on the corner of the driver's side window, in the thinnest diagonal crook between glass and frame, so that only the last inch of the barrel protruded outside into daylight.

The rifle's notched iron sights aimed at the spine of Lena Nguyen, the one and only Lena Nguyen, whom he'd been summoned to collect like a dogcatcher, standing now beside Corporal Raycevic in the bridge's northbound lane thirty feet away. She didn't see the gunman in the truck. Her pistol was in her right hand, trained on Ray. Her attention was on something in her left. Ray's diversion, whatever it was, seemed to involve his billfold.

As Lena inspected it, Ray took another furtive step back, creating five feet between himself and her. Enough room to miss. Furtively, he turned to face the truck.

Shoot, he mouthed.

The gunman disengaged the rifle's safety, and in his sights, Lena glanced sharply toward Ray. She couldn't have heard the click. Maybe she saw his lips move. Or she was noticing he'd moved. Could she know? She glanced back down at the billfold in her hand (what kind of distraction was that, anyway?) and took a timid step backward. The rifle's front sight followed her, smoothly recentering on her back.

Red-faced, Ray mouthed again, furiously: *Shoot. Shoot.*

The gunman squeezed the trigger.

But Lena took another step backward. His gunsights followed her another wavering half step, and she dropped Ray's wallet. It hit the pavement.

One more step. The front sight bobbed after her.

Finally, she stopped, her foot raised birdlike in a moment of pause, and the pinpoint of floating death found her spine. He had her. The girl's head cocked, as if straining to hear a faraway noise. As if, too little, too late, a whisper in her mind warned of the growing danger behind her.

Still squeezing the trigger, farther, farther . . .

Shoot now—

Then the girl spun sharply, whirling in a blur to face the Winchester's sights—and the eye behind them—directly. Her black pistol spun into view, her second hand clasping around it, raising to aim. The entire maneuver took less than a half second, and by the time he comprehended this, she'd already fired with a smoky flash.

The driver's side window spiderwebbed with cracks—a brittle, glassy impact; the snap of displaced air; the shattering thud of lead impacting metal. The gunshot arrived a microsecond later, a tinny pop chasing the sound barrier. By then the man was already ducking on reflex, half crouching, half falling behind the door.

The Winchester fell to his lap, his hands now clumsy mittens.

The pistol's echo thinned. It had happened so fast. On his ass now in crunchy fast-food debris, he looked up, blinking, at the fresh hole punched through his window. A crystalline star shape against white sky. Based on its location in the glass, she'd missed his face by barely an inch or two. Across thirty feet of distance, fired in a split-second quick-draw spin.

As he shouldered his rifle and rose to return fire, he mouthed astonished words of his own: "Where in the *hell* did she learn to shoot like that?"

CHAPTER 16

CAMBRY'S STORY

"Get her. Get her now—"

Cambry recognizes Corporal Raycevic's urgent voice in the darkness, nearby but far from her mind, as huge fingers clamp around her windpipe and squeeze. The plastic-shrouded man has already closed the distance with shocking speed.

She tries to scream, but her throat is already pinched shut. His gloved index finger and thumb clench tight. His plastic is cold against her skin. The fierce pressure crowds the blood up into her brain, making her thoughts swim.

Voices swirl around her: "You got her?"

"Yeah."

"You're sure?"

"I said I got her, Ray-Ray." The second voice comes from directly behind Cambry's right ear, muffled by a mask. The voice is deep, full of warmth and moisture. She smells something fragrantly sweet, like tea. "She just surprised me. You could've warned me she was so close—"

As he says this, he tightens his grip on her airway, wrenching her jaw painfully up and out of alignment. Her sinuses swell behind her face, about to explode. Her eyes well with stinging tears. Her chest balloons with pressure, a frenzied scream trapped inside her ribs.

"Careful." *Raycevic's voice rises with alarm.* "Careful. You're going to bruise her skin—"

"For Christ's sake, Ray-Ray—"

"No finger marks. No bruising. No evidence at all. If you crush her windpipe, that's a dead giveaway. Just steady, indirect pressure. Easy does it. Okay?"

The Plastic Man's choke hold doesn't loosen. But the uncomfortable grip relieves a bit under her jaw. Her elbows are wrenched achingly upward, like bird wings—she can't even remember how he did this. Whatever this wrestling hold is, he's done it before. They've done this before. This entire night has been one awful calamity after another, but to these bickering men, it's routine. And this gives way to the ultimate, most visceral disbelief of all: I'm being murdered. Right now.

By a man dressed like a condom, who talks like the Lucky Charms leprechaun.

Nightmares do come true, but never in the shape you expect. The man tugs her backward, as if easing her into a recliner. She kicks the ground in blind frenzy, searching for traction to brace against. Just yards of slippery, frustrating plastic. Like the sloped floor of a bathtub.

This is it, Cambry.

This is how you end.

Out here, off a desolate road in Howard County, Montana. Murdered by a crooked cop and a fat trucker. Strangled to death by a man wrapped head to toe in Saran wrap, with his crinkly mummy hands clamped around her throat. She struggles anyway. Her heels scuff plastic. Squealing, squeaking.

His warm voice returns by her ear. "Hey. You know how a boa constrictor suffocates a rabbit?"

I don't fucking care, *she'd say if she could.*

But it's been twenty, thirty seconds now. Her trapped breath burns inside her chest. She can't hold on to consciousness much longer. The oxygen dwindles in her brain, her thoughts going indistinct. Blood cells withering, going dark and blue.

"Sorry. I was expecting you to answer for a moment, there." The Plastic Man sniffles, a deep and snotty huff. "See, a boa constrictor has a whole pink mouthful of curved needle teeth. It grips the rabbit with them, dozens of little fishhooks, while it wraps its coils around and around and around—"

His hold on her left arm is weaker, she realizes. She squirms, twists, pivots. She can slip her left shoulder against his grip. Slowly, though. One sweaty inch at a time, and she's running out of it—

"And those coils tighten, oh so slowly, into a noose. Not a hard squeeze—just gradual constant pressure. Like a firm handshake. The rabbit might even have a full breath left in her chest from before the attack. Maybe she thinks she'll be okay, and she can just wait it out. Until she exhales."

Almost . . .

Cambry twists harder. But to her terror, there's a new and powerful darkness around her, rising, lapping at her thoughts, and a putrid taste in her teeth. River water. Green algae.

"See, the instant she lets that breath out, her chest shrinks a bit, and the boa's grip tightens, and her lungs won't ever inflate fully again. Against that gentle, constant squeeze, every breath is a little smaller, a little weaker—"

She keeps twisting her arm toward freedom, inch by torturous inch, outrunning her own fading thoughts, but she's already back in the Yakima River under the railroad bridge again, trapped far beneath the water's glassy surface, her lungs bloating with horror. Thrashing and flailing under a heavy blanket of cold water, with no one coming to help.

"And after three or four or ten breaths . . . the rabbit's lungs can't expand at all."

Cambry Nguyen's muscles turn to jelly. She goes limp.

His rotten voice in her ear as she slides deeper into the river's crushing darkness, sinking, sinking: "You aren't the first. You aren't the last.

You're nothing special to the boa. You're just satisfying his need, and he won't remember you at all when you're gone."

Lena, *she thinks as she plunges.*

Lena will remember me.

She'll come in after me.

She's jumping in right now . . .

CHAPTER 17
LENA

I hit the water and for a split second it feels as solid and unyielding as asphalt. I swear I'm splattering against it the way an insect streaks against a windshield. The air punches from my chest. My shins and knees instantly bruise.

I don't remember deciding to jump in after her.

I just did.

But I remember the fall itself, how Terrible Guy #11 and all the others vanished behind me under a turbine-engine roar of racing air. A disorienting tumble as sky, trestle, and water rearranged wildly. Upon landing, I know I did everything wrong and hit the river sideways. I definitely, certainly, one hundred percent did *not* clench my butt cheeks.

And now I don't know which way is up. I'm still whirling, slowing now under icy water clouded by a rush of bubbles. My teeth hurt. There's a ringing in my ears. I open my eyes but see only a glaucoma of dimness pierced by faraway rays of sunlight. I sweep my sore fingers to my sides, exploring, feeling for my sister in all this darkness. Finding nothing.

But I know where the sky is, at least—I orient myself—and I wait for someone else to shatter the shimmering surface above, to come pummeling down on me feetfirst and break my neck. It takes a few more moments of icy quiet to realize that I'm alone, that not one of Cambry's friends—not even her boyfriend—is jumping off the bridge to follow my sister down.

It's just me.

I'm the only one who jumped.

I'm alone under a heavy blanket of cold. My lungs burn with pressure. I've lost my breath upon impact. I know I should thrash upward through the layers of warmer water, to break the sun-stippled surface and take a gulp of air before diving again. But I won't. I can't.

I'm a lousy swimmer. My form is sloppy. I can't dive more than a few vertical feet. So this moment, right now—this ten feet or so of depth, gained by my thirty-foot plunge off this trestle—is my only chance to find her. I'll never get this deep again. And she's running out of air, wherever she is down here in the blackness of the river's bottom. Somehow I've already made up my mind: if my sister drowns down here—well, so do I.

I find gnarled tree roots. Slimy alien plants tangle between my fingers. I sweep them away but keep finding more, clinging in heavy knots. And my lungs are on fire now, and my brain is screaming for oxygen, and even my own body—in its stupid desperation—urges me to open my mouth, to try inhaling this dark water.

I'll be honest. I don't remember much of the searching in the crushing, cold vault.

I know only that I found her.

We explode to the surface together. I gulp a breath on a raw throat, gagging green water, fiery sunlight in my eyes. I don't remember daylight ever being so bright. I hold my sister. I can't tell if she's conscious or even alive.

Struggling to keep both of our heads above the surface, I lean back and begin a lurching backstroke. I can't see the shore. Only a vast blue sky and the tar-black skeleton of the bridge we leaped from, blurred by surges of water. I time my breaths between them. My chest throbbing, my bruised arms and legs melting with every kick and stroke. I'm running out of energy. I'm fading. We're sinking.

Cambry's head is on my shoulder, the lapping water coming to cover her face, and I'm afraid to look at her. I'm afraid she's already dead, and I would apologize if I had the breath, because I'm failing, letting her down, and we're both vanishing under the pull of the slurping waves—

Rocky ground scrapes my back.

We're ashore.

I heave onto the cold bank with her in my arms, rolling onto wet sand. I cough up water, spitting grass and twigs, and now the others show up—her boyfriend and friends followed the railroad tracks and took the long way down—and only now do they crowd us, asking if we're all right, a forest of arms and legs and shoulders blocking the sunlight. Cambry is just beside me, sprawled on the sand, and Terrible Guy #11 is tugging her upright, and I dread seeing her face—oh, God, if she's unconscious, none of us know CPR.

Her eyes are wide open.

She's in his arms, but she's staring over his shoulder at me with perfect razor-sharp awareness. There's an awed terror in her gaze, like she's met the Reaper and witnessed her own end in the black water. And it's hard to describe, but I feel like I've already lost her to it in some intangible way.

A fresh red rivulet runs down her eyebrow, beading on her eyelashes. She blinks it away. Only now do I get it, that the smack I'd heard wasn't her wrist hitting the beam.

I wish I hadn't been rooting against her.

We didn't speak at all. We just sat in shivering, exhausted silence, as others spoke for us. Clapping our backs, complimenting, joking. Someone cracked another PBR and shoved it in my face. We left the river soon afterward. Her friends went their separate ways in the evening. Most I never saw again. One of them died last year, I learned via Facebook. Overdosed on something.

Cambry and I never spoke of this afterward, either. We took

separate cars home, and by the next week she'd moved out in a tornado of slammed doors and thrown suitcases. I don't think she visited the Yakima River or that wooden railroad bridge ever again. To be harshly honest, I don't know if she ever knew it was me who jumped in after her and dragged her out. I think she might've assumed it was her boyfriend. I'm sure he liked it that way. Who knows if any of her people told her? Because I never did.

I'm not sharing this to brag. I just need to write it down, because there's a decent chance that by the time you read this, I won't be alive to tell it myself. I like this memory, I always have, and I privately hold to it when people urge me to remember the good. Not out of vanity—just because, in a small way, for a few terrified moments, our incomplete relationship as sisters felt whole and meaningful. She needed help, and I was there.

I hope she knew it was me.

Not her shitbag boyfriend, long forgotten.

That I loved her. That I *still* love her. She may be a stranger to me, but for all the miles of unknown space between us, now and forever, if she needed me, I'd follow her without hesitation.

So tomorrow I'll jump into that dark water again.

And this time, whatever happens, I know I won't be able to pull her out. God, how I wish I could. I wish the ghost stories of Hairpin Bridge would turn out to be real tomorrow, that I'll discover the fabric of space and time to be thin there and I can slip from present to past, to the moment Raycevic killed her. I'd tug a cosmic string to change her fate. I'd fix it so she never stopped at that bridge and could be that racing girl in my mind forever, exploding down highways and back roads from White Sands to the Everglades, the running girl with a notepad and her wits, who never, ever stopped. I'd trade places with her in a heartbeat. I wish I could.

But maybe when I confront her killer on that bridge, I'll make sense of what happened to her. Maybe I'll learn a little more about who she really was. Maybe I'll sleep better. Maybe the night terrors will end, and

I'll stop seeing the plastic bags and throaty screams and unraveling intestines on the ceiling of my bedroom.

And if I succeed at none of that . . .

There's always revenge.

I'll settle for revenge.

SHE DOUBTED HER SINGLE HASTILY AIMED SHOT HAD HIT THE gunman inside the cab. She saw the half-open window go opaque with cracks. And the rifle barrel swung up, falling back inside.

Silence.

Her Beretta's report flattened across the open land, rolling like thunder. Brass pinged off concrete. She dropped her purse and corrected her shooting stance, bringing her gunsights back up on the truck's driver's side door. The old man had ducked out of view. He'd crouched, or perhaps he'd been hit. She hoped she'd hit him but knew her luck wasn't that good. Not today.

Her thoughts raced. The Beretta's sights wobbled in her hands.

They murdered my sister.

Both of them.

It came down to this: a one-eyed trucker with a silly accent and a corrupt highway patrolman. She'd been prepared to capture Cambry's killer. But not Cambry's *killers.* For all her strategizing, she'd made a critical assumption that she recognized now: she'd never, until earlier today, considered the possibility of facing multiple enemies on Hairpin Bridge. She could hold one man at gunpoint. But not two. Certainly not this rifle-wielding stranger in the truck and Raycevic . . .

Raycevic, she remembered with a jolt of terror. She'd forgotten about him and given him the opening he'd been waiting for.

She spun to her left, aiming at the handcuffed cop. She feared he'd be midcharge already, tackling her to wrench the Beretta from her fingers, but no—he'd dropped to the pavement. He was twisting his cuffed hands behind his back. Sliding them to his ankles, under his raised boots—

"Hey!" she shouted, unsure of what else to say. "Stop."

The echo of her gunshot still crackling in the distance. An odd time to feel socially awkward.

On the concrete, Raycevic kept twisting his hands around his feet. Vaguely pathetic, like a flipped tortoise. He threw his head back toward the semitruck and shouted, "Shoot her."

Lena aimed at him instinctively. For a split second, her nerves buzzing with wild panic, she almost shot Raycevic. Right there. Right in the stomach.

His voice rising, a string of saliva on his lips: "Shoot-her-shoot-her-*shoot-her*—"

The truck, her mind screamed.

The fucking truck with the fucking man with the fucking rifle—

The air went syrupy. Adrenaline mired in quicksand as Lena whirled back to face the semitruck—yes, the man's rifle was back up on the door, nestled right there between the window's corner and her fresh bullet hole. The barrel pointed directly at her. A pulse of fiery light—

Lena hurled herself down to the concrete under a deafening cannon blast. A powerful disturbance of pierced air, startling in its *closeness,* a whine over her head as his high-caliber bullet came and went. Sprawled belly down on the road, she twisted and aimed and fired again.

A bad shot. She wasn't even sure she hit the truck.

The rifle bobbed, repositioning. She couldn't see the man crouched inside—just flickers of dark motion, a few inches of exposed scalp, as he aimed at her again. The concussive blast must have blown out the damaged window; safety glass poured down the door in a glittering blue-white shower. Whatever weapon he held in that nest of darkness, it was huge. It was loud. And he was ready to fire it again.

I'm exposed.

She needed cover. She needed to get behind something solid. Twenty feet back, to her left, was Cambry's Corolla. It would have to do.

She scrambled upright.

Raycevic's voice: "She's running."

On her palms first—the Beretta's barrel scuffed pavement, a gritty scrape—and then up into a runner's crouch, launching forward. *Get to the car. No time to stop—*

The trucker fired another blast. Again, she *felt* the bullet rupture the air as it struck to her left, peppering her with chips of concrete. She stumbled through it, dust in her eyes, as the rifle's report boomed in the sky. Still running, she twisted her head left to check on Raycevic. He was upright, too. Crouching, one pant leg hiked up, still shouting: "Shoot her, *just shoot her!*"

Her heels high. Palms slicing air. *Don't stop.*

Her sister's blue car came up fast. Lena kicked up her toes and hurled herself backward to slide the final five feet, slamming down hard on her back, sliding on the rough surface. Her tailbone mostly shielded by her jeans. Her right elbow skinning raw, as if chewed by a cheese grater.

She cried out, still sliding.

A rifle round struck the Corolla—the license plate frame exploded off—and she slid past it, slamming her knee against the bridge's guardrail. Safely behind the car. She made it.

Her dust cloud caught up with her and blew past. Her heart slamming in her chest. None of this seemed real. The entire last twenty seconds, the visceral alarm of both shooting and being shot at, couldn't have really happened. She realized her right hand was now empty.

No, the Beretta was in her left now. She couldn't remember changing hands, but she must have. Her kneecap throbbed where she'd knocked it against the railing post. Her chewed-up elbow stung. She felt blood racing down her sleeve, hot and sticky under the fabric. And the sun in her eyes was so strangely, unnaturally *orange*. The wildfire smoke was darkening the air. Like a strange dream, the sun looked like a dying star on some alien planet.

Focus. Her brain was tugging in a million directions. A million sensory details, all distractions. She rolled onto her stomach and crawled against the Corolla's front quarter panel, her back to the metal, shielding herself behind the engine block. The densest, most solid part of any car.

Across the bridge, the rifle fired again. A metallic thud as the Corolla took a bullet. She felt the concussive shock in her bones. She almost dropped the Beretta between her knees.

Okay.

She wiped dust from her eyes. Her fingers shaking. Tried to collect her thoughts.

Okay, Lena. Think.

The trucker was firing from a sniper's nest in his cab across the bridge, but he couldn't hit her without relocating. She was protected by the bulk of Cambry's car, lengthwise. She'd barely made it there, and shredded her elbow badly enough to need stitches, but yes, she was temporarily safe.

Although his thunderous weapon—whatever the hell it was—clearly outmatched her Beretta Px4 in range. And power. And accuracy. And noise. And pretty much everything.

Focus. What would Cambry do?

She peered up over the Corolla's hood. Sideways, exposing one eye. She couldn't see the trucker in the shaded interior. She caught something, though—more motion—the rifle's barrel moving on the door. Aiming. Preparing to fire again—

So Lena fired first.

She raised the Beretta over the warm hood and shot a staccato string at where she guessed the asshole's face was. She couldn't be sure. She was panic-firing at glimpses. Her shots went fast and without conviction, and she counted down in her mind—*Twelve left, eleven, ten, nine, eight*—knowing that all she was accomplishing was sailing harmless bullets over his head, through one window and out the other, making him crouch behind cover and wait. Still, she hoped she'd get lucky, that she'd nail him with a ricochet, or that he'd stupidly peek over the door and take one to the forehead.

A distant voice shouted, tinny in the crowded air, and she recognized that silly leprechaun accent and her heart sank with embarrassment: "She's wasting her ammo."

Despite herself, she fired one more furious shot (*Seven left now, for fuck's sake*) and smacked the truck's lantern-shaped mirror, spilling crunchy shards to the road. Not even close. An embarrassing miss. How many playing cards was that? At Sharp Shooters she would never, *ever* miss like this.

"Think she . . ." The trucker's voice burbled with rotten laughter. "Think she has a second mag?"

She stopped firing and ducked behind the hood.

Raycevic didn't answer the question. But the answer was yes. She had brought a second seventeen-round Beretta magazine to Hairpin Bridge, but her waistband holster didn't have a mag pouch and her jeans pockets were too much of a giveaway, so she'd kept it in her purse. And her purse was back in the center of the bridge, twenty feet away, where she'd dropped it after the first bullet snapped over her head.

She was pinned behind the Corolla's engine. More than half her magazine gone already. *Shit.*

She wanted to punch the concrete.

"Dumb bitch." A breathy laugh from the cab. "Must be her first gunfight—"

She hated him. Whoever this man was, she *loathed* him. And she loathed herself, too, for giving in to the pressure. For wasting precious ammunition. For living down to their assumptions, for revealing herself to be the frightened amateur they thought she was. She was better than this. She had to be.

A sour thought made her cheeks flush: *What would Cambry think?*

She'd tell me to be tougher. Be smarter.

Fight harder, Ratface.

Another rifle round thudded into the Corolla's engine block. Flinching behind it, Lena glimpsed motion in her periphery— Raycevic had moved. He was now standing in front of his black Charger, with a clear view on her left. Unprotected, in the open, like a shell-shocked soldier. For a surreal moment, they made eye contact.

No emotion in his eyes. No urgency. Just blank calm tinged with despair, like when he'd begged her to walk away. How long ago that seemed. It was strange—something like Stockholm syndrome—but seeing Corporal Raycevic gave her a flicker of relief. Familiarity. Maybe it was the lesser danger he posed hand-cuffed and unarmed, but she was almost *glad* to see him, like greeting an old friend.

Then Raycevic raised both cuffed hands together, and in them, a stubby shape her gut recognized immediately as a com-pact revolver. His eyes still blank, cold.

She thought: *Oh, come on—*

The weapon barked and the Corolla's side-view mirror ex-ploded over Lena's shoulder, showering her with glass and plastic. She was exposed again, now lengthwise *beside* her car. She dove to her stomach, thrust the gun toward Raycevic with knuckled hands, and fired back twice. No trigger control, no sight picture, all reflex.

A starfish of cracks appeared on the Charger's windshield, to Raycevic's right. He ducked behind his car. Out of sight.

He'd be back.

I have five shots left now.

She scooted back against the car, a frenzied voice in her mind: *This is bad.*

She was squished up against a compact car, pinned by a devastating rifle on one side and a cop with a revolver on the other. They had her at a ninety-degree cross fire. The Corolla couldn't shield her from both angles. She knew it. They would know it soon. She pressed herself against the car's hot metal, her ankles pulled in, her shoulders flat, but it wasn't enough.

They have you from two sides, Lena.

Simple geometry. She was exposed. Raycevic would pop out again from behind his Charger on her left, on her unprotected side, and take another shot at her.

This is bad.

This is so, so bad.

Her right elbow crunched against the car, full of gravel. Blood beaded between her fingers, bright as ketchup. The chemical smell of gunpowder. More details, more distractions. She urged herself: *Be like Cambry, living like a rover in her car. Focus on the important things. Dump everything else.*

She caught herself absently curling strands of hair around her index finger and twisting violently. She couldn't believe herself. Hair-pulling, even now?

Even during a *gunfight*?

The rifle boomed again. The Corolla shuddered, and engine fluid splashed the road. It had been a few moments since the last shot from that direction—maybe he'd been reloading. If so, that meant his rifle held five shots. But this, too, was a distraction, because the danger wasn't the fat bastard camped across the bridge. The danger was Raycevic. To her left.

She aimed back at his cruiser and waited for him to reemerge. Salty sweat stung her eyes. The Beretta rattled in her hands, her sight picture veering. She couldn't keep the front and rear sights together. She couldn't focus.

Bad odds, she knew. He had cover. She didn't. He had her entire unshielded body to shoot at. Her target would be a sliver of his exposed face. Half a card in her deck of fifty-two.

Don't miss.

Her index finger crawled to the trigger and squeezed it halfway. Down to a millimeter, a muscle twitch from firing. The guys at Sharp Shooters called this *staging the trigger.*

"Ray-Ray." From across the bridge, that familiar Irish accent rang in the pressurized air, so strangely alien in Montana: "*Oi. Ray-Ray.*"

Behind his car, Raycevic's voice was alarmingly close. "What?"

"Did you see her?"

"Yeah. I saw the little bitch."

They're working together. It was chilling to hear them communicate. They didn't care if she overheard. They outnumbered her. They'd encircled her.

"I've . . ." Raycevic's voice lowered to a growl. "I've got a clear shot on her."

She held her aim and waited. She had no choice. Moving anywhere else was instant death. The trucker's rifle boomed again, but Lena tried to ignore it. She knew it was another distraction, just suppressing fire. Meant to pin her down while Raycevic fired the killing shot.

She glimpsed him now, a blurry shape peering around his cruiser's taillight. She fired again, too late. Another waste.

Four left, you idiot.

She held her aim. Bit her tongue hard. Blinked away another drop of sweat.

You're losing.

"She's wasting her ammo," Raycevic hooted. "She's pissing herself."

She wanted to shout back—*Speak for yourself, asshole*—but it was a waste of breath. He had her. It was a losing engagement, him versus her forced lengthwise against her car. He knew it.

"She knows she's pinned," the cop crooned. "She's got nowhere to run. Nowhere to relocate to. I've got her. She's completely exposed from my side, with no cover. There's nothing between us—"

Lena grabbed the Corolla's door and opened it—between herself and him.

"Oh, *goddamnit*—"

She scooted low. Now shielded from Raycevic's revolver by the open passenger door. Shielded from the trucker's rifle by the engine block. A wedge of safety.

The trucker shouted, "What? What happened, Ray-Ray?"

"Nothing. It's fine."

"Did she block you with a door?"

"I said it's *fine*."

She laughed a hot gasp. She hunkered against the Corolla's lifesaving passenger door, nearly bumping it shut. She held it open with one palm to the blue paint, slipping her knees underneath herself. To better crouch and return fire.

She was still in this fight, protected on both sides, dug into cover like a tick. Her Beretta in her right hand, noticeably lighter as its ammunition depleted. Her situation was still terrible—she was still cornered, outgunned, with four shots left—but hell, she was rolling with it, adapting, proving to be a royal pain in their asses. Would spartan, scrappy Cambry approve? She hoped so.

Good move, Ratface. Keep it up.

"Hey." The cop shouted to his buddy abruptly, a jarring question: "What's the difference between cover and concealment?"

Bizarre silence.

The trucker answered: "I don't know, Ray-Ray. What?"

Lena's blood chilled.

Cover versus concealment. This stirred another memory from Sharp Shooters. Something written. Where did she see it? A poster? Yes. A cartoon poster by the restrooms—just to the left of the drinking fountains—posed that very riddle, with pictures of ordinary objects sorted into two columns. *Cover* was boulders, cement, brick. *Concealment* was things like bushes, walls, furniture . . .

"Ice the bitch—"

. . . And car doors.

The painted metal exploded inches from her face. Shrapnel slashed her cheek, stung her eyes, peppered her front teeth. She screamed with shock, slapping a hand to cover her face and slamming down low to the road. Raycevic fired again—a second hole punched through the door, shattering the handle into plastic shards.

His gunshots echoed. Crisp thunder.

Lena stayed flat. Her cheek pressed to the concrete. Blood in her teeth, the taste of copper.

"She screamed!" the trucker giggled. "I heard it. Sounded exactly like Cambry—"

Hunched fetal below the pierced door, she caught her breath. Still alive? Yes. Crunchy flecks of Toyota paint on her tongue. Her cheek turning warm, a dozen tiny paper cuts soaking with blood. The window disintegrated above her, showering her with blue-white fragments. Yes, the door had been concealment, not cover. Raycevic's bullets had punched right through it, like it was paper.

Stupid, she thought. *Stupid, stupid.*

I should have paid more attention to the posters.

And she realized her hand was empty. In her panic, she'd dropped her Beretta.

Piggish laughter from the cab. "I . . . I love that scream—"

She found her pistol on the concrete to her left and grabbed it with numb, blood-slippery fingers—accidentally slapping the trigger—and it fired sideways into the Corolla. *Three shots left. Three left now, you fucking clumsy idiot.*

"Ray-Ray. Did you hit her?"

"Can't tell."

"Then shoot again. Lower."

"Okay." His voice focused—he was aiming at the door again.

Lena's stomach heaved with terror.

She was already pressed as low to the concrete as she could possibly flatten. No space to move. No escape. All she could do was close her eyes, cover her face, and wait for it.

In her awful, dwindling seconds she tried to picture Cambry's face, to sear it into her mind. She couldn't. Her thoughts were water. She tried to hold on to something. Anything. Only the bad. Fights. Plastic. Steaming guts. Barbies with molten faces. Twelve-year-old Cambry's knife sliding through the doe's fur with a splash of warm blood. The deep ache of last night's dream, of being shoved away and scolded and rejected from the grave: *Go, Lena. Please go.*

Just go—

Raycevic's revolver barked again and a third hole pierced the blue paint above her in a gritty blast. She held her breath as the echo faded—waiting for a bone-splitting bolt of pain, for non-existence, for the bright tunnel of death, and experiencing none of those things.

The echo faded.

Still alive? Yes. His third bullet had hissed over her head. She had gotten lucky. She held the Beretta in livid knuckles in a bed of glass kernels, listening, blinking sweat from her eyes.

"Did you get her?"

"I don't know. Hopefully." Raycevic audibly smirked. She couldn't see his face, but she knew it was the same venomous grin she'd seen once today, an hour ago.

Because she did toss herself.

Catching her breath, her heart slamming in her throat, Lena made a desperate promise: She would kill him. She would kill them both. Forget bringing them to justice. Forget the audio record. Forget writing a book. Today wasn't about building a case or taking the proper channels. Today was about *killing* the men who took Cambry's life.

And right now they were winning.

Raycevic shouted, "Still alive, Lena?"

She didn't answer.

"You came all this way to find the truth. So, what do you think? Was it worth it? I gave you a chance to walk away, Lena. You should've taken it."

She wouldn't have. Even now.

He darkened. "You're all that's left of your sister, you know."

She said nothing.

"So, when we kill you today, Lena, it'll be like she's really, truly gone. Erased."

He's goading me, she knew. *Trying to make me talk.*

"You should know, Lena." His voice lowered: "I fucked her."

She wouldn't take his bait.

"She loved my cock, Lena."

Still she said nothing.

She waited. So did they. The silence built and built.

A shadow darted over the bridge. It was a vulture crossing

overhead, its black wings stuttering through a flash of sunlight. Its flaps sounded like sighs.

Wait, Lena. She held her breath.

Wait, and force them to make a move.

"You could've fucking warned me she had a gun, Ray-Ray," the trucker finally shouted abruptly. "I wouldn't have parked so close—"

Raycevic sounded defensive. "I didn't know she brought one."

"You didn't pat her down?"

"It was just a meetup."

"And you *wonder* why you're the one that flunked academy selection?"

The trucker's words were vicious. Hateful.

She enjoyed hearing the men bicker. She kept her breaths controlled, in and out, and waited. She didn't dare move—even the lightest crunch of glass would give her away. She gripped the Beretta, sticky with her own blood, and aimed up at the door. If she played dead, she'd force Raycevic to come in close to verify his kill, and then she could surprise him with a bullet to the face.

The trucker again: "She could be playing dead. To lure you in close and surprise you."

"I know."

For Christ's sake. She could do without the commentary.

"Be careful, Ray-Ray."

Ray-Ray. And she hated the man's singsong nickname for Raycevic. There was no affection or humor in it. It was a taunt—sarcasm and cyanide.

She heard a dry click. Then another. Another. Her eardrums still cottony from the gunfire, it took her a few moments to recognize the small sound of footsteps on pavement. Raycevic's boots.

He was coming.

This was her chance. She elbowed upright into a better shooting position, glass kernels crunching beneath her. Her heart slamming vivid blasts of color in her eyes. She listened as the cop's boots clicked closer and closer. Every sound seemed magnified. The sigh of the wind. A faint ring in her ears.

His footsteps changed course. Moving right. She understood—rather than approach the open door directly, he was moving to encircle her from the right.

She repositioned, her back touching the punctured door. She aimed right.

"Passing through your line of fire."

His voice moved, one footstep at a time. The shooter in the truck was doing his job, keeping Lena fixed with covering fire while Raycevic maneuvered. Executing a pincer move. It was unfair, but gunfighting isn't about playing fair. Duels are for the movies. Gunfighting is about *advantages,* about stacking the odds in your favor, and fighting dirty and smart.

His footsteps slowed with anticipation. He was circling the Corolla's front now, sidestepping the headlights with his revolver aimed. Rounding the corner a few degrees at a time, clearing the space beyond it inch by inch.

Crouched beside the front tire, Lena raised the Beretta and drew a shaky bead where she estimated the cop's face would appear. She held her aim exactly there, on that unremarkable patch of smoky sky, staging the trigger with her index finger and focused on his footsteps. The creak of flexing leather. The click of the sole touching down.

So close now.

The trucker shouted, "Ray-Ray, is she dead?"

He didn't answer. Another footstep. Was he ten feet away? Eight?

"Ray-Ray?"

She held her aim and waited.

Sweat dripped into her eye. She blinked it away.

"*Ray-Ray*. Hey. Talk to me."

A small consolation: Raycevic had to be getting just as annoyed with the old man in the truck as she was. Predator and prey were mere feet apart on opposite ends of the car and drawing closer, guns up, trigger fingers rigid, a heartbeat away from instant death, and the faraway asshole would *not shut up*—

Ray's sunburned face entered Lena's sights.

Six feet away.

Right over the Corolla's hood. Her blocky sights were right on his sweaty forehead, right between his surprised eyes as they found her, too—*dead center,* as sure as a shot can be—and as he thrust his gun back down at her, she was already pulling the trigger.

Nothing happened.

No kick, no noise. Nothing. The Beretta suddenly inert in her hands—

Jam.

Her mind screamed with white-hot panic—*jam, jam, jam*—and she kicked and scooted backward as Raycevic fired at her. Concrete chips exploded off the road, inches to her right. This close, she felt the revolver's blast rattle her teeth.

The big man crouched behind the Corolla's grille, huffing with adrenaline. This close, she could hear his panting breath, smell his sweat. "Holy shit."

She kept scooting back, back, knocking the bullet-riddled passenger door shut, but there was nowhere to go. She was pinned behind her sister's compact car. The gun useless in her hands. She recognized Raycevic's throaty laugh, alarmingly close. "She almost got me."

"What?"

"I think she's jammed—"

Yes, the Beretta Px4 was jammed and slide-locked in Lena's

hand. She already knew what had happened: a stupid amateur mistake. She'd broken a cardinal rule of shooting. When she'd grabbed the weapon with her finger on the trigger and accidentally fired it off the ground, the slide had skimmed the pavement. Interrupting the cycle. She saw a gleaming brass casing pinched inside. *A failure to extract,* the rangemaster had called it at Sharp Shooters. *They can be fussy.*

She tugged the pistol's slide—firmly stuck.

"No more chances." She heard Raycevic lick his lips, crouched at the front of the car. His voice was calm, coaching. "She's behind the vehicle's front doors. You're shooting the .30-30 big boy, right?"

"Yeah."

"*Front* doors. Not the back ones."

"Okay."

Lena understood. *Oh, come on.*

She scrambled farther back on her elbows and knees, the slide-locked Beretta clattering in her hand, as another high-caliber round exploded through the passenger door behind her, slamming it violently back open. It left a crater, dwarfing Raycevic's three pea-size holes.

She cursed through her teeth.

The Corolla was becoming Swiss cheese, leaving her unprotected. Only the steel engine block could reliably stop a bullet. That was why Raycevic had moved there—to cut her off from it.

"Did I get her?"

"She moved."

"Where now?"

"Rear doors."

She crawled farther back, a racing animal scramble, stopping at the Corolla's trunk because there was *nowhere else to go.* She hunched up in a fetal position, covering her face, waiting. She knew it was coming. For a nerve-shredding second, nothing happened.

Then it did: another tooth-rattling detonation behind her, another crater blasted through the rear passenger door. Glass kernels fell out of the windows. Whatever this rifle was, it tore gaping, illogical holes into everything it touched. Like taking fire from a Civil War–era cannon.

A dreamy yellow substance wafted down around her. Snow? Ash?

No. Obliterated seat foam.

She gripped the Beretta with both hands and fought the weapon's jam under the surreal blizzard, twisting the slide in her bloody fingers, but it wouldn't budge. The 9-millimeter brass was smashed inside the mechanism's teeth, a wicked metal clog.

Shit, shit, shit.

"Nowhere to hide." That rancid smirk in Raycevic's voice. "She's behind the trunk now."

She knew he was right; she was out of space. Trapped behind a perforated car. Struggling with a jammed pistol, useless and slippery in her hands.

She was tugging her hair again, wrenching her scalp hard, like pulling up carpet. It had all gone to shit so fast. Fifteen minutes ago, she'd had Raycevic handcuffed and alone at gunpoint. She *knew* he'd radioed someone. How arrogant she'd been, to believe she could handle it alone. She'd brought a gun when she should have brought backup. From the very beginning she'd assumed Corporal Raymond Raycevic was an outlier, a single rogue cop operating alone. Serial killers are always loners, right?

She thought about Cambry in her dream, heartbroken and defiant. Refusing to let her in, refusing to say *I love you,* or explain anything.

I'm sorry, Cambry.

Fighting the locked pistol in her hands, she felt it coming—a wave of hot tears welling in her eyes—and she hated herself for it. It felt fundamentally wrong to cry here, while crawling behind a shot-up car with blood and scorched gunpowder on her hands. This was a gunfight. There's no crying in a gunfight.

I screwed up, sis.

I underestimated him, and I'm so sorry.

This was it. The assholes who murdered her sister would kill her, too, on this very same bridge. All because she had the audacity to challenge a law enforcement officer to a *shootout,* of all things. To something he was literally trained for. And now she was pinned, encircled, almost out of ammunition, and she couldn't even fire her three remaining shots, as the gunmen's withering fire pierced the car's flimsy metal, corroding it before her eyes—

Then she froze.

Meaning . . .

It hit her now, a quiet bolt: *Meaning my bullets will, too.*

She pictured that smug asshole in his cab, crouched behind the shelter of his own door. She gave the Beretta another twist in her hands, harder, *harder,* straining with pinched fingers and watery eyes—and with a gasping release, the mechanism finally opened.

A squashed shell casing fell in her lap.

She let the gun's slide rocket forward. It clacked home on an oily spring, chambering a fresh round. Ready to fire.

Yes.

She exhaled a hot, shivery breath, and across the bridge, a matching dead-bolt click-clack echoed from the truck's cab. As if in unison, the trucker shouted, "Ready to fire."

"She's right behind the trunk."

"Gotcha." She imagined the one-eyed man taking aim again with that devastating rifle, leveling his scope on the Corolla's trunk. His grubby fingernails crawling over the trigger, squeezing.

Raycevic panted: "Blow her guts out."

Lena had an idea. A bad one. She sat still with her back to the metal trunk and waited, the noise and sun and gritty discomforts dissolving away, last night's dream slipping back to clarity. The way Cambry had refused to even look at her. The piercing heartbreak in her eyes when she finally did. Her cold sidelong whisper: *Just go.*

She waited.

Lena, go.

No. Not yet.

Please, go.

Still, she waited. No second chances. Her timing needed to be exact. Her sister's eyes watering with tears now, Cambry shoving her with an open palm, her voice twisting with frustration.

Go. You're running out of time—

Now.

She whirled left, rolling away from the Corolla and into open space—another concussive crack as a bullet punched through the trunk, ripping through her sister's folded clothes and tent inside and exploding out through the panel she'd crouched behind a half second before—and as she hit the concrete, she brought the Beretta up in knuckled hands and aimed straight across Hairpin Bridge's lanes, at the semitruck's cab. This time Lena didn't aim through the truck's shattered window, at the glint of a rifle barrel and a few half-glimpsed inches of scalp.

She aimed lower.

Lower. Directly at the truck's door. Squarely at the Kenworth logo on the red paint. Exactly where she estimated a human occupant would be crouched.

She fired three shots.

They came out like three heartbeats, as controlled as a Tuesday afternoon at Sharp Shooters into a fresh deck of fifty-two: Crack. Crack. Crack.

Three silver holes pocked the door's red paint. Exactly where she'd aimed.

Her third shot had felt different—if you spend enough time at the range, your muscles can identify the abridged recoil when the slide locks empty—and she knew this was it. She was out. But she stayed frozen there on her stomach, her empty Beretta's sights still pin-sharp, aimed in a suspended moment on that truck, at the tight grouping of holes in its door.

Silence. The world seemed to catch its breath.

She waited for the man's rifle to reappear over the door. For the next fiery muzzle blast.

She waited.

And waited.

She was sorely aware of Raycevic somewhere to her right. Aware that she was now vulnerable, that she should scramble back to her dropped purse, reload, and reengage—but strangely she sensed Raycevic was waiting, too, on a lungful of breath. A realization was building, coalescing in the air. She resisted it. She wouldn't, *couldn't* allow herself to believe it.

I got him.

THREE PINPRICKS OF DAYLIGHT HAD APPEARED IN THE TRUCK'S door, right before his eyes.

The old man slumped back, the cowboy rifle falling crookedly in his lap. He blinked in the sudden silence, the air still thick with scorched powder and smoke. He realized he was splashed with a warm liquid he couldn't identify. It drenched his hair. Droplets cooling on his cheeks.

He stared stupidly at those three holes.

Then, with glacial dread, he rotated his neck and inspected the cab's interior around him—trying to trace the three bullets' paths, if any had hit him—as more liquid dribbled down his eyebrow, gumming his eyelashes. It was sticky. Body temperature.

Blood, he realized. *My skull is blown open.*

He fought a scream. He'd always wondered why women screamed when he smothered them in his plastic. There was never anyone nearby to hear. It was a waste of remaining oxygen. It was a strange and helpless animal thing that puzzled him, like why they moan during sex. But now he had a scream swelling inside his own chest, so maybe he finally got it. It gnashed against his ribs, threatening to burst.

I'm dying. Oh, Christ, I'm dying.

He tried to focus on straight lines. He thought in lines, vectors, angles. He'd been an A-plus geometry student. He never used Google Maps or Waze like the other drivers. No, sir—give him a map and a graphing calculator, and he'd find his way to Eureka, California, like a homing pigeon. And now, reconstructing the three bullets' paths was how he processed his shock. Like a computer rebooting.

Bullet number one? It had entered the door just below the handle and pierced a folded map before skimming his belly just above the pelvis. His white T-shirt was soaked with blood. It didn't hurt, exactly—more of an uncomfortable, hernia-like tightness. But it wasn't fatal. It was a purple heart.

More warm blood dribbled down his forehead and into his eyes. Too much to blink away. That panicked scream thrashed inside his chest again.

I'm dying. That bitch domed me through the door, and oh, God, I'm dying.

Don't scream. Bullet number two?

My brain is runny egg yolk, leaking out of my skull.

Bullet number two—he tried to focus—was farther forward. The 9-millimeter slug must have nicked the steering wheel, passed under his armpit, and then hissed over the dashboard and—presumably—out the window like the others. Bullet two had missed him. A small relief.

This left bullet number three.

The one that killed me . . .

Bullet three had penetrated the door six inches higher, to his left, and ripped a cottony gouge out of the driver's seat. He followed its path to the cup holder, where it had struck his sweet tea bottle. Glass blades glimmered. The seat was sticky with running droplets of tea, warmed by the sun—

Wait.

Tea?

He ran his tongue over his upper lip. Tasted it.

I'm splashed with sweet tea. Not blood. Thank Christ, it wasn't blood and cerebrospinal fluid and chips of skull running down his face. He was okay.

He'd still taken a ricochet to the hip, of course, and it hurt royally. Blood bloomed over the belly of his shirt, livid red in the sunlight. But short of sepsis it wouldn't be fatal, and he knew a veterinarian who'd fixed him up with some quality painkillers for his eye back in June. No, Lena's three bullets through the door weren't half as awful as he'd feared. He was down but not out, and he still had his Winchester cradled in his lap, and yes, even immobilized in his cab, he was still in this fight.

He twisted, feeling knives of pain above his crotch. From the floor space, he couldn't see over the door. But sounds carried. If Lena approached his truck, maybe hoping to grab his rifle to fire at Ray-Ray, he'd hear her footsteps. He certainly wasn't in much shape to run or duck or properly gunfight. His ass was planted here, in the sun-cooked nest where he spent sixteen hours a day anyway.

This didn't bother him, but something else lingered at the edge of his thoughts. He feared he was missing something. Forgetting something.

Where did the second bullet go?

Didn't matter. It missed him. Just like the one that had exploded the bottle of sweet tea in his face, and the five or six she'd fired through the windows that snapped harmlessly over his head.

It was lower than the others, his mind whispered.

It went somewhere.

Fine. He looked again, wincing through another stab of pain, and retraced the bullet's trajectory as it punched through the door, gouged through the steering wheel, passed by his shoulder, and continued above his Quadratec CB radio, directly into—

He froze.

Kitty.

She wasn't coiled into her familiar ball shape. Her pose was strange, arched. Her neck cocked backward, her jaw grimaced to show pink gums and needle teeth. A rivulet of blood ran down the dashboard. Kitty and him—they'd seen thousands of miles of highway together, from the white peaks of Colorado to the muggy wetlands of Louisiana. Sometimes she rode on his shoulders like a cold, clammy scarf. She'd seen him through three trucks, a divorce, a prostate cancer diagnosis, and the suicide of his son. Next week would have been Kitty's twenty-third birthday.

Now, finally, Theo Raycevic screamed.

CHAPTER 18

LENA HEARD IT ECHO FROM THE TRUCK'S CAB. A SURREAL wailing cry that rose like a siren. It punched her gut—the raw *consequence* of it. The violence of discharging a firearm, watching it tear painful and irreplaceable holes into the world. Paper targets don't scream.

For a split second she felt a pang of sympathy for the man she'd shot inside the truck, who'd been trying to kill her just moments ago.

She swallowed it.

The Beretta was slide-locked in her hands. Empty and sadly light, like a plastic toy. And Corporal Raycevic was still armed, still crouched a car's length away. She heard his breathing, a soft and patient huff, as he weighed his next moves. The fight was still on. She'd injured one of her assailants, perhaps fatally, but she'd spent the last of her ammunition to do it. There's no half credit in a gunfight.

With a quivering hand, she twisted a finger around her hair and tugged hard.

The man's screams intensified, building like a migraine as Lena tried to think. Forcing her thoughts upstream against the noise: *I'm defenseless. I need to reload. Or I'm dead.*

"Dad!" Raycevic shouted. "Dad, are you hit?"

The asshole in the semitruck was Ray's *father.* She pushed the revelation away. Another distraction, not relevant to her current problem.

"Say something, Dad. Please—"

But the trucker's cries had already tapered off, leaving a strange vacuum.

"Dad?" His voice hardened. "I'll get her. I promise."

Cold terror seized in her gut, a wave of trapped-animal panic. She urged herself to focus. Ignore the distractions. *My second magazine. Where is it?*

In her purse.

Where's my purse?

In the center of the bridge. Where she'd dropped it.

In the open.

"Shit—"

She could see it from here. Twenty feet away? Thirty? She steadied herself against the Corolla's dusty bumper and considered running for her purse. Could she bolt the distance, grab the mag, slam it into the Beretta, and return fire—all before Raycevic shot her? No. No chance.

Worse, with a single car's length between them, the silence cast a microphone to every footstep. He'd hear her very first step. She wouldn't make it halfway. She'd die with bullets in her back.

"I'll kill the little bitch, Dad. I promise—"

She gripped the empty pistol, exhaling through shivering teeth. Bad ideas shuttering through her mind, one hopeless dead end after another. *Run for my purse?* Get shot. *Stay here?* Get shot. *Hide under the car?* Get shot.

She'd backed herself into a hard corner. She didn't know what else to do. She kept looping her hair between her fingers, falling back to that terrible mindless habit and twisting until the pain was unbearable. Her eyes watering with stinging tears as the ideas turned more desperate.

Charge Raycevic? Get shot.

Throw the empty gun at his face? Get shot.

Another knot around her index finger. Twisting harder. Harder.

Beg for mercy? Get laughed at, then shot—

Her hair tore from her scalp with a sharp, crackling rip. A rush of fresh warmth.

It startled her, the sickening sensation of her own body coming apart. All of her senses caught up to her at once and the world went thick, gauzy. Pain flared from her shredded elbow. And to her right, beside the Corolla, she heard a gentle, leathery click. Then another.

Approaching footsteps.

He was coming.

He might kill me tomorrow.

I know this. I'm not stupid. And in case he does, I need to set the record straight on something about Cambry.

Here it is.

One summer in Oregon, when Cambry and I were twelve, we came across a whitetail doe that had been hit by a truck. Her legs were broken. Her eyes lolled up at us and she made this strange rumbling noise from low in her throat, like a cat purring. And if you went to our school you've already heard the next part a thousand times: that to my horror, I watched young Cambry Nguyen wordlessly kneel, pull out her butterfly knife, and slit the doe's throat.

And it's all true. She did it.

But only because I *asked* her to.

When she refused, I begged her. I promised I wouldn't tell. I couldn't stand to hear the purring anymore or see those awful bent legs, and I knew it was miles to the farmhouse, hours until an adult could get there, and I was too much of a coward to do it myself.

So finally, Cambry did it.

I watched.

Then she rinsed her hands in a creek and we didn't speak at all on the rest of the walk back. It started to hail. I remember sobbing the whole way, the two of us walking on opposite sides of the highway under the pelting storm. I know now that ending the animal's pain wasn't enough. I'd needed someone to blame, and you can't blame a truck.

When we got home, I didn't just break my promise. I told my parents it was *all* Cambry, that twelve-year-old Cambry murdered a dazed animal for no reason at all. I showed them the blood on her secret folding knife, which it turns out is illegal to own under eighteen. They believed me. Not her. To this day, they still believe my version.

Cambry Nguyen. Deer Slayer.

I'm the reason she was the only seventh grader at Middleton Junior High with her very own psychotherapist. I'd relished being the victim with the nutcase sister, so I kept retelling the story with new details and gore. She'd lost most of her friends by October—none of their parents allowed her in their homes. Someone filled her locker with a can of red paint. And as she grew up, Cambry lived down to her reputation and kept acting out—the stunt with the toilet and the sponge was a highlight—but it wasn't until high school that the psychologist finally pegged her: *schizoid personality disorder.* To this day I don't know if she had always been there or if I pushed her.

The psychotherapist was a drunk, too. Sorry, but he was. He came in for house calls with a red sweater and red cheeks like a shitfaced Mr. Rogers. I remember snippets of overheard sessions, and the one that lingers most is Cambry's pained, pleading voice, muffled by a door: *You're not listening.*

You're not listening to me.

And now I wonder—if I'd kept my promise to my sister twelve years ago, maybe we would have had a functional relationship as adults.

Maybe Cambry wouldn't have felt the need to painfully uproot herself every few months from a world she could never relate to, living like a nomad in her Toyota with sea glass in the console and a tent in the trunk. Maybe that moment was the first domino, my only chance, and I lost her. Maybe I pushed her to that bridge in Montana.

Maybe it's my fault that my sister is dead.

Maybe.

I'll never know.

So there it is, in writing. It's out of my head now. I can't describe how much of a relief it is to see these words on a screen, a single click from posting on *Lights and Sounds,* from becoming history. If I die tomorrow, this won't die with me.

I've let it go.

Maybe, if tomorrow goes wrong, this will give me some final comfort while Corporal Raycevic walks in close to finish me off.

HE CREPT FORWARD WITH HIS .38 UP.

One careful step at a time. Glass kernels crunched like egg-shells under his boots—he knew it didn't matter. Every sound and every footstep was magnified in the double-edged silence. She certainly heard him coming. And if she moved, he would hear her, too.

He'd heard nothing.

Where could she go, anyway? She was crouched behind the Corolla's trunk with nowhere to run. And she was low on ammo, if not empty. If she'd had a spare mag, she would have reloaded, and if she'd reloaded, he would've heard the click of a mag sliding home.

Again, he'd heard nothing. Just sun-blasted silence.

He kept his sight picture in focus as he advanced closer. He gently elbowed the passenger door aside. It clicked shut on a warped hinge.

Another crunchy step. Another.

"Hang in there, Dad," he shouted to the truck. "I'm finishing her."

No reply.

He held his revolver with the sights canted, in the textbook "high" position. His dominant hand up, his support elbow low. His support-side foot at a ninety-degree angle. Center Axis Relock, the system is called. A brutally pragmatic answer to Lena's quaintly old-fashioned isosceles shooting stance, founded on the radical notion that gunfights don't occur in shooting ranges. Real-life shooting scenarios are sudden, harrowing, and unpredictable, and an operator must be able to both retain their weapon from hand-to-hand attack and fluidly transition between close (unaimed) and ranged (aimed) fire. There's a poetry to it, watching a user rotate their body to efficiently engage threats.

Yes, smug little Lena Nguyen might shoot tighter groups on paper, but she'd already learned that her rehearsed skills didn't translate to the sweat and terror of real life. She'd already missed numerous shots, suffered a malfunction, and taken fire through cover. And she was about to receive her final lesson.

He came up on her. He sidestepped left around the Toyota's trunk, weapon up in a bladed stance. Sights aligned. With perfect focus, he cleared the hostile space beyond the vehicle's tailgate inch by careful inch, like slicing a pie, gradually revealing . . .

Empty concrete.

She was gone.

He blinked. *What?*

Left behind, a pair of empty Chuck Taylors. Slipped off and set neatly aside.

His brain struggled to process this. As jarring as three months ago, when Cambry had seemed to abruptly vanish into the night behind the bends of the dark highway, as if she'd evaporated. Where did she possibly go? And why would she take off her—

Something pressed into the back of his neck. A small circle of hot metal.

"Drop the gun, Ray."

Christ, he marveled.

They really are twins.

LENA CHANGED HANDS TO TRAIN HER NEWLY TAKEN REVOLVER on Raycevic, and then she walked him at gunpoint to her purse. There she quickly knelt, grabbed her backup magazine, and reloaded her Beretta.

He watched sullenly. "Wait. You were *empty?*"

She smiled, thumbing the slide stop. Seventeen new hollow-point rounds, loaded and ready. She was getting the hang of this.

"Come on." She tucked his revolver into her back pocket. "Let's go see if Daddy is still alive."

He sighed, beaten.

As they approached the semitruck, she made him walk in front—so if the old man in the shaded cab was still alive enough to lift his rifle and shoot again, he'd be forced to shoot around his son.

His *son,* Raycevic. She was still getting her head around it.

"You flunked academy selection?" she jabbed. "I thought you were Supercop."

He said nothing.

"What was it? Push-ups? Couldn't memorize the radio codes?"

No answer.

"Unless there's a test for not getting outsmarted and disarmed by a woman half your size? Because I think you fucking *tanked* that one, Ray-Ray."

Ray-Ray. His father's hateful taunt.

Still, Raycevic remained morosely quiet, giving her nothing, and they walked in silence through smoky air. She realized she didn't have the stomach to tease him further. She didn't have the energy to be cruel to a man who'd just lost his father. She knew what loss felt like. For an uncomfortable moment, Lena forgot all of the sweat and terror of the past ten minutes and felt like the aggressor. The bad guy.

I'm not the bad guy. I'm just trying to find justice for my sister.

Right?

A breath of wind slipped over the bridge, turning the sweat cold on her skin. She shivered. It occurred to her that the first shot fired in this gunfight had been hers, not theirs. It wasn't self-defense. Not exactly. Whatever the truth was, she needed to secure both son and father—and then she could finally get her answers. She could hear the truth from their lips, that these sick assholes strangled Cambry to death and then dumped her body off Hairpin Bridge to feign suicide.

Right?

She knew it. She just needed to hear it.

She was so close now.

They reached the cab. To Raycevic, she ordered: "Stand here."

He did, staring up at the semi's tall cab with dread. At the three holes punched through the red door. With a shaky voice, he called, "Dad?"

"Shut up." She approached with her Beretta raised. The screams inside had long fallen silent, but that didn't mean the old man was dead. He could be waiting in ambush. If he was still alive, she decided, she would try to reason with him. If he was dead, she'd confirm it. And whatever happened—there was a devastating rifle in there that she couldn't allow Raycevic to get his hands on.

She wiped grit from her eyes. Her cheek stung and itched, peppered with shrapnel buried in her skin like bug bites. Her chewed elbow throbbed, too. But she couldn't lose her focus. Not now. Not when she was this close to the truth.

She climbed the truck's smooth silver footrail. It was slippery, scorching hot from the sun. It burned her feet through her socks.

"Dad," Raycevic said hoarsely, "she's coming up on the door now . . ."

She snapped back to glare at him, but he'd already finished his sentence: ". . . so *please,* Dad, don't shoot her."

She studied him, now deeply uncertain. The handcuffed cop didn't meet her gaze, staring down to the road with defeat. His jaw quivered. He blinked and a falling tear glinted midair in the sunlight. Some persuasive acting—it was acting.

Please don't shoot her meant nothing, she knew. But as for *She's coming up on the door now*? That sure meant something.

Perched on the cab's footrail, keeping her body back, she extended her free hand and reached for the door handle. It was a thin, polished latch. She feathered it with blood-slick fingertips. Then slowly closed them around it. She held her breath, her stomach clenching into a ball, bracing for another thunderous gunshot to explode from the darkness within, blossoming the painted metal inside out, severing two or three of her fingers in one nightmarish blast.

It never came.

The handle clicked. She tugged the door open. It swung

hard, creaking the frame, and a few leftover shards of safety glass hit the road. She stayed back, her socks precarious on the slippery rail. She considered saying something to the man inside but decided against it. Raycevic had said enough.

She took a breath.

Then she peeked once inside the cab, a birdlike pecking motion, and glimpsed a single occupant collapsed in the floor space. Head down. And blood. Lots of blood.

She leaned back out, exhaling.

"Is he dead?" Raycevic whispered below.

She ignored him, passed the Beretta into her left hand, and peeked a second time, slower now. Her index finger curled around the trigger, ready to fire, as the cab's shaded interior rotated into view. The man inside did appear dead, as Ray feared. His white T-shirt—*I Believe in Bigfoot*—was stained with blood, bright and Technicolor-red. He'd clearly been hit by her gunfire. He was slumped against the stick with his head lolled down, facing his lap. She could see the brown strap of his eyepatch digging uncomfortably into his gray hair. Gunsmoke still tinged the air. The odors hit her all at once. Fetid, bacterial. Dried sweat, bad breath, stale farts, the inevitable result of a man in his sixties confined to a single location for days without showering.

She breathed through her mouth. She saw the rifle he'd been firing at her—vintage in its design but immaculately maintained—in his lap, barrel-down. Within her reach.

Take it, Lena.

She started to lean inside but stopped herself. It felt like a trap. She'd be turning her back to Raycevic outside. And what if the old man was playing dead? He could thrash to life and grab her wrist, wrestling the Beretta away, and she'd be too close to twist away and shoot him again—

Grab the rifle from his lap. Take the chance.

She didn't. It didn't feel right. She had two guns already. Why get herself killed for a third one she didn't know how to operate?

Throw it off the bridge, then.

No. Not worth the risk.

It's a risk just sitting there, too. In the lap of a man who might not be dead.

She tried to weigh equally bad options. Her stomach gurgled. She squinted in at the man's bloody shirt but couldn't tell where she'd shot him. Chest? Probably fatal. Stomach or hip? Less so—

"*Hey.*" She realized Raycevic was moving to her left. "Get off my flank, Ray-Ray."

He froze. Caught red-handed.

She pointed beside the front tire. "Back there. Stay."

"Is he dead?"

She didn't answer. She didn't know. Her skin prickled with goose bumps as she stood perched in the truck's doorway, orienting herself so she could see both of them. She was afraid to take her eyes off the blood-drenched old man inside, and equally afraid to take her eyes off Raycevic. Even handcuffed, he was deadly up close. In a heartbeat, he could sweep her ankles off the footrail, slam her down to the concrete, and stomp on her windpipe before she fired a shot. How many ways could a man like Raycevic kill with his bare hands?

Stay alert, Lena. More distractions.

He asked a third time: "Is he dead?"

"Yes."

"Are you sure?"

"Yes," she lied, watching the old man's body closely.

"Can I see him? Please?"

Somehow that felt like a mistake, too. Lena shook her head and the world wobbled. For a swirling moment, she felt nauseated. All of the sensory horrors came back at once—the racing panic of being shot at, the dense odor of gunpowder, the thunder of the blasts, the coppery taste of blood. The strange whining sound bullets make as they slice overhead. The dead man here in the cab, the stranger she'd personally *killed* through a door.

"He . . ." She said it aloud, like she had to justify it. "He shot at me."

"You shot first," Raycevic whispered. "We were defending ourselves—"

"Bullshit. One of you strangled my sister. Wrapped up in plastic, so you wouldn't leave any skin cells or hair or fibers. And you asphyxiated her, just gently enough that there'd be no bruising or marks on the skin or burst vessels in her eyes—"

"Lena, you're *not listening.*"

"Tell me now. Was it him or you?"

"It was neither of us."

"You're lying."

"Cambry jumped off this bridge." The cop treaded closer as he spoke—too close. "I'm trying to tell you the truth, Lena. You keep asking, expecting a different answer—"

On the dashboard she noticed a browned dirty sock coiled in a knot. It took her a few seconds to realize what it actually was. Stomach acid climbed her throat and she shook her head again, feeling the precarious situation thrash from her control. "No, no, no. You assholes killed my sister. You threw her body off the bridge and pretended to—"

"We couldn't catch her."

A hard stop.

"What . . . what are you saying?" She forced the pieces in her mind, trying desperately to make them fit. "What do you mean, you *couldn't catch* Cambry?"

Raycevic took another step. He was close enough to be dangerous now, close enough to grab Lena's ankles with his cuffed hands, if he chose to.

He didn't. He looked her dead in the eye. "Lena. She *got away.*"

CHAPTER 19

CAMBRY'S STORY

Cambry hasn't lost consciousness—not yet. She's only pretending. Letting her limbs go limp and sagging helplessly in the Plastic Man's arms is just an act.

He buys it.

His lips move beside her ear. "Gone already?"

My knife. It's been there in her right pocket, a faint pressure against her thigh, skimming the edge of her thoughts. It's right there. Inches away. And now, as the Plastic Man loosens his grip slightly to check her pulse, it's finally, finally within her reach.

Unseen, she closes her fingers around the KA-BAR's handle, sliding it out of her pocket. She peels open the three-inch blade with her thumbnail. Tightens a fist around it.

"Huh." He huffs, disappointed. "You know, kiddo, I thought you'd last longer than—"

Over her shoulder, she stabs him in the face.

The blade finds soft tissue and it feels like piercing jelly. Easier than she'd dared hope. She can't see where it entered, but she has a pretty good guess. At first the Plastic Man barely reacts. He just inhales sharply through his nose, crinkling plastic. Like the buildup to a sneeze.

Then he lets go.

Cambry rockets forward, hitting her palms on the slick tarp. She has let go, too—of the knife—and left it planted in the man's face behind her. She springs upright, shoes slipping, recognizing the tall shadow of the truck. The night air is shockingly cold, stinging her raw throat. Blinking, searching for Raycevic, for his red and blue lights, finding only darkness.

She spins, looking back at the Plastic Man.

He hasn't moved. He stands dumbly with both hands raised to his face. He's afraid to touch it. A double flash of lightning reveals the KA-BAR jutting above his respirator mask, pierced between his cheekbone and eyeball. His eyelids jerk open and shut, as if trying to blink away a grain of sand, waggling the knife's handle up and down.

He touches it, patting it with light fingertips. Feeling out this new development with a profound and terrible awe.

"Oh," he says. "Oh, wow."

She tastes vindication—then fear. He's not dead. Not even close. He's an injured animal, stunned by the sight of his own blood. In another moment he'll be enraged by it. She backs away from him, away, away, until her back thuds against the trailer's chilled metal.

"Oh." The crinkle of flexing plastic in the darkness. She can't see him. Behind her: "Dad?"

Her heart seizes in her throat—it's Raycevic's voice—but it's recycled, electric. It came from a radio unit. Meaning the cop isn't nearby. Not anymore.

"Dad, should I turn around?" The radio chirps again. "I'm at the bridge—"

The Plastic Man stomps furiously now. Hands clenched, hissing with exhaled pain. She can't see details without another flash of lightning, but she knows he's pulling the knife from his eye socket. With racing thoughts, she considers attacking him. Right now. Charging, tackling him, landing on top of him and mashing both palms downward against the jutting knife with all of her weight and tunneling it directly through his brain—

This is your chance, her furies urge. Your one chance. Now.

Fight him, Cambry.

But it's already too late. He screams and his knuckles tear juicily from his face. The knife flies and claps against the tarp somewhere. An enraged grunt.

"Dad. Come in—"

Invisible in the darkness, the Plastic Man lunges at her now. But Cambry feels the rush of displaced air and ducks under his whooshing arm. Then she twists on her ankles and skids below the semitrailer, crawling for the other side.

"YOU BITCH." *He crashes down on all fours behind her.* "YOU FUCKING BITCH—"

She scrambles between the giant tires on her elbows and knees, pushing through the dangling chains. She can't see the Plastic Man, but she hears him scuttling close behind her, panting, lunging for her ankle with a crinkly, grasping hand.

"Gotcha—"

But she slips between his closing fingers. He's too slow. She's too fast. She's born to run. Cambry has always been a speed demon, untouchable and uncatchable, always a heartbeat ahead, making her graceful French exit before the party rolls and the cops show up. She's already somersaulting out from the trailer's other side, pivoting hard left under a kicked spray of gravel.

She can see her Corolla now—there it is, lit by another strobe of lightning—and she breaks into a sprint as the Plastic Man howls behind her, in bloodcurdling rage: "FUCK!"

On the radio: "Dad. What did she do?"

"SHE . . . OH, JESUS FUCK. I CAN'T SEE OUT OF MY EYE—"

"What?"

"SHE POPPED MY EYE."

Good, *she thinks as she reaches her car. She tugs the door open—it's still ajar—and crashes down into the driver's seat. Home again. She twists the key and the engine coughs, taking a few sputtering seconds to turn. Just fumes in the tank.*

But the interstate can't be far now.

You'll make it, Cambry. Don't look at the clock.

The time is 8:58.

She cranks the car into gear. You'll get somewhere, and you'll find a well-lit public area, and you'll call the police. The real police. And both of these assholes will burn—

"SHE'S IN HER CAR—"

"Wait. What happened to your eye?"

Cambry stomps the pedal and the engine roars. An exhilarating sound she's always associated with freedom. The Corolla surges forward, barreling past the eighteen-wheeler. She flicks on her headlights, flooding the empty road with light and scans for the half-blind bastard, hoping to clip him as she careens past. No luck. Their voices fade in a blast of air: "SHE'S GETTING AWAY—"

It's all vanishing behind her. The Sidewinder truck. The Plastic Man. Their bickering voices, the choking pressure on her windpipe, the musty odors of sweat and snake shit inside the cab. All of it going, going, and finally gone.

Her speedometer hits sixty, seventy, eighty. The road bends and weaves. The night air races through her windows, tearing her hair back. She shivers and laughs, giggles as hard as stones in her throat. The assholes' trap failed. She witnessed something she wasn't supposed to see, and she's slipped their clutches and soon the whole world will see it, too. She'll make them famous. They'll be arrested, strung up, sentenced. Maybe the fat one will need a double-wide electric chair.

Now the road twists, ribbonlike, into an incline. A final patch of foothills before the interstate. Then she's home free. She checks her rearview mirror for pursuing headlights. Nothing. Another bolt of lightning confirms it. She's alone.

A straightaway now and she floors it. More cold air flecks the tears from her eyes. She can't help it—she's crying, laughing, screaming, all at once, because every breath is new: Mom and Dad and Lena, she *thinks with aching joy.* I'll see you again. When I get back to Washington, I promise, I'll see all of you again, and we'll be a family.

I'm sorry. I should stop.

I'm being wishful. The truth is, I have no idea what was in her mind at this point.

I should stick to the facts while I write this.

But I like to imagine my sister thinking warmly about us as she drives for safety. How she'll make amends with Mom and Dad. Maybe she'll get an apartment, stop living hand to mouth, take night classes in graphic design. Maybe—I hope—Cambry even thinks about me as she drives: I miss you, too, Ratface. I'm sorry we never speak. I'm sorry we're strangers.

I wish I had spent my time with you differently.

It's also possible that I never entered her thoughts at all on that cold night in June. I can't prove it. Based on Corporal Raycevic's account, I know only that my sister eluded the Plastic Man's attack and kept driving north, toward the interstate. Which means...

Ahead of Cambry, the road twists sharply.

Revealing a bridge.

It comes up fast. It emerges from the blackness, gaunt and skeletal and hideous. Erector-set beams stand in spidery fractals, bolted solidly into rock. A rust-eaten sign catches Cambry's high beams, and she glimpses black spray paint as the Corolla whips past:

ALL OF YOUR ROADS LEAD HERE.

CHAPTER 20

LENA

"WHAT REALLY HAPPENED TO MY SISTER?"

Theo Raycevic sat perfectly still with the Winchester barrel-down in his lap. He kept his head down, his breaths glacial, and just listened. He knew, based on the volume and bearing of Lena's voice, that her question was directed at Ray-Ray.

Listening is everything.

Eyes? Overrated. Most boas have near-useless daytime vision, relying instead on an almost supernatural awareness of smell and vibration. Theo understood this. His best moments are in the dark, when he's draped in painter's tarp and standing like a hanging coat inside a motel closet. Ignore your vision and your other senses take over. The tiny room becomes an intoxicating tactile buildup. The woman's gentle breaths. The jingle of her purse. Her padding footsteps from the bed to the bathroom sink, blithely unaware that she's sharing oxygen with her killer.

This was almost like that.

Ray-Ray must have hesitated, because Lena's voice rose: "*Talk*, Ray."

Her breaths were hitched, shivery. Theo reminded himself:

This wasn't a Super 8 unit, and she wasn't a dumb stray with heroin needles in her purse. Lena was a fighter, a scrappy little Asian like her sister, and she was still high on the adrenaline of the shootout. In her world, she'd survived the O.K. Corral. But Theo had gained some breathing room by playing dead, and now he would choose his moment to counterattack. She'd already made a cardinal error by not confirming her kill.

You don't have the instincts for this, he thought. *Not like Cambry did. You're just a shadow of her.*

He smelled the girl's sweat. Green apple in her shampoo. Maybe a deodorant of some sort, something breezy and floral. They always did smell nice.

Finally, Ray-Ray spoke. "He's . . . he's not a good man."

"Your dad?"

"I know he's not a good man."

Speak for yourself, Ray-Ray. This was like listening to his own eulogy.

"He, uh . . . he murders people."

No shit.

"Not just people. He targets women."

Oh, is that worse? So much for gender equality.

"He'd take them . . . uh . . . ." Ray-Ray's voice quivered with discomfort. "Off the roads. He haunts the highways, from Chicago to Austin to Memphis, like a roving demon in an eighteen-wheeler. He'd offer to help stranded girls, hitchhikers, drunk kids who just needed a ride home. If he couldn't get them inside his truck, he'd find out where they were sleeping that night. He called them his *strays.* Anyone young, tormented, living in her car, outrunning a rough past . . . who could easily disappear without a last known location."

Don't shit in your own backyard. I taught you that.

"I remember once when I was five or six, my brother and I were playing Nintendo and he walked in from his workshop.

And he was cloaked in this big raincoat. Head to toe, like a walking corpse in a body bag. Terrifying us both. I asked him what he was doing. And without missing a beat, he beams this huge crocodile smile through his respirator and says in a goofy voice: *Why, son, I'm the Plastic Man!"*

Theo barely remembered this. But it was oddly heartwarming that Ray-Ray did.

"Like a superhero," Ray-Ray said. "Like Clark Kent disappearing into a phone booth. It became normal to me, that sometimes Dad would disappear because he was being the Plastic Man."

His tone darkened. Like the sun passing behind clouds. "My brother and I learned the extent of it later, when we were eighteen. We each coped differently. He put a Mossberg under his chin, like I told you. And meanwhile, I'm about to start the academy in Missoula, my lifelong dream, and I've just lost my twin brother, and my father—my *only* surviving family—is a pathological killer. What do I do?"

Theo sensed motion. Three feet away, the girl was adjusting her stance in the doorway. She was focused on Ray-Ray outside and not on the slumped corpse down in the floor space.

This was as good a time as any.

He slid open his good eye. Breathed through his nose. Slowly, he crawled his right hand down to the Winchester's polished walnut stock. A reassuring familiar shape, sticky with blood and iced tea. He mentally rehearsed his attack: He would raise his head, lift the rifle, and blow the girl's lungs out. All in a microsecond, before she turned her pistol on him. He could do it now, if it weren't for one problem.

One major problem.

A round wasn't chambered. He would need to first crank the rifle's lever action to cycle a fresh .30-30 round, and that would make a distinctive noise. Lena would hear it.

Shit. He'd forgotten about that.

"I offered my father a deal," Ray-Ray continued. "That if he promised he would never, ever do it again, I would . . . help him cover his tracks."

"He did it again, didn't he?"

You bet I did.

"He relapsed, yeah."

"Poor guy."

As they spoke, Theo applied slow, constant pressure to the rifle's action. Opening the scissor jaws, millimeter by millimeter, to cycle the weapon as quietly as possible.

Then he would thrash up and shoot her.

"Seventeen years," Ray-Ray continued. "I've cleaned up my father's messes. Everything he's needed. Any hour. I've made bodies disappear. I've torched evidence. Buried vehicles. Misfiled records. For my entire career, he's been my ugly secret and I've been his guardian angel in blue."

My guardian angel in blue. Theo remembered saying that— those exact words—one morning while they poured cement. Father's Day, it had been. You can't make that shit up. Under his belly, he felt the Winchester's hinged mechanism open farther, farther, the firing spring's tension building—

"But," Ray-Ray added, as if this was important, "I only did the cleanup. Only the aftermath. I never had the stomach for the . . . you know."

This was true. How shattering it must have been for his young son, who'd idolized the boys in blue, who'd dreamed of being a cop ever since he'd first arrested his brother with plastic handcuffs—only to find himself grown up and playing for the wrong team. Life comes at you fast, huh?

The rifle's action opened to its apex and pushed out a spent .30-30 casing, which Theo silently guided out into his palm. He couldn't let her hear it hit the floor.

"You didn't try to stop him?" Lena asked.

"I-I *always* tried to stop him," Ray-Ray stuttered. "I threatened to turn us both in. Many times. But he always called my bluff, because he knew I was as committed as he was. And I had more to lose."

This would be the risky part.

Theo adjusted his two-handed grip and closed the lever a fraction of a degree at a time, slow and steady pressure, sealing a fresh round into the Winchester's chamber like closing a vault. Finally finishing with the faintest, most muffled click.

A whisper of motion. It was Lena, turning her head to face him. *She heard.*

Theo sat in jagged, sweaty silence. His pierced belly clenching, the hairs prickling upright on his skin. He wondered if she'd recognized the sound as a lever action closing. She knew her way around guns, didn't she? Unusual in a female. The temperature inside the cab seemed to change, hanging on a knife's edge. If Lena leaned in and inspected closer, she'd notice that the corpse's bloody fingernails were now clasped suspiciously *inside* the rifle's trigger guard.

A second passed.

Two seconds.

He waited in darkness with his good eye clamped shut. A drop of sweat trickled down his nose and hung from his nostril. It faintly tickled.

Finally, he heard the girl exhale and speak again. Back to Ray: "That's it? I'd been so fixed on you. But you're not even the killer." She sounded disappointed, like this whole shootout had been a waste of her time. "You're the killer's little *cleanup boy.*"

His son sighed, audibly hurt.

Theo felt an amused chortle well up from his gut, somewhere near where her 9-millimeter round was lodged. Maybe he did like her. Maybe she was worthy of Cambry's DNA after all. Not that it mattered: the Winchester was now cocked and ready between his knees. His index finger crawled around the trigger.

Lena hesitated, as if she dreaded saying it: "Was she . . ."

"What?"

"Was my sister one of his victims?"

This was a big question. It would receive a devastating answer, so Theo knew this was his moment to attack, to snap open his eyes, thrash upright, and raise the now-loaded .30-30 to fire into her chest. He waited in his private darkness for Ray-Ray to clear his throat and respond, and then he would give this little bitch the biggest surprise of her—

———

LENA SHOT THE OLD MAN IN THE FACE, JUST TO BE SURE.

He thrashed, a thin spray of blood filling the cab like sunlit powder. His skull thudded off the radio and he slumped against the stick shift, cranking it forward. The rifle clattered. Maybe it was Lena's imagination, but she swore she saw a split-second expression flash over the corpse's face.

It looked like *surprise*.

The gunshot reverberated in the confined space. Raycevic cried out in shock.

"I had to be sure," she said. "He could have been playing dead."

She'd fired the revolver bullet right through the man's upper lip. A little low on her usual deck of fifty-two, because she'd drawn and fired left-handed. But a solid hit nonetheless. She thumbed out the revolver's cylinder—all primers punched now—and dropped the empty weapon.

Raycevic stared with baffled horror. "Why . . . why would you *do that*?"

Gut feeling, she almost said.

And now her gut sensed something else—an uneasy motion. She realized the truck was moving. Below her footrail, the pavement inched under. Like standing over a receding tide.

Raycevic noticed it, too.

The old man's body slumping against the gearshift must have kicked the rig into neutral. Ten tons of machine and cargo now rolled down the slight decline of Hairpin Bridge. Air brakes whined softly—fighting, but not hard enough.

Lena decided this was fine. She'd spent enough time perched in the doorway of this vessel of sun-cooked sweat and snake shit. They would continue this conversation by the cars, near the Shoebox, so the rest of Raycevic's confession could be captured for history. If this rig had a date with the bottom of the valley, she sure as hell didn't want to be there for it.

"Back up, Ray."

As he obediently stepped back from the rolling truck ("Back . . . back"), Lena kept him at gunpoint and descended the footrail, jumping the final few feet, landing hard and twisting an ankle, squinting in the blazing daylight. Raycevic stared transfixed at something in the distance. She saw it, too.

East of Hairpin Bridge, the nearest hill—and its bristly coat of pines—was now consumed by a roiling wall of apocalyptic flames.

The Briggs-Daniels wildfire was here.

CHAPTER 21

"WE'RE RUNNING OUT OF TIME, LENA."

She clicked another ninety-minute cassette into the Shoebox recorder and ignored Raycevic. She slapped the record button, leaving a bloody thumbprint. She'd come too far and fought too hard today to let that forest fire sweep in and interfere.

"Lena," he whispered. "We need to *go*—"

"Not yet. How did my sister die?"

"You're insane."

"Was she one of his . . ." She grasped for the vile word. "One of his *strays*?"

"No. Cambry was different." Raycevic watched the distant trees go up like seventy-foot candlewicks, feeding pillars of oily fire. "She wasn't a victim. She saw my burn pit firsthand, and it was too much for her—"

"Your *what*?"

"My burn pit."

"What does that mean?"

He struggled to organize his thoughts. "Out that way, on Pickle Farm Road, there's . . . right behind the burned-up barn, if you follow the dirt road south . . . my uncle gave my dad some land when his logging company went under. We call it the Raycevic Estate. The family legacy was supposed to be a big house, something grand, but it never came together. Roads kept washing out in the winters. Trucks never got the materials there. Then the foundation cracked and the groundwater well dried out and it eventually just became a place where I . . . uh . . ." He trailed off and stared shamefully at the concrete between them.

His burn pit.

Lena tasted stomach acid in her throat. "She . . . saw you burning a body?"

"There's more to it than that."

"And you had to make her disappear, too?"

"I wish it never happened, Lena."

He means it. Somehow she knew: this was not a lie.

The idling semitruck had inched a hundred feet down the bridge now. With Ray's daddy inside, slumped beside his dead snake. The human predator who stalked highways and gathered souls like a crow collects glass. He was the dark heart of this mystery—perhaps the one most responsible for Cambry's death—and he was already dead. Unreachable. He couldn't be punished any further. Was shooting him supposed to feel good? Was that the sugar high of revenge, already spent?

Lena felt her eyes water in the smoky air. "That's the whole reason Cambry had to die?" Her jaw quivered, but she fought it. "Because she saw a stupid fire? *I don't have a sister anymore,* and it's because of that?"

"What were you expecting?"

She didn't know. A conspiracy, maybe? Ghosts on Hairpin Bridge? Anything was better than this. The true monster was already dead inside an eighteen-wheeler inching down the bridge, and all she had left here was Ray-Ray, the killer's sniveling little assistant.

Cambry died. All because of a fire.

Answers can let you down. Lena knew this as well as anyone. Your friends can move away. Your expensive English degree can qualify you for a career in retail. Your dream about your dead sister, the night before you avenge her murder, can end with her refusing to look at you, refusing to speak, basically telling you to fuck off from the grave. *Go, Lena. Just go.*

Please go—

A scream reached her ears. Gritty, metallic, screwdriver on a chalkboard. It was the semi's right flank scraping against the bridge's guardrail. Two hundred feet away now.

"She was running. I had to stop her. I'm sorry, Lena."

"Are you?"

"Yes. For everything. I deserve you. You know that? My dad and I, we had this coming. You came in like a gunslinger in a Western, to clean up this place and stop its resident serial killer, and you did. He's dead now, and you've caught me." His voice broke. "And I regret what happened to Cambry."

"Don't say her name."

"*Cambry Lynne Nguyen.* I have all of their names. I had to remember them, because Dad wouldn't. It's like you said: When you're dead, you're not a person anymore. You're an idea."

Down the bridge, the grinding metal shriek intensified. The bridge's guardrail warping, sagging, about to snap—

"Anna Richter. Molly Wilson. Kara Patrick. Ingrid Wells." He inhaled, a jarring speed rap. "Janelle Ross. Ellie Erickson. Erin DeSilva. Megan Hernandez. Mary Keller. Sara Smith."

She stepped back. They kept coming.

"Karen Fuller. Alex Ford. Kelly Sloan. Melanie Lopez." He glanced at the Shoebox. "Did you get them all? All of those people, erased. Dad operated mostly in the summer months, when women travel late and alone. There was no master plan. No strategy. He just indulged his whims, like a kid ordering toys from a magazine. He'd call me up when he was done with them. And I'd be at home with Liza or lifting weights at the station, and my phone would ring—*I've got a stray for you,* he'd say, and then that was my part. I'd step in."

She imagined him *stepping in* and dutifully charring some stranger's body to black bones. And Cambry, poor wayward Cambry, stumbling across the macabre scene on her journey, witnessing the Raycevic family secret, and being marked for death.

The screech reached an anguished peak. The railing sagged under ten tons of cargo, rivets bursting like gunshots, the semi-trailer leaning over Silver Creek, inches now from tipping irreversibly.

His voice lowered. "I killed a *kid* this week."

She looked back at him.

"Dad called me one day and told me he had another stray to disappear. And her car. And . . . he said there was a *situation* to deal with in the back seat."

His eyes glimmered.

You didn't, she thought. *You didn't—*

"Age three, maybe four." His voice broke. "This brown-haired little boy, looked just like me or my brother when we were kids. In a car seat covered with superhero stickers, Captain America and Thor and the Hulk. He was crying because he'd just seen his mama taken. That's what Dad's *situation* was. That's what I was expected to clean up."

Lena wanted to shut her eyes, to make it all stop. The truck's screech was intensifying.

"I took the boy to our shed and kept him there. Dad told me it was a bad idea. But I didn't know what else to do. I brought him food and clothes and old toys I snuck out of my attic. Built Marbleworks with him. He got an ear infection and I brought him some of my dad's antibiotics. I thought . . . fuck, I don't know what I thought. That we could raise him, I guess. But my wife could never know. So then I thought maybe I could drive him down south, to Arizona or New Mexico, and leave him outside a fire station in the middle of the night. They'd process him back to his surviving family. Right?"

He paused, as if waiting for Lena to agree. She wouldn't give him the validation.

"But he'd seen our faces. He remembered *everything*."

As if *he* were the victim.

"I had no choice." He swallowed, letting it all out. "I spent three months ruling out all of my other options, okay? And finally, this week, I blindfolded him and told him that once the T-shirt came off, he'd see his mama again. And I carried him to the groundwater well. It's long dry, a forty-foot drop down to solid shale. And I just . . . dropped him headfirst and heard him hit the bottom. It was fast. Too fast to hurt, just like Cambry. I think he died instantly on impact, which is good, because a slow death by dehydration down there would have been far worse . . ."

He trailed off again. He was only trying to convince himself. He glanced up at her, a pathetic overgrown child in a uniform himself, like he expected her to pull the trigger now.

She considered it.

"That was two days ago. You asked why I haven't slept since Thursday? *That's* why."

Thursday. The day Corporal Raymond Raycevic fully lost the battle for his soul.

"There you go." He sniffed. "Congratulations. You just solved fourteen cold cases reaching a decade back, missing persons from California to Philly. It'll make a hell of a book. You'll be famous."

So will you, she thought.

The kid killer forced a tortured rictus grin, all teeth. "Are you satisfied, Lena?"

Three hundred feet away, the rolling semitrailer continued its grating scrape, the railing groaning, the trailer leaning, the whole rig finally tilting, submitting to gravity—only to unexpectedly halt. Ten precarious tons, hanging off Hairpin Bridge by a tangle of railing.

It felt unresolved.

A painful incompleteness, a hole in her. Something was absent. Something had always been missing here, all day, and she couldn't explain it. Across the valley, she watched the distant wildfire leap from tree to tree, surging sheets of orange. The campfire taste of ash in the air.

If they killed Cambry, why did they fake her suicide? Why not just burn her and erase her tracks, like they did everyone else?

"You can kill us both, Lena, but you can't change the past. Your sister still *chose* to jump off this bridge," Raycevic said. "Right over there. That railing."

He lowered his voice. "I was there. The minute she jumped."

CHAPTER 22

CAMBRY'S STORY

She stomps the brakes, her heart plunging hard.

No, no, no—

Ahead, Raycevic's familiar police cruiser is parked on the bridge's far end. Sideways. Waiting for her. She can see the apelike man sitting on the Charger's hood with that same black semiautomatic rifle in his lap. He glances up at her, squinting in the glare of her high beams.

She sees his trap, too: Clawed black shadows lie neatly in front of his patrol car, arranged railing to railing. Like lurking crocodiles half submerged in river water. They're spike strips, designed to shred tires into black gristle. Police issue.

No, *she wants to scream.* It's not fair.

I got away—

Raycevic waves at her. A weary smile, workmanlike.

She punches the steering wheel. The horn bleats. She screams at nothing, at everything, at him, at herself—because she knows her fate was sealed the very instant she escaped the Plastic Man and chose to drive north. She'd had two options—north or south—and she chose wrong. Like the owl shepherds the souls of those soon to depart, like the Grim Reaper surely finds his prey in that cave, she's already made an inescapable appointment on this bridge.

There's no undoing it. No resisting it.

The digital clock reads 9:00 P.M.

She catches her breath and considers—could she drive over Raycevic's spike strips and keep running? Not for long. Not on four mangled, flapping tires. He'd catch her easily.

He shakes his head. Like he's read her mind.

Tears cloud her eyes. "No. Please."

Then he lifts the rifle to his shoulder, the deadly muzzle finding her through the windshield. Her mind races with panic: Turn the car around, Cambry. Go back, toward—

Headlights in her rearview mirror, too. Those familiar lantern lights of the Plastic Man's eighteen-wheeler, returning like a nightmare. Even after he's lost an eye. How is that possible?

She's trapped here. On Hairpin Bridge.

At her front Raycevic approaches, stepping over his spike strips and aiming that rifle at her. He snaps the barrel left, a stern gesture: Get out.

She shakes her head. Warm tears on her cheeks.

He waves the barrel again, harder. His finger on the trigger.

Get out. Now.

"Please, Ray." *She hates using his name.* "Please. Just let me go."

In the harsh glare she finally sees his eyes. For the first time since nightfall, he isn't a towering Hulk-like monster, biceps and buzz cut drawn in silhouette. He looks human, flesh and blood and fallible and right now, so damn tired. He doesn't want to be here. He hates his life.

His voice is tired, too. "Cambry, I will shoot you if you don't exit the vehicle."

She does. She has no choice. The Corolla's door creaks open. She finds the bridge's concrete with shaky feet. Her chest heaving with hitched gasps.

He points. "Stand there."

He's aiming at the bridge's guardrail, ten feet away. Prickled with flakes of rust that glow like embers in the headlights. She approaches it with slushy knees, certain she'll die here. It's a wretched and powerless sensation, sleepwalking where you're ordered to. Leaving the car is a mistake, she knows. She should have stomped the gas, driven right at Raycevic, and taken a hail of armor-piercing rounds to the chest and face. Again, she considers: I need to run for it. Down the bridge.

I'll die running, at least.

But Cambry Nguyen has always been a runner. She's been running her entire life—from therapy, from going to the dentist, from saying I love you to her family. In a strange, sad way, she's sick of it. There's peace in being caught.

She can almost smile. This bridge has been waiting her entire life.

"By the railing," *Raycevic instructs gently.* "Please."

"Why?"

"I'll explain in a sec."

He's oddly polite. It terrifies her.

She looks back toward the Plastic Man's eighteen-wheeler, which blocks the bridge's entrance. The fat bastard himself stands silhouetted on the truck's footrail, watching them with a hand clasped to his face. In his other hand, an old-fashioned rifle.

Raycevic is closer now. "Your name," *he says,* "is Cambry Lynne Nguyen. You're twenty-four. A bit of a wildcat. I saw a trespass. Malicious mischief. Vandalism. Shoplifting. One DUI, knocked down. You grew up in Washington—"

My driver's license, *she realizes.* Back when he pulled me over.

He ran me in his computer.

"Your parents are John and Maisie Nguyen, and they live at 2013 West Cedar Avenue in Olympia. The Eastside neighborhood, looks like. Ages fifty-four and fifty-nine—"

"Please," *she whispers.* "Please stop."

"And let's not forget your sister. Lena Marie Nguyen. Same age and birthday as you, so she must be a twin. Are you close? Her photo looks exactly like yours. She lives in an apartment called the Biltmore, on Wabash Avenue in the White Center neighborhood of Seattle. Unit 211."

She can't speak.

He draws closer. She smells his sour sweat.

"It's a shitty deal, Cambry, and you have my sympathy, but let me tell you." His voice lowers, like he's letting her in on a grim secret. "It's the only deal you're getting tonight."

"What are you talking about?"

"Help me out." His smile looks like a grimace. "See, everything depends on you now. Your family depends on you. You can save their lives. John, Maisie, and your sister, Lena, will never, ever meet me or my dad. If you just do this one thing."

He points. "This one little thing, Cambry."

With inching dread, she realizes he's pointing past her. Over her shoulder. Over the bridge's blistered guardrail, into the vast and pristine blackness beyond.

"Jump."

PART 3

THE LAST WORD

CHAPTER 23

Cambry can't remember climbing the bridge's guardrail. In a watery blink, she's just there, as if teleported, lifting her numb ankles over the railing one at a time. Her breaths hitched and sore. Her arched shoes on the two-inch concrete ledge now, perched by her toes.

"Don't look down," Raycevic whispers. "Just let go."

With her knuckles on the chilled metal, she glances down anyway—a vast and formless night yawns below—and the sheer, frightening depth of it rips the air from her lungs. She can't jump. She won't. He'll just have to shoot her in the head. She collapses against the guardrail, feeling her cheeks burn red under running tears.

"Do it, please." The cop's voice softens. "For your family."

The Plastic Man's voice echoes, a distant holler muffled by adrenaline. It takes her a few moments to understand what he said.

"Just shoot the bitch."

"No," Raycevic shouts back. "I'm giving her a chance first."

Giving her a chance. The ghoulish backwardness of it. She clenches tightly to the guardrail's outside edge, digging her feet into it. She swears to God, to the voided sky, to anyone who's listening that she'll never, ever let go of this bridge. They'll have to snap her rigor mortis fingers off it. Even after Raycevic puts a bullet through her skull and slaughters her family one by one.

"Ray-Ray. Just shoot her."

Shaking the hair from her eyes, she looks back at Raycevic. "Please." Her voice is a dry croak. "Please, just let me leave."

He shakes his head.

"I won't say a thing about your fires."

"You won't. Because here's what's going to happen, Cambry. I'm going to count down from ten. When I reach zero, I will shoot you in *the head. And then, this weekend, I'll take some PTO and drive out to Washington."* He flashes that toothy smile again. *"You can save them, Cambry. You can ensure they never, ever meet me. But you're running out of time."*

"You don't have to do this."

"Ten."

"Please—"

"Nine."

"No." Her voice breaks. *"Let's talk. Maybe we can—"*

"We have nothing to talk about. Eight."

Another bolt of silent lightning, and the Plastic Man's voice again: "She's not going to jump. I need to get to a hospital. Just shoot her, Ray-Ray. Or I will."

"Seven." His dark gaze never leaves her. *"Make a choice, Cambry."*

"That's not how it happened, Lena."

"You didn't have to throw her off the bridge," she whispered with building horror. "You *terrorized* her into jumping off herself. You have a police computer. You threatened her family. Me, my parents—we were your hostages—"

"No, I tried to save her." He softened now. "You're in denial."

"Keep lying, Ray."

"You'll write an exciting book about her, I think. It's got a chase. A desperate heroine. An evil cop on her tail. A surprise second villain. It's got all the thrills and spills."

She almost pulled the trigger. *Let those be his last vile words—*

"But . . ." He licked his lips. "There are some plot holes."

Plot holes? The phrase enraged her.

"Let's start with Bob the Dinosaur. Remember him?" He nodded back at his cruiser. "How did Cambry's cartoon character get scratched into the vinyl of my vehicle? You say I forced her at gunpoint to jump off the bridge. Answer me this: In your version of June sixth, was she ever inside my vehicle? And would she take the time to *doodle,* anyway, during a life-and-death chase?"

She tried to think. For a moment she was lost, rudderless, before she made the incongruity fit: "She carved it as a clue, maybe. For me to find—"

"When?"

"I don't know."

"That's vanity, Lena. It doesn't revolve around you." He came closer, licking his lips. "Tell me. In your version, why is Cambry running out of gas, anyway?"

"What?"

"You heard me."

"Her tank was empty. When you said you found her body—"

"That's not what I'm asking. I'm asking: Was your sister in the habit of driving around aimlessly, alone, on less than a *quarter tank,* up and down Montana back roads?"

"Maybe. If she was low on money—"

"How convenient."

"She stole. She siphoned gas when she had to—"

"No. When you need to siphon gas, you go to town, Lena. Take it from a cop, okay? You go to Super One or a bowling alley or an apartment complex. You don't siphon gas in the middle of nowhere. Out here you can go hours without seeing another person—"

"That's being desperate."

"No, that's being a *dumbass.* Your sister wasn't a dumbass."

"You knew her?"

"Better than you."

Again, she almost shot him. Right in the throat.

"I couldn't have coerced her into jumping, anyway." His grin widened. "The database doesn't work like that. There's no

Wi-Fi out here. I would've had to radio it through Dispatch, which would've been suspicious. And all I could have gotten is Cambry's address, which would have been hopelessly out-of-date. Maybe if your parents were on a no-fly list, I guess?"

"You bluffed, then—"

"And that's not even the biggest plot hole, Lena."

Ash flakes fluttered between them. Stinging her eyes.

She knew what was coming.

She waited for it.

"Answer me this: Why didn't I just burn Cambry's body like all our others? I have it down to a science at this point. That's the simplest, safest solution. Living off the grid like a nomad, she should have been just another of my dad's strays, easy to disappear. What made her so special?"

"You tell me."

"Why would I force her to jump, even? Instead of just shooting her on the spot?"

"Because you're an asshole."

He counted on his fingers: "Staging a death. Burning her notebooks. Scrubbing her vehicle for evidence. Faking a suicide text. Claiming I pulled her over. You really believe I did all of that for *fun*?"

She took a step back. "Maybe."

"You didn't know your sister." He smirked with adolescent cruelty. "You have no idea who she was. Meeting me here on this bridge today wasn't really about revenge. Revenge is just an excuse. This is about learning something, *anything,* to fill the aching hole in you, because the truth is: you had almost twenty-four years to know her while she was alive, and you wasted every minute you had."

He spat at her feet. A stringy, hateful glob. "You were a shitty sister," he said. "Face it."

Another breath of wind carried ash between them. For a moment, his words rang in the silence and she said nothing in answer.

Fine, she thought. *We're doing this.*

He was right, too. Everything he'd said was true, and she felt effortlessly and efficiently dismantled. He'd cut her to pieces and laid them out and now understood every private inch of her. Every word hurt her down to her bones. There was no outrunning or outsmarting it.

But she remembered twelve-year-old Cambry slicing that injured doe's throat. Doing what needed to be done. Lena knew she shared that DNA, that the same blood ran through her veins here and now. The same furies and flaws and fight.

You can hurt me, Raycevic. And he had. He knew exactly where to cut. But now so did she.

I'll hurt you worse.

With a still voice, she whispered, "I think I know your secret, Ray."

"For the last time, we didn't kill her—"

"Not Cambry. *You.*" She watched him over the Beretta's sights. "Who you really are."

"Oh?"

"You're not a cop."

"What?"

"You're not a cop," she repeated.

"You're not making sense—"

"You're *not a real cop,* Ray. You're a fraud."

He blinked.

"Because you're not Ray," she whispered. "You're Rick."

Stunned silence.

"You're Rick, aren't you?"

Under the roar of distant fire, a tree fell with a splintering crash.

She studied his eyes. "You stole your brother's identity after he shot himself, didn't you? He—the real Raymond Raycevic—was the one accepted into the Missoula academy at eighteen. Not you. You were the screw-up twin who couldn't make selection. You flunked. Disqualified. And then, when you both found out your daddy was a serial rapist and killer, your brother Ray shotgunned his head off. He was a good man who couldn't cope. But you could."

He said nothing.

She mimicked Theo's accent: "And you *wonder* why you're the one that flunked the academy?"

His face reddened with blood. Taking it all in. Staring back at her hard. His fingers kneaded the air, like he was rehearsing how he'd break the small bones in her neck.

Lena got it now. The subtle venom in his father calling him *Ray-Ray.*

And she loved it.

"So, did Ray really shoot himself? Or did you talk him into it, like you talked my sister into jumping? I mean—he was Daddy's favorite, and he looked just like you, and he had a bus ticket to Missoula to be trained for your dream job. Must have hurt, huh?"

He glanced at the Shoebox as it listened. Logging every damning word.

"You're *not a real cop,* Rick." She couldn't hold it back, snarling now, her words cutting her throat like glass. "You snuck in on your brother's name. You have the training, the badge, the uniform. But you're unworthy of it, Rick, and you're an insult to all the thousands of people who get up in the morning every day and do the hardest job on earth. All of your heroes—you'll revolt them when they learn the truth about you. You're not the good guy. You're a kid killer and a fraud, and your father is using you. How's that for *a personal attack, asshole—*"

He attacked.

The man who took the life of Raymond Raycevic charged Lena midsentence like a linebacker, coming in with startling speed. His big hands up and out for her pistol, to wrench it skyward so he could snap her neck or stomp her windpipe or force the weapon under her chin and pull the trigger. However he planned to do it, it didn't matter, because she'd spent three hours studying him today. She'd noted all of his mannerisms, his tics and tells. She was ready.

Before he could reach her, Lena shot Corporal Raycevic squarely in the chest.

Three times.

———

THREE DISTANT GUNSHOTS JOLTED THEO RAYCEVIC'S WORLD. Like whipcracks.

His good eye snapped open, finding focus. At first all he saw was red, a withered terrain of browned redness soaking into sunken channels, until he recognized Marilyn Monroe's tits and realized he was facedown in a blood-drenched *Playboy*. Not sweet tea this time. His blood. Quarts of it.

She shot me.

He couldn't believe it.

In the face.

He shouldn't be alive. It was impossible.

Well? Here I am.

He couldn't see a mirror, but he reckoned Lena's bullet had punched through his upper lip. Coppery blood filled his mouth, drooling through his lips. His jaw was all wrong. His teeth grazed, snagged, and crunched together in ways new and sublimely awful.

That little bitch.

The truck had stopped rolling at least, raised askew on a tangle of crunched guardrail. He was grateful for this—the ten tons of weight could have just as easily snapped through the bridge's thin bars and plunged. But the railing held. Barely.

The cab wobbled in a precarious seesaw. A metal groan. One tire hung over the void.

He lifted his Winchester rifle from the floor, still warm. Still locked and loaded. He hoisted it weakly into his lap. "Yes." His tongue explored the new contours of his harelipped mouth.

Yes, yes, yes.

Twins share a soul, they say. It's an abomination when one dies. The other is cursed to wander the earth incomplete and alone. Ray and Rick were doomed to be apart forever and nothing could change that, but the Nguyen sisters should go together. They would, here on Hairpin Bridge.

Theo would make sure of it.

CHAPTER 24

"TEN-FOOT DOCTRINE, LENA."

She felt his hot breath on her face. Stinging the cuts on her cheeks. His huge hands were clamped over hers vise-tight, fighting for control of the Beretta.

It fired into the sky. An earsplitting blast.

For a man who'd taken three bullets to the sternum, Corporal Raycevic was still shockingly strong. He thrashed the weapon against her two-handed grip, rag-dolling her body left and right, forcing her to backpedal on scraping heels. Like the thrashing jaws of a pit bull. Lena's only advantage: she'd already fatally wounded him. She just had to hold on to the gun long enough for the handcuffed giant to bleed out, to watch his big eyes go flat inches from hers—

They didn't.

His smile grew. Another warm breath hissed through his teeth. The sickly sweet odor of his sweat. Something was wrong.

Click. A small object hit the concrete between them. A coin? She was afraid to glance down—she kept staring into his eyes. Trying not to blink. Trying to appear fearless. All that mattered was the firearm in their clenched knuckles. She wouldn't let go of it.

Two more strange sounds—click, click—and moth wings of terror fluttered in her chest. Raycevic's smile widened until she could count his teeth and see their gritty tartar. He was daring her to look down now. He wanted her to see it.

Don't look down, Lena. It's a distraction.

She had to.

Don't—

She did.

At three metal objects on the pavement. Flattened into mushroom shapes. Crushed upon impact against a solid and impenetrable shield; something under his uniform, and she remembered the strange tungsten click she'd heard hours ago when he tapped his chest.

He's wearing a—

Raycevic swung her with full strength. Lena's feet left the concrete, a wild and weightless centrifuge—like the way her uncle used to twirl her as a little girl with the summer air rushing in her ears—until she crashed spine-first into the door of his Charger. She felt her ribs pop with jagged pain. The air blasted from her lungs and she cried out in a wheezing voice she didn't recognize.

He was already lifting her by their interlocked hands and slammed her again. Again. She felt the door dent inward. The window crumbled. The Beretta fired another concussive blast inches from her face and her ears rang. She didn't let go. She held the pistol with both hands between his, refusing to budge, her index finger locked behind the trigger.

His furious breath in her eyes. "Let go, Lena."

Before she could answer, the huge man lifted and spun her again, whiplashing her into the cruiser's front panel. Face-first. She felt her cheekbone crack. She bit into her tongue with a spurt of coppery blood. The car shook with the impact.

The Shoebox recorder slid off the hood and clattered to the concrete. Still running, still listening, recording every hit and gasp and cry.

"Mom and Dad," she screamed at it, "I love you so much—"

"They can't help you, Lena."

"Cambry *did not kill herself.*" Her voice heaved as Raycevic lifted her again and slammed her against the cruiser's hood. "I found her killers."

"Why bother?" he grunted. "I'm just going to smash it."

"I'll always be with you, Mom." She struggled as he raised the gun high in their locked hands, wrenching hers upward. "Whatever he does to me, Cambry is not in hell."

His strength nearly lifted her, too. Tugging her elbows straight. For a moment, the gorilla shoulders of Corporal Raycevic blocked the red sun—his biceps nearly bursting through his sleeves—before he smashed the Beretta's aluminum heel down on her temple like a bludgeon. A piercing white flash behind her eyes. A glassy crack inside her skull.

"Mom," she burbled, her mouth filling with blood. A front tooth wiggling loosely now, whistling to her last words: "*Mom!*"

Raycevic raised the Beretta in their hands again. Like a club, directly above her face—

"Mom, Cambry is *not in hell*—"

He shattered her nose with a sickening wet crunch. Her sinuses detonated like firecrackers behind rubbery cartilage and she saw scalding red. Her grip loosened on the gun and Raycevic almost tore it from her clenched fingers. Almost.

She held on.

"Let go," he huffed. "Just let go—"

"Let go, Cambry."

She grips the bridge's guardrail with her toes at the edge, blinking away cold tears as Raycevic's voice softens behind her, becoming almost sympathetic. Almost soothing.

"Please. Let go." He's closer now, his black rifle lowering. "I don't want to go after your family this weekend, okay? I don't want to shoot your parents in their bed. I don't want to slip into Lena's apartment like a shadow and cut her throat. That's not me. I'm a good guy."

She shuts her eyes. His voice creeps closer.

"Please, Cambry. Please don't make me do all of that ugly stuff. I'm not a bad person."

No. She tightens her grip on the railing. No, he's lying, most of all to himself. Raycevic isn't a good guy. He's not even a bad person—he's a rancid person. He's worse than evil. He's a virus with a social security number. He's a walking, talking, six-foot insect.

"Six," he counts. "Cambry, you can save them—"

With her elbow hooked around the guardrail, she looks down. Her eyes must have adjusted to the blackness by now. She can see the plunge below her perched shoes in awful vivid clarity, two hundred vertical feet to a gravel creek bed studded with boulders and pale drift-wood. Not many people get to see the very thing that is about to kill them.

What went through my sister's mind, before she died?

I have a guess.

The wild girl who sabotaged a toilet in junior high, who boondocked across the country with a dirtbag and boondocked back without him— she doesn't give up. She's too hardheaded. Too fierce. Not even now, with a rifle at her back and a fatal drop at her feet. She thinks, I can't let go. If I do that, the Raycevics win. I have to force him to shoot me. I have to be a pain in the ass. I have to fight him, with every dwindling breath and heartbeat, and even when I'm dead, I have to fight him—

He urges: "Let go. Please."

Nope. I'm never, ever going to let go of this railing, and I'm going to force him to shoot me in the head. And then, if he's not bluffing, he'll come after my family. He'll probably come for you first, Lena. Your Seattle apartment will be on his way to Olympia.

I'm sorry. It's my fault.

He's coming for you, sis, with all his guns and training and muscle. So you need to fight him. You need to fight Raycevic head on. Don't be afraid of him. Fight smart. Fight dirty. And above all, no matter how bad it gets, don't let go, Lena.

Don't.

Let.

Go.

He ripped the gun from her clenched fingers.

I'm sorry, Cambry. He's too strong.

She knew it was over, even while the inertia of Raycevic's throw carried her over the Charger's hood. She bruised her tailbone on the windshield, kicking off a wiper, and slammed mouth-first against the railing. Then she landed on hard concrete, sprawled half over the bridge's edge. She caught herself by an elbow, both legs dangling over the terrifying void. Two hundred feet down.

"Finally," the cop huffed.

He had the gun now.

Lena's thoughts came slowly, taking odd shapes in her dented mind. She blinked away starbursts of rotten color. Fresh blood pumped from her broken nose, clogging her throat.

Get up, Lena.

"This bridge . . ." He wheezed. "The Suicide Bridge isn't really haunted, by the way. Never was. My daddy's first few kills were here. He'd fake car trouble, flag down a passerby, and then push the poor fella right off the edge. Didn't even know he'd made the bridge famous. Apparently *four* is all it takes."

She heard a car door open, then a click. He was unlocking his handcuffs.

She heaved herself away from the precipice and pulled her legs back up. Each one felt like a log. She tried to stand up but could only crawl. The world hurtled dizzily around her, brown sky and smoke and rocks and concrete in nauseous orbit. She tried to focus her blurry eyes and realized her contact lenses were knocked out. She couldn't see him.

"Want to hear the funny part?" His rancid voice on the other side of the car, coming closer. "I've been wanting to kill my dad for *years*. Can you believe it? And you just saved me the trouble—"

Her mind screamed: *Stand up. Fight him. Now.*

But she was spent. Muscles burning. Every bone ached. Legally blind without contacts, one eye already swelling shut, her teeth clicking in her gums. She couldn't stand up, let alone try to fight two-hundred-fifty-pound Corporal Raycevic. Not again.

I'm sorry, Cambry. I'm failing you.

"I wanted to, but I'm not like him. I'm a born cop." He roared, hoarse with smoke: "I'm a *good guy*—"

She looked back, blinking away blood and tears. She saw the blurred shadow of Corporal Raycevic approaching around his car, like an executioner silhouetted by fire. His wrists were free. He carried a gun. *Her* Beretta, in his hand.

She heaved her body to crawl away. Not fast enough.

"Two days ago, the little boy in the well—never again." His footsteps followed her. He forced a barking laugh. "I love my dad, but Christ, I have forty more years to think of. He doesn't."

She kept crawling. Closing her eyes. Bracing for the gunshot.

I'm so sorry, Cambry.

"And now it's over." His voice was so *close* now. She could feel his breath on her neck. "My dad will never take another stray. Which means I'll never have to burn another . . ."

It took Lena a few breaths to realize Raycevic had stopped midstep.

He'd noticed something.

CHAPTER 25

HE'D FORGOTTEN ABOUT THE AUDIO RECORDER. HE LIFTED IT from the pavement now.

Lena turned and saw. "Wait—"

He hefted it—large but surprisingly light. It had studiously recorded every word, every accusation, every gasp and gunshot. It was Lena's ultimate backup plan, containing the admission of Corporal Raymond Raycevic to aiding and concealing fourteen homicides, plus the murder of a little boy. And once this shit-storm of a day was cleaned up, it wouldn't exist at all.

Just like his dad's body. Just like Lena's body. Just like their bullet-riddled vehicles.

He watched Lena pull herself upright on her elbows, drool-ing blood. Christ, her face was a grisly Halloween mask. Her skin was swelling purple. The cartilage of her nose was dented in, her lip split and leaking heavy globs.

"I've been making things disappear my entire life." He grinned, feeling the world align just for him. "You think you're special? You're just one more skeleton with meat on it. You solved the biggest problem of my life, and I'll be back to work on Monday."

She gurgled, "Please, wait—"

He raised the Shoebox high.

"No, no, *no*—"

And he hurled it against the pavement. The gadget exploded into plastic fragments before Lena's helpless eyes. For good mea-sure, he found the cassette tape and crunched it under his boot.

The entire day's conversation, every detail and admission—all instantly, irreversibly gone.

"You didn't stop me, Lena. *You set me free.*"

———————————

Tomorrow, one of two outcomes will happen.

1.   <u>I am killed by Raycevic.</u> This is possible, and even likely. I'll be confronting an armed killer alone, with only a concealed gun and my instincts. If either of those things fails me, there will be no cell signal and no backup to help me.

And the second outcome?

2.   <u>I win.</u> I record Corporal Raycevic's confession to the murder of Cambry Nguyen. He ends up dead or handcuffed, and I'm a hero.

Then what?

I'll . . . drive back home, I guess.

I'll stop at a diner, maybe, and have one of those stupid banana split sundaes Cambry and I used to share as kids. I'll rejoin life. I'll sell my gun. I'll go back to work, pay bills, and try to be the person I was before she died. The Lena Nguyen who twists her hair, who's never had a boyfriend, who hides behind online personas and rarely leaves her apartment.

That terrifies me.

I guess I'm realizing that I have very little interest in surviving my date with Raycevic tomorrow. If I make it out alive, it's not really a victory, because my problems will continue and his will end.

I've absorbed this mission, internalized it, externalized it, obsessed toward it with every cell in my body—the endless trips to the shooting range, exhaustively punching five-round groups into every card in every deck of fifty-two—and once I set the record straight and bring Raycevic down, I have no idea who I'll be afterward. Am I me anymore? In a way, I think Lena Nguyen died at the same moment you did, Cambry. Raycevic murdered us both.

You committed suicide, they say?

I guess I will, too.

I think my plan is to die on Hairpin Bridge tomorrow. I didn't request the days off work. I didn't pay this month's rent (practice ammo is expensive). I didn't tell anyone where I'm going or what I'm doing, because they would surely try to stop me.

I guess, in my usual roundabout way, this makes my blog post here on *Lights and Sounds* my suicide note. The final writing of Lena Nguyen. English major, absentee sister, sandwich enthusiast. April 11, 1995—September 21, 2019.

Sorry, dear readers.

There probably won't be a book review next week.

Be honest. You had to have figured it was heading this direction. Do I seem okay? Are the prior 5,000 words the thoughts and observations of an emotionally well person? And if (or when) I die tomorrow, just know, dear readers, that I do have a backup plan. And it's a good one.

I'm suicidal, yes.

But not stupid.

"TAKE ANOTHER LOOK AT IT," THE GIRL WHISPERED.

"What?"

"The thing you smashed. Look at it."

Are you serious? He kicked a fragment with his boot.

"No, Rick." There was a condescending sharpness to her voice—*Rick*—that made his guts stir with rage. "Really, actually *look* at it."

"You're concussed."

"I'll wait." She spat red on the pavement, still gazing up at him with an eerie calm. Brain damage, maybe? Her cheekbone swelled under her eye, taking the color of rotten pumpkin.

He knew he didn't have time for this. He had to move fast, to kill Lena and pack the bodies into his trunk and move the vehicles off the bridge before the approaching wildfire drew firefighters. He had two bodies, a semitruck, and a Corolla to disappear in the middle of a *forest fire,* for Christ's sake. He'd have a hell of a busy weekend—but somehow his pride was tangled up in this, and he had to indulge her, just to prove her wrong.

The first piece he picked up was a green circuit board. Nothing. He lifted another fragment—a white plastic spoke. Nothing special there, either. Just a standard outdated digital cassette, like the kind they still used at the Howard County hearing office.

He looked up. "Satisfied?"

She kept staring with dreamy calm. Not at him—not anymore—but down at the road, at the scattered debris. At one particular piece.

He followed her gaze. To a black polymer casing, shell-like, fractured down the middle. Made of a different material than the Shoebox recorder. It must have been fastened to the back with electrical tape. There was white lettering stenciled on the side.

He turned it over with his boot. It spun on the concrete and twirled to a halt, the blocky letters rotating into view: *Motorola.*

A chill wriggled up his spine.

Lena looked up at him and smiled a wicked grin with blood-stained teeth.

———————

This *Lights and Sounds* blog post will go live on a delay, set to auto-publish on Sunday, September 22, at midnight Pacific time. (So if you're reading this, that means it's already too late to stop me.) Sorry, but it's necessary.

And since Hairpin Bridge occupies a well-documented cellular dead zone, I'll record Raycevic with Cambry's old Shoebox recorder and—as a backup—via a walkie-talkie duct-taped to the back. The companion walkie will be digitally linked to my laptop, recording to the cloud. It'll all upload automatically. It'll all cache. And, come midnight, it'll hit the internet embedded in this post. With or without me.

Don't believe me?

Well, here it is.

If you'll simply click the hyperlink below, you can listen to it. Wow! You yourself can download my entire September 21 conversation with Corporal Raymond R. Raycevic:

Corporal Raymond R. Raycevic: <u>SS9.21.19Raycevic.gxf</u>

Enjoy!

But listen responsibly. It might contain my murder.

———————

RAYCEVIC LOOKED UP AT HER. EYES WIDE. "WHERE'S . . ."

She grinned. It made the muscles in her cheeks ache.

"Where's the other walkie-talkie?"

She shook her head, dropping more red blots to the concrete. She turned away, watching the wall of fire in the distance. Lodgepole pines going up in flamethrower jets, feeding billows of roiling cauliflower smoke. Ever since she was a girl, she'd always loved watching things burn.

He roared: "*Where* is it?"

"Really?" She looked back to him. "You still haven't figured it out? You were there. Back at the Magma Springs Diner. Remember?"

His eyes narrowed. He didn't.

"I didn't go in there to buy *water,* asshole. The second walkie is linked to my laptop. Every word you and I have spoken here is already uploaded. The big cassette recorder was just a redundancy. It'll all auto-publish, embedded in my blog, tonight at midnight. No force on earth, short of an EMP blast, can stop it." She spat a glob of heavy blood at his uniform. "You could drive back to Magma Springs right now and smash my laptop, too, if you'd like. Won't matter. It's already done. Your confession is up there in space, right this second, waiting to drop."

He took it all in.

Lena couldn't fight it. She laughed, her cheeks taut and swollen: "Did you really think I'd be that naive? That I'd be so certain you were a murderer, but then I'd gamble it all on a *gunfight* with you?"

The kid killer said nothing.

"I'm willing to risk my own life. To throw it away, even. But I won't risk the truth. The truth is too valuable. For the truth, I took precautions, to ensure that whatever happened on this bridge today, the world would hear it."

And you gave me shit for working in an electronics store, she almost added. Gripping the sun-cooked handrail, she tried to stand up. Better to die on her feet.

"The edge is right there," she said, pointing. "In case you want to . . . you know. Before your department finds out you dropped a child down a well this week."

He looked smaller. He was slouching, shrinking, an impostor in his uniform. The gun rattled in his hand. A feverish shiver. Maybe it was all coming down on him like a wheelbarrow full of cinder blocks, that by this time tomorrow, he would be the target of a nationwide manhunt.

"But . . ." Lena caught her breath. "I can say one thing for certain."

He looked back at her.

She smiled. "You *won't* be going back to work on Monday."

The cop smiled, too. But not entirely—the edges of his mouth curled like a grin caught on a snag. The muscles in his face seemed to disagree. Then in another blink he'd gone eerily blank again. His mind was made up. She read it easily.

"You can shoot me," she added. "It won't change your outcome."

"It'll change yours."

He pressed the Beretta to her forehead and pulled the trigger.

The gunshot is earsplitting.

Cambry screams against a blast of pressurized air. Her shoes lose traction on the concrete precipice and she catches herself with fingertips on the guardrail. She can't hold on much longer.

"Five. That was a warning shot, over your head." He aims the semiautomatic rifle lower. "The next one explodes right through it. And then your problems are over, but as for your mom and dad and sister's problems? Oh, boy howdy, are they just beginning."

Cambry sags against the railing. She's strong and scrappy, but her muscles must feel like dead flesh by now. Her fingers are slick with cold sweat. She's slipping, surrendering to gravity, every inch a slow slide to free fall.

"Four. Just let go, Cambry." He softens again. "Don't worry. I'll write a nice suicide note to your family. I'll text it to your sister. Okay?"

The Plastic Man mocks in a girlie voice: "Please forgive me. I couldn't live with it—"

A hoarse sputter rattles behind them. The Corolla's engine finally going dead. The last of its fuel burned. How much farther could she have driven it, even if she'd tried to run? Another mile? Estimates vary. No one knows the exact quantity she'd started with.

The creek bed is a black void, calling her under. And Raycevic's voice is a venomous whisper in her ear: "No one will miss you, Cambry. You know that, right?"

God, I hope she didn't believe him.

"You're just a basket-case loner running from her problems. Thousands of you die every year. You're a statistic—"

What was my sister thinking in that moment as she looked down off Hairpin Bridge? This part is difficult for me to write.

Who can possibly say?

"Three."

Christ, I wish I knew.

"Two."

I know what I believe, in my heart: She decided she would save us. Cambry Lynne Nguyen assessed a no-win situation and made a rational choice to protect our mother and father and me from the revenge of that psychopathic cop. She must have known we'd never know the truth. We would trust Raycevic's lies, that she fell victim to her own furies on a desolate Montana highway, that Mom would believe her daughter was sentenced to hell.

She did it for us. On June 6, she became our guardian angel.

"Ray-Ray, shoot the bitch."

Raycevic's voice rises, and he aims. "One—"

My sister lets go.

I'm dead.

It took Lena an airy moment to realize she wasn't.

The distant flames were still roaring, seconds still racing, her heart still slamming in her chest, and the Beretta in Raycevic's hand—*her* gun, in his hand, pointed at her forehead—had abruptly failed to fire. He jerked the trigger again, harder, and then stared wide-eyed at the malfunctioning weapon.

This thrilled Lena. Exhilarated her. She wanted to laugh again in his reddening face—because Corporal Raymond (Rick) Ray-cevic, who'd already confessed to concealing fourteen homicides and murdering a child on tape, who would be a national head-line by this time tomorrow, couldn't even execute the woman who'd make him famous.

Cambry, she thought with a chill.

She knew better. She knew what had really happened. But still: *Thank you, Cambry, thank you—*

She rolled away from Raycevic and scrambled upright, her blood-drenched hair whipping. Her Toyota keys in her fist. And she broke into a heaving, wounded run toward her Corolla.

Thank you, sis, for one last assist.

I'll take it from here.

RAYCEVIC RACKED THE BERETTA'S SLIDE IN HIS FIST, EJECTING brass.

It was no miracle. Nothing supernatural. During the scuffle, their hands had been locked around the pistol, and when it fired, the action had failed to properly cycle. An easy fix, and one of the first malfunctions the instructors train you for.

He let the weapon's slide clack forward with satisfying power. He raised it again smoothly to draw a bead on the running girl's back. She was just reaching her vehicle twenty feet away, skid-ding on her heels and twisting open the door—

He fired as she dove inside. The side-view mirror shattered.

He sidestepped right for a better angle and aimed through the Corolla's lined back window. She was still exposed. A flimsy seat wouldn't protect her. He saw Lena through the glass, her frantic movements in the driver's seat as she jammed in the key.

The Corolla's engine thrummed to life. The taillights glowed red. But running away wouldn't save her, either. As he aligned the pistol's black sights on the headrest, he couldn't help but feel a twinge of disappointment in the girl he was about to kill.

Really, Lena?

You came all this way, he thought as he squeezed the trigger. *You found me.*

And now you're running?

————————

SHE SLAMMED THE SHIFTER INTO REVERSE.

I'm not running, motherfucker.

She stomped the gas pedal and the Corolla whiplashed backward on screaming tires. Straight back. Straight at Raycevic.

He opened fire.

She ducked as bullets pierced the rear window and shredded her seat, spewing gouts of yellow foam. The gauge cluster exploded. The windshield spiderwebbed with cracks. She scooted low, low, as low as possible under the steering column and jammed the pedal with her knee, and the car kept barreling backward, and she knew that all of this deafening gunfire was a good thing—because Raycevic had spent his valuable seconds shooting instead of moving, and it was now too late for him to dive out of her way.

She felt the car's tailgate ram into him with a solid thump.

A satisfying, fleshy impact. She loved it. She twisted her neck back around the seat and saw his huge shoulders sprawled over the Corolla's rear window, the big man winded by the hit. Riding the moving car atop its trunk, his left hand grasping the spoiler—

His right hand raised. With the gun.

Aimed directly at her. Too close to miss now. Grinning cruelly at her through the cracked glass. He wouldn't have been grinning if he knew what was behind him, coming fast.

Lena did. And she braced.

As the Corolla plowed trunk-first into Corporal Raycevic's cruiser.

————————

HE FELT HIS KNEES SNAP LIKE DRY STICKS.

The human brain is supposed to shut down as a shock response to bodily trauma—that's what every medical class had assured him for two decades—but somehow, the man who called himself Raymond Raycevic experienced every sensory detail in IMAX clarity. The detonation of colliding metal. The screeching, live-wire pain. The shocking visual of his legs vanishing from the knees down. They were still somewhere down there between the crumpled metal jaws, hopefully still attached.

Then a violent whiplash as momentum sprawled him over the hood of his own Dodge Charger, cracking his skull with a glassy thud.

Time dilated here. He remembered staring into the Mars-like orb of the sun, low and alien. He saw embers riding thermals like fireflies. He'd lost the pistol in the crash—but somehow, impossibly, his right hand was still full. He was holding something else. He twisted his neck to look.

A cloth child's shoe with a Velcro closure.

His guts churned. *No.*

Yes. There in his palm, its rubber soles porous with detail in the hard sunlight. It had slipped off its owner's little foot purely by accident—

No, no, no.

As he stood over that dried-up groundwater well, hearing the little boy's trailing scream vanish down a tunnel of dark stone. Then far below, a reverberating thud, sickening in its heaviness. Like a bag of flour. The scream ended instantly and that was it. It couldn't be undone. His stomach gurgled with acid. With nothing else to do and sensing the awkwardness of a task left half-done, he dropped the small shoe in, too, to join its owner forty feet down.

It had to be the well. He couldn't burn such a small body. It was too ghoulish to even imagine the specifics of where he'd cut. In the lonely vault of his thoughts last night, six inches from his wife's head on the pillow beside his, he'd resolved to fill the well with wet concrete on Sunday, to bulldoze the stonework and bury it forever.

This brown-haired little boy who came to him in a car seat covered with Marvel stickers was the first human being he'd ever personally killed. Forty-eight hours ago.

I should have just left him at a fire station, he'd decided last night with teary eyes under the rumble of Liza's snore. *If he grows up and ID's us someday, fine.*

I made an evil choice.

I'll never, ever balance the scales for it.

His legs ignited now. A rolling, crashing wave of pain as frayed nerves sparked and fizzed to terrible life. He thrashed and screamed through locked teeth, but he was trapped between Cambry's vehicle and his own. He tried to hoist himself up and felt his left kneecap pop messily inside a broken socket. Through watery eyes, he glimpsed a bright knuckle of exposed bone.

Ahead, he heard the Corolla's door creak open. Glass fragments sprinkled on the road. Another jangling pain on his pinched nerves—the vehicle's suspension relaxing—as someone climbed out.

Judgment was coming for him.

Wearing Cambry's face.

———————

That's it, everyone.

Blog over, I guess.

It's past midnight as I type this in my apartment, so I guess it's technically *today* now—September 21. The day I face him.

Everything is in place. My letters to my parents, my coworkers, and my friends are all written and sealed. Some went in the mail today. Some are digital. The rest are neatly arranged on my coffee table. And now I need to crawl into bed to secure at least five hours of sleep, to be decently well rested for what will be the most important day of my life on Hairpin Bridge.

But before I go . . .

One final letter. To you, Cambry. Because I'm realizing I never wrote anything for you. Not officially.

So, to my twin . . .

Whatever our differences, whatever the distance between us, I'm proud to wear your face. At one point in the womb, we were even the same person. We shared atoms. And someday, when our bodies are dust, we will again. I'm sorry I lied to Mom and Dad about that deer. I'm sorry I never told the truth for all those years. I'm so sorry we barely spoke. I could have been there for you and I wasn't. It's my fault you ended up on that bridge.

Tomorrow, I atone for it.

I'm going to bed now. And when I wake, I'll drive to Montana and fucking destroy the man who murdered you, sis.

Ratface, out.

9/21/2019 12:11 A.M.

CHAPTER 26

SHE WATCHED HIM WRITHE, PINNED BETWEEN THE COROLLA'S tailgate and the grille of his own cruiser like a mashed insect. She couldn't see his legs below the knee, and she didn't wish to. The spreading puddle of blood on the pavement was enough.

She picked up her Beretta.

"I . . ." He struggled to speak. "You need to know this . . . before you kill me—"

She checked the chamber and aimed. "Talk fast."

"It's not your fault," he gasped. "What happened . . . to Cambry."

She stopped. Her finger on the trigger.

She'd expected venom from Corporal Raycevic, more lies and taunts and hate. More gory details. Maybe a final *I fucked your sister* or *She loved my cock* through gnashed teeth. Anything but this, as the ruined man took another long breath, bracing his crunchy legs between the cars, struggling to turn air into words. His slacks were shiny with blood.

She waited.

"Cambry was her own person." He forced a guttural whisper. "I learned . . . when Ray shot himself, that you have to let the dead share the blame. Hating yourself won't bring her back."

Her eyes watered. The gun growing heavy on her wrist.

"Lena, it's *not your fault* Cambry died. Her choices brought her to this bridge."

She twisted her head away.

She wouldn't let him see her cry. She stared out into the horizon, blinking hard, focusing on the spurts of flame. The smoke bleeding into the sky like brown paint. The bleak beauty to how things char and wilt and scatter. She remembered staring entranced into the campfire for hours as a girl, while Cambry searched the dark for insects for her jar.

Restless Cambry. Always moving. Always searching.

It's not your fault.

Finally, she looked back. "Thank you, Ray."

"Call me Rick." He smiled gently, and for a moment she saw the man he must have wished he'd grown up to be, not the one who threw kids down wells. "God, you look . . . *exactly* like her."

"I know."

"Like seeing a ghost—"

"I know."

"She never mentioned you," he whispered. "Not once."

Wait. This piece snagged in Lena's mind. Refusing to fit.

What?

He was unbuckling his belt now, tying a crude tourniquet above one knee. He winced with pain as he tugged the knot tight. She waited for him to speak again, replaying his words in her mind—no, that was incorrect. It was still wrong. He was lying again. More mind games.

She remembered his wallet.

In the road. Like a hockey puck. Right where she'd dropped it an hour or two ago, the instant she called Raycevic's ruse while his father trained a rifle on her back and squeezed the trigger. To distract her, he'd been lying. She'd been certain of it. So certain.

Now a sour chill crawled up her spine. One vertebra at a time.

She paced back to the center of the bridge on numb legs. She knelt, lifting the billfold in trembling fingers. She opened it sideways, letting his cards spill out and hit the road—

In the back. The very last photo . . .

This time she tucked the Beretta under her arm and used both hands. She found it inside a hidden pocket. Thick paper, like card stock. She peeled it out with her thumbnail and turned it over.

She didn't recognize Raycevic in civilian clothes—ripped jeans and a salmon-pink shirt, aching in its humble dorkiness. He sat in a two-seater canoe with a fishing pole across his lap and glassy water behind him. From the other seat, the boat's second occupant had leaned in close for the self-shot photo, jutting her neck into frame with her palm resting on Raycevic's thigh, and she was—

Lena thrashed her head away. She wanted to drop it. Throw it off the bridge, let the fire take it.

He watched. "I *told you*, Lena."

She stared up into the dirty sky, blinking hard. She cried out, a long and strange moan. There was no unseeing it, and this time no gunfight to change the subject. Finally, with a pounding heart, she looked back down at the photo.

At her own face.

"I knew I liked her." Raycevic smiled wistfully. "Ever since I first caught her stealing gas outside the Super One and convinced her to stay in town awhile. That was March, I think—"

No, no, no. It didn't make sense. It contradicted everything.

She searched the picture for Photoshopping errors, for incongruous shadows or snipped edges. Signs of duress, maybe, like a gun against her ribs, because there was no way Cambry could look so effortlessly happy with this man, fishing with him, kissing him, talking by firelight and drinking from the same bottle. Her skin was tanned, her mouth curled into that familiar smirk. Aglow with mischief.

"You didn't know her, Lena."

She forced herself to speak. "But you chased her."

"I did."

"After she saw your burn pit—"

"It's all true. You know every minute of the chase, and why we chased her." His eyes shimmered, holding something back. "But you don't know why *she ran*."

The pause was excruciating.

The silence before the drop of a guillotine blade.

"Cambry and I spent that afternoon on the lake. We had a good time. Our last good time. She caught a cutthroat trout the size of my arm. But by the end she was noticing that my heart wasn't in it, because all I could think about was the little boy in my shed. It tore me up, being a secret monster. And Cambry knew I was hiding something from her. Lying just made it worse. We had a fight. She left angry. And I left, too, with a cooler full of fish melting in my boat, just drove back to my dad's property, so fucking *furious* at him, at what he's twisted my life into. I really could've killed him that time, I think. But of course he wasn't home.

"And then I . . . I heard this gentle clanging sound, coming from inside my dad's truck trailer. Like a metal chain, softly swinging side to side. And I'm just realizing what it is—empty handcuffs—when a rifle touches the back of my neck."

Empty handcuffs.

He swallowed.

"It's my dad's latest stray. A mother, thirties, abducted from the interstate. She's just freed herself. Slipped her cuffs somehow, or maybe Dad was too drunk to lock them fully the night before. And she stole the rifle from his cab and crawled out and ambushed me with it. Just my luck, right? She's blood-soaked, in a frenzy, snarling at me with her finger on the trigger: *Tell me where you took my son. Or I blow your head off.*

"And I'm telling her, with that .30-30 barrel jammed into my throat: *I'm not the Plastic Man,* I just clean up after him. And I promise her that her little boy is fine, that I took him for his own protection, that she doesn't have to kill me, that we'll figure something out—"

He exhaled.

"Then Cambry shot her."

———————

NO.

Lena's thoughts dropped into terrible free fall.

No, no, no—

"She'd followed me. And then she saw a stranger holding a gun to my head. Okay? She *acted.* Your sister saved my life."

His words were tinny. Far away.

"But then she sees inside the trailer. The handcuffs. The camcorder. She notices the woman she's just shot in the back still has *duct tape* hanging off her. It's all dawning on her. And I have to look her in the eye and explain the truth. What my father is. What I do for him. And now what she's just done."

The coldness of it.

"And she's . . . she's *mortified*—"

Lena felt the bridge wobble dizzily underfoot. Nearly losing her grip.

". . . kissed her on the head and told her she was safe, that she was part of the Raycevic tribe now, that no one will ever know what she did—"

Her stomach turned.

"I showed her how I cut up the bodies and drain them—"

She hit the pavement on her palms and coughed. Acid in her throat.

"I loved her, Lena. I *loved* her. I told Cambry I'd take her out for a sundae the next morning. I wanted to cheer her up. That's the sad part. I felt like I was *celebrating* something. Like all my life, I've carried my dad's burden alone, and maybe now I didn't have to—"

He forced a smile. No malice. Heartbreak.

"So I showed Cambry the little boy in the shed. I had this brilliant idea—me and her, we would raise the kid ourselves. Right? I'd already decided I would leave my dairy cow of a wife for her, and we'd become a little family of our own. It was fucking *perfect*. We'd make some good from this wrong. We'd save the kid. She could atone for her sin. Balance the scales. But Cambry wasn't listening. She just sat on the hill and watched me burn the woman's body. I didn't get it back then, but I think I understand now, how seeing the little boy broke whatever was left to break inside her. She didn't just kill an innocent woman by mistake. She killed a *mother*."

With Blake's gun, Lena realized. *She did steal it.*

Raycevic spat a blood glob. "She played me, too, okay? She asked me if she could go to her car and roll a cigarette and think about everything. I said fine, because at this point I'd already taken her gun and siphoned her gas. What could she do? But I'd forgotten about the reserve in the tank. About a gallon."

That's why she ran.

"She started the engine and *drove like hell*."

Tears welled in her eyes.

"I only wanted to talk to her, to calm her down, before she got to Magma Springs. I didn't want to hurt her. But she could destroy us. She was in tears, her car running on fumes, trying desperately to call 911, to escape and turn us all in—"

In Lena's mind, the chase replayed. Cambry tricking Raycevic after he stopped her. Losing him at the junction, then the unlucky lightning flash. Dodging his fishtail maneuver by inches and sending him spinning off the road. Chasing down the semitruck, fighting the Plastic Man—

"We cornered her here on the bridge. My dad was furious about his eye, hollering at me to just shoot her. And Cambry had nowhere to go. No options. She knew I couldn't possibly protect her now. She tried to send a final text message and exited her car and climbed that railing, right there, and before I could stop her, she—"

Lena kept shaking her head with battered, powerless horror. She wished he could stop, that he would *just please stop*—

"She jumped, Lena."

"Stop talking—"

"She killed herself. It's true. You've been putting her on a pedestal." He smirked, as if remembering something funny. "Hey. Will that be in your book? Some heroine she makes—"

"Stop—"

"Won't that just break your mother's heart? Cambry didn't just kill herself—she killed *someone else,* too. So she's definitely in hell—"

"Please, stop—"

"Her suicide text was the problem. When I took her phone off-site, the message auto-sent to you. Can you believe it? If it weren't for that one little text, I could have just burned her body like any other. But now there was a message straight to her family, with *my name* in it, so I had to make up a story—"

Lena's heart tugged with bruised hope as she remembered the text's final sentence: *Please forgive me. I couldn't live with it. Hopefully you can, Officer Raycevic.*

"Revenge," she whispered.

"That's not it—"

"Cambry texted me your name, so I would come for you—"

"No." He looked reluctant. As if this revelation was too cruel, even for him. "That text wasn't meant for you, Lena. Cambry was apologizing to *me*. She couldn't live with murdering that woman. And maybe she was a little disgusted that I could. But when she tried to send it on that clunky flip phone, I think she selected your number accidentally in the contacts list. *Ratface* is right above *Ray*."

A hollow cavity opened up inside her stomach.

"I don't . . ." He shrugged weakly. "I don't think she had anything to say to you."

In the trembling photograph, her sister smiled up at her. The grin of a stranger wearing their shared face, impenetrable, unknown.

"You thought . . . what, her ghost sent you here in a dream? *Grow up,* Lena."

She turned away.

"Wait. There's more—"

She left him there. Shooting the vile man didn't even enter her mind. Maybe he'd bleed out. Maybe the heat and smoke would broil him alive—

"Hey," he called out. "Want to know her last words?"

She didn't.

"On that railing, before she jumped—"

She ignored him, twisting open the Corolla's door.

"Your sister begged me with teary eyes: *Ray, please don't tell my family*—"

She hit the seat, slammed the door.

"*Please.*" His voice rang through broken windows. "*Don't tell Mom and Dad what I did*—"

Lena set her gun in the cup holder and shifted into drive. She couldn't execute Raycevic like an animal, but she took a visceral pleasure in the way he screamed as she separated their cars and spilled the kid killer to the pavement behind her on his own exposed kneecaps.

CHAPTER 27

EXCRUCIATING PAIN.

Theo was hoisting himself the final agonizing inches up to the cab's door when he heard his son's echoing screams. In the side-view mirror's broken glass teeth, he glimpsed the two cars separate. Ray-Ray sprawling to the concrete. The Corolla pulling away and leaving.

Driving toward Theo.

He was almost out of time. His ruined jaw pumped rhythmic squirts through his fingers. He was leaking, losing himself to his fatal wound drop by drop as that blue car drew closer in the mirror. Inside, little Lena Nguyen thought it was all over, that she was leaving Hairpin Bridge victorious. In another few seconds her path would take her past his truck, and for a magic half second, Theo Raycevic would have a perfect angle on her.

So he made a choice. The only choice.

For Kitty.

He lifted his sticky hand from his throat and heaved the Winchester .30-30 to prop the barrel on the door. One final time. Raising the weapon was a Herculean effort, but he groaned and pushed through. He pressed his cheekbone to the stock and took aim as the car approached.

One last stray. One last ambush.

He steadied the rifle. *Kitty, you'd love this one.*

Without his fingers to his throat, hot blood spurted freely down his shirt. He would die putting Lena Nguyen down, and it was a perfectly fair trade. Why fear death? Oblivion is painless, the default state of everything is nothing, and hell, it solved the prostate issue. The world swam around Theo, all sickly oranges and whites. He guessed he had maybe thirty seconds of consciousness left.

Which was fine, because Lena had fewer. Three seconds, maybe?

The Corolla came up. Her face took shape through the cracked windshield. She was pale, haunted, drenched with blood. She had no idea she was to be the Plastic Man's final victim. The tension was delicious. This was the climactic moment of Theo's life, as good a note as any to go out on: like a stray nonchalantly approaching the slatted closet door of a Super 8 to grab her bathrobe, Lena drove closer and closer, slipping into beautiful alignment, granting him his shot through the glass.

Two seconds now.

He didn't even need to move his rifle. He let Lena's face slide perfectly into his gunsights. And carefully, as all vectors aligned, he squeezed the trigger.

One . . .

Death is painless.

Her brain is instantly destroyed.

After approximately three seconds of free fall from the railing of Hairpin Bridge, Cambry impacts the rock floor headfirst at almost a hundred miles per hour. It's all over in a thousandth of a second. The soft matter of her brain liquefies, every synapse explodes like a million strings of ruined Christmas lights, and everything that is Cambry Lynne Nguyen is instantly, irretrievably gone. All of her secrets, her jokes, her passions. Bob the Dinosaur, her favorite lyric of "(Don't Fear) The Reaper," the unknown reason she called me Ratface. Electrodes in a shattered circuit board, their data gone forever.

Right?

That's how I imagine it happened.

The medical community agrees with Raycevic's testimony—falling from such a height, you can't possibly feel the pain of impact. So that's how I wrote it. But the truth is . . . I have no goddamn idea. And I hate saying that. Who can possibly know how it feels to die? All I know, dear readers, is that my sister's story ends here, and I wish it ended differently.

More than you will ever understand.

I've written this account as accurately as possible, based on the verbal testimony I recorded on September 21 during my confrontation with Corporal Raycevic and his father, Theo—the serial killer now more famously known as the Plastic Man. After I crushed Raycevic's legs between our cars, he told me one final thing: that he was sorry he murdered my sister. The walkie unit was destroyed (by him) at this point, so there is no audio record of his confession. But it's important to note that after hours of bullying and lying that day, he did finally confess to my sister's murder.

I'm sorry we killed Cambry.

Those were his exact—and final—words to me.

I couldn't give him the validation of forgiveness. I couldn't execute him. I didn't know what to do. I left him there, got back in my car, and drove away.

No. Drove *is the wrong word.*

I ran away.

And in my weakness, I left an evil man with a still-functional car and a semiautomatic rifle in its trunk. Even injured, he could have fled, taken hostages, or ambushed first responders. The incoming wildfire wouldn't have killed him—Hairpin Bridge stands to this day, blackened with soot but unscathed.

As I left it behind me, I remember glancing up to the rearview mirror and seeing Cambry's bruised, bloody face. A clear thought entered my mind.

Earlier in the day's transcript, I repeat something from her service: when you die, you're transformed from a person into an idea. Back in June, I only thought I'd understood, but now I fully grasp it—the cruelty of what death is. My sister has lost her physical membership to this world. Cambry has no voice, no body, no self. She exists only in the ways we remember her. We carry her entire being within ourselves now, the way nomadic tribes used to carry fire inside a horn to keep the embers alight.

As I drove past the crashed semitruck containing the Plastic Man's body, I decided that only one person would carry the fire of Cambry's memory. And it won't be her sole surviving killer.

The final hours of my sister's life aren't Raycevic's story to tell. They're mine.

That's why . . .

That's why I turned around, I think.

The Corolla swerved hard, out of Theo's gunsights.

What?

Shock became disbelief—

No, no, no—

The blue Toyota whirled a skidding one-eighty, denying him his perfect shot on Lena Nguyen. In a blink, her face was gone, now obscured by the body of her car. Moving away.

He couldn't believe it. He'd had her. He'd *had* her. How could she have known to turn around, at that exact moment, at that exact place?

The rifle wobbled in his hands. Sights blurring. He wanted to lean outside and fire at the girl's car anyway—now racing away from him, back up the bridge—but it would be pure guesswork at such a severe angle. He was too weak to hoist himself up over the door anyway.

He'd already paid his price. Blood pumped down his shirt

to the slowing metronome of his heart. His mind went sludgy and dark as she left his cracked mirror, and a single disbelieving thought echoed against the shrinking walls of his brain: *I had her. I had her. I had her.*

I always get my strays . . .

LENA ACCELERATED BACK UP HAIRPIN BRIDGE.

Back to Raycevic's cruiser, coming fast through smoke. The kid killer himself was on the ground, leaving a slug trail of blood as he dragged himself away on shattered legs. Not fast enough.

She hit her brakes, lifted the Beretta from the Corolla's cup holder, and ejected the magazine into her palm: empty. Just one 9-millimeter round left, seated in the chamber.

She needed only one.

Fifty yards ahead, Raycevic saw her coming. He knew. He crawled faster on crunchy bones. Panicking, trying feebly to stand, scrambling for the back of his cruiser.

Lena clicked the empty mag back into the pistol. The few ounces of added weight would help steady her aim. She lifted her sister's eyeglasses from the dashboard and slipped them on. She mashed her eyes with her thumbs, took a deep breath, and exhaled a final heartsick promise—*Mom and Dad will never,* ever *know*—before stepping outside into the scorched air and slamming the door hard behind her, to face Corporal Raycevic one last time.

I promise, sis.

Mom will never know.

Up the bridge, Raycevic reached his Charger's trunk— unlocked now—and pushed it open with bloody handprints on the tailgate, and reached inside . . .

———————

AND LIFTED HIS AR-15 INTO DAYLIGHT.

It had waited in darkness all day, and now it was finally, *finally* in his hands. Black and shiny with beaded oil, pungent with the sweet candy odor of solvent. He fought burbling laughter—"Surprise, *bitch*"—as he looked back at Lena.

She was out of her car now. She calmly stopped beside her door with her feet shoulder-width apart. Her elbows came up, forming a perfect practiced isosceles grip as she raised her Beretta to aim at him. She wasn't even using her vehicle for cover.

More perplexing was the distance. They were still fifty yards apart.

Raycevic slapped the bolt catch to chamber a round. He brought the rifle up on her, resting the barrel shroud on his Charger's bumper. The red holographic reticle found her easily. Hungrily.

Cambry stood tall. Aiming back at him.

No, *Lena*. Wearing Cambry's glasses. She was a statue a half a football field away, pinned in the glassy bowl of Rick's rifle scope, staring back at him down unmagnified pistol sights of her own. For a surreal moment, he felt like they were making eye contact over their weapons. Something about this—this straightforward duel under a fiery sky—frightened him. No cover. No words. No excuses.

Really, girl? he wanted to shout. *This isn't like trick-shooting a sign.*

Fifty yards—a hundred and fifty feet—was easy for his AR-15 and its magnified optic, but it was twice the effective range of her handgun. Pistols are close-range weapons, extraordinarily difficult to accurately fire at range. Low-velocity rounds are much more vulnerable to wind and gravity. Certainly, this was farther than whatever air-conditioned shooting range Lena had practiced at back in Seattle. He still had his ballistic vest, too, shielding him from anything short of a head shot. She was a good markswoman. But she couldn't be *that* good. Right?

Right. He thumbed off the safety.

Maybe Lena was realizing this now—her fatal error in returning to finish him, that he'd lured her into an unwinnable gunfight—as Rick Raycevic centered his rifle's magnified reticle on her chest and prepared to fire, while she aimed her Beretta back at him two-handed with hard eyes unblinking, taking a deep breath and doing the same.

She's not that good, he thought, squeezing the trigger.

She can't possibly be that goo—

He saw a flash in her hands as she fired first. At fifty yards, the light reached him instantaneously, then a tenth of a second later the bullet, and a sixth of a second later, the sound.

He never heard the sound.

FOUR MINUTES LATER, THE NGUYEN SISTERS' COROLLA LEFT Hairpin Bridge for the final time and, on its way out, again approached Theo Raycevic's stalled semitruck at the south ramp.

There, in wait, his Winchester lever-action rifle rested atop the door with a .30-30 steel-jacketed cartridge chambered. A dirty fingernail held the trigger staged. The Corolla appeared first in the truck's broken mirror and then entered the weapon's iron sights. But the rifle didn't fire, because the man holding it had succumbed to blood loss minutes earlier.

The car passed through the gunsights.

And drove on.

Theo's truck continued to hang by a knot of tangled guardrail for another forty-eight minutes. Then a final rivet blew under the suspended weight and the entire rig—and inside, the body of the serial killer who would become posthumously known as the Plastic Man—plunged to the creek bed in a meteoric crash of accordioned metal and igniting diesel, heard and seen by no one.

CHAPTER 28

As I left, I swore you were in the car with me, Cambry.

You rode shotgun. Right beside me. It's so vividly clear in my mind—I saw you sitting there with your toes up on the dashboard, chewing gum, sketching in your notepad, glancing up and smiling at me between the strokes of your pen. You always loved to draw.

I smiled, too.

I can't describe how I felt in that moment. God, I'm trying right now, and failing. All I can say is that it was the warmest, most content feeling of my life. A hard-fought peace.

Your spirit can finally rest now, sis, because your killers will never take another innocent life. Mom knows you're not in hell. As I drove your bullet-riddled car back to Magma Springs, I couldn't help but let that dumb, joyful smile take over my face, and I turned your Toyota's volume dial to full blast and listened to your old CDs as loud as the speakers could go.

Lena drove in silence.

She was past screaming. Past sobbing. Past throwing up. She'd done it all already, with red eyes and a raw throat, and she felt exactly nothing now. A barren cavity had opened inside her chest. She pulled the rearview mirror down, because she couldn't stand to look at her sister's face anymore.

Hairpin Bridge vanished behind her. She promised herself, as the skeletal structure shrank against a mile-high wall of smoke, that she'd never, ever set foot on it again. She wished metal could burn. She wished she'd never come to Montana at all.

A jagged lightning bolt crossed the sky. No thunder, no storm. Just friction in the ash.

On her knee rested Raycevic's wallet photo of himself and Cambry, smiling together on the lake. Its very existence was a loose end, and a last-ever glimpse of her sister's crooked smile, and she was so deeply sick of looking at that, too.

She held it out the window and let the wind take it.

CHAPTER 29

I need to say this one last thing.

Then I'm done.

As I type this, dawn is breaking, it's September 21, 5:31 A.M., and I'm about to depart for Howard County on my suicide mission to confront Raycevic and learn the truth about Cambry's death. I have a thermos of black coffee and my Beretta locked and loaded.

I had a dream last night.

And I need to write it before it vanishes. Before I go.

In my dream, we were eighteen again. You and me, Cambry. We're up on that railroad trestle over the Yakima River with your friends, and you've told me that you didn't believe in an afterlife before you jumped off. That terrible smack as you struck your head on the beam. I've leaped in and found you, somehow, in all that cold and dark. And then we're collapsing ashore on chilled sand. Chests heaving. Green river weeds in your hair.

And you turn your head and look at me—and I know this is the dream now, not memory, because in real life your friends had already surrounded us—but in my dream, it's just us and the lapping water, and you look at me with piercing sadness in your teenage eyes. I've never seen such heartache before.

I wait for you to speak.

I know this isn't a normal dream. This isn't another nightmare with slit throats and glistening intestines. Somehow I know: This is my chance, maybe my only chance, real or imagined, to speak to you ever again. After this dream evaporates, you're gone for good.

I wait for you to speak. This is it.

Please. Say anything, sis.

LENA REACHED MAGMA SPRINGS UNDER A TOXIC ORANGE SKY. The highway was blockaded with evacuees going east and fire crews coming west. She reached the familiar gravel parking lot shared by the Magma Springs Diner and the Shell station. Gray ash speckled the windows like apocalyptic frost.

She shut the Corolla's door and locked it. Mindless habit— the windows were shot out.

She entered the diner and found her booth undisturbed. The recording had uploaded to the cloud exactly as planned. The connection was uninterrupted. The .mp4 file had recorded for three hours and nineteen minutes before Raycevic destroyed the walkie unit. By tomorrow, the two criminals she'd slain would be national news.

Watching wildfire coverage on the flat-screen, the lady at the counter didn't even glance up. She absently asked how Lena's project went.

Fine, she answered.

Would you like anything?

No. Then she reconsidered. *A sundae.*

As the lady ducked back into the kitchen, Lena noticed a newspaper clipping framed on the wall. A local trooper honored with an award. She recognized a younger Raycevic's smile and studied his face, his white teeth and action-hero squint, wondering how many bodies he'd made disappear at the time that photo was taken. What did her sister see in him, Terrible Guy #18? Was he another bug for her jar?

Cambry would never answer. If hell existed, she was probably there.

Or she was gone completely. Which is worse?

On the tabletop, Bob the Dinosaur stared up at Lena. She'd drawn it earlier today while she waited for Raycevic. Now she pulled a pen from her purse and began scribbling it out in hard, grinding scrapes. Her mind returned to Hairpin Bridge, to the version carved into the vinyl seat of Raycevic's cruiser—another loose end. But with a sinking heart, she knew he'd been right, that Bob the Dinosaur really was a facsimile of the lizard from that old Nickelodeon cartoon, and thus anyone could have drawn it. Not everything Cambry drew was brilliant.

The sundae arrived.

Lena ate three bites, but her loose teeth ached in her gums. The chocolate syrup was thin. Everything tasted like blood. Her stomach turned again, and she dropped the spoon, her cheeks burning, her eyes welling with tears.

The waitress watched, petrified. She hadn't left. It took Lena a moment to realize why—her broken nose, the blood hardening on her clothes and hair, the rotten purple knot over her left eye.

Can you call the police, please?

The waitress nodded and hurried away.

Lena waited at her booth. She slipped the empty Beretta from her holster, field-stripped it, and placed the oily black parts on the tabletop. Then she sat on her hands and wondered if she'd ever truly loved her sister, or if she'd just loved *the idea* of her. Does it even matter, if the person no longer exists?

She stared forward, into the seat opposite, until her eyes fell out of focus.

You look back at me.

Your eyes brim with tears, and your lip curls, and I don't recognize it at first, because I've never seen it on your face before: Shame. Deep, aching humiliation. It's heartbreaking. I can tell you're terrified of me, somehow. What I must think of you.

I ask you what's wrong.

You won't answer. You snap your head away, blinking through tears, and look out at the Yakima River.

I still don't understand. I touch your shoulder. You shake your head, whipping your slick hair. You keep staring purposefully ahead, out over the water that nearly took you, out at the far shore and even farther. And you part your lips and finally speak through shivering teeth, your words floating on shallow breath:

Lena, go.

——————————

SHE BLINKED.

She was alone in the diner. The flat-screen was muted. No jangling silverware or running dishwashers in the kitchen. The waitress had ushered the staff out after seeing the disassembled handgun on the table. All Lena had to do now was wait for the police—the *real* police—to arrive and take her in for questioning. But something wasn't right.

Not yet.

In the tabletop's wood grain, Bob the Dinosaur was still partially visible. She hadn't fully scratched out his cartoon eyes.

She didn't touch her pen. She sat rigidly on her hands in a blaze of red sunlight as last night's dream took sharp focus.

Go where?

——————————

You don't answer me. You just stare out over the rippled light of the river, shaking your head.

Go, please.

I don't understand.

You turn to face me and a tear darts down your cheek. Something new in your glassy eyes—urgency. Rising alarm.

Go, Lena.

Just go now.

Still, I can only stare.

I can tell you're getting frustrated now that I don't get it. And truthfully, Cambry, I'm getting annoyed with you, too. I jumped into dark water after you and risked my life, just to be pushed away like this? What was the point, then? Why did I even bother?

I shake my head, still confused. I don't want to go, anyway. I want to stay with you. I miss you. Please, God, let me stay here a while longer on this half-remembered shore of the Yakima River and talk to my dead sister—but then you shove me. Hard.

Why are you doing this?

I hit my back on the wet sand, stunned and hurt, staring up at you. Tears in my eyes. I can't help it.

Go, you hiss through your teeth. *Now.*

You're running out of time.

———

SHE LEFT MAGMA SPRINGS DINER.

At her booth she left her laptop, her barely eaten sundae, and the five disassembled parts of her handgun. The door clapped shut behind her and she returned to her Corolla under a darkening sky. Beside the Shell pumps, the waitress watched her drive away with a cell phone held to her ear, reading her license plate to 911.

She merged back onto the highway. Driving fast. The engine rattled and coughed.

Lena, go.

She wove between fire trucks and twenty-ton water tankers, feeling the air lash her fresh cuts. Highway 200, then Pickle Farm Road. After a few miles, the mournful whine of a police siren came up behind her. She didn't look back. She knew she was being followed by a Dodge Charger identical to Raycevic's. It didn't matter, because she was nearly there.

Go. Now.

She almost missed the driveway. But yes, it was there, a right turn past the burned-out barn, exactly as Raycevic had described. Another half a mile over washed-out gravel, and she reached a modest double-wide and a workshop over a vast cement foundation. She parked and left her door ajar, her headlights fighting the falling darkness, and on foot she entered a strange wasteland, past the rust-eaten body of an ancient semitruck, around piles of excavated rock, orderly rows of lumber starting to rot, and to her right she spotted the ghastly sight that had started it all: four firepits stacked with pyramids of heavy stone. They were empty now. Dry coals exhaled dust in the wind.

She kept walking. To her left, trenches and exhumed earth. A red tractor caked with grit. The ground was stirred and sunken underfoot. She wondered how many buried cars she was walking over. How much of the soil was cremated human bone.

Red and blue lights strobed. The police cruiser parked behind her Corolla, casting wild shadows across the Raycevics' property.

She kept walking deeper, deeper. The cop chirped his siren, calling her attention. Still, she didn't turn around. She couldn't stop. She wouldn't, under the intensifying thud of her heart.

You're running out of time—

Then I woke up.

That was my dream, dear readers.

I hope to God that it was really you, Cambry, and not my wishful imagination. I hope it was really your soul visiting me in my sleep, urging me out the door this morning in your own gruff way. To not lose my courage, to *go* and confront Raycevic on the bridge you died on, to prevent what happened to you from happening to anyone else.

But something doesn't fit—the despair in your eyes. The way you shoved me away. Why were you so upset? I wish you'd had something nicer to say, like *I love you.*

I guess I just don't understand.

And it doesn't matter, because whatever you did when you were alive—I don't care. I forgive you in advance, sis.

For anything. For everything.

Whatever it is.

I woke up before I could say this to you, but if you wanted my response? You know me. I'll make it as nerdy as possible. Think of it like an inverted version of the evil AI from "I Have No Mouth, and I Must Scream." Just: Love. Love. Love. Love. Only love for you. Nothing but love here on earth, in the crater you left behind. Love of unthinkable depth, unknowable vastness, stretching east and west and north and south to infinite horizons of unceasing, untiring, unconditional love. Cambry, my twin, I love you so fucking much.

And whatever you did in life that you wish to atone for, that you fear my judgment for, I don't care. Rest warm, sis, because I will always love you.

And . . .

That's it. I'm out. Montana-bound. I'm shutting this laptop and walking to your car and starting the engine and going. *Going,* just like you asked. But I'll ask something of you, too.

Today on Hairpin Bridge, please watch my back. Be my sixth sense. Be the whisper in my mind, the raised hairs on my neck, the subtle edge that helps me survive today's battle. Let me borrow one of your furies for a day. But most of all, if it was really you in my dream, and not just my heartsick imagination . . .

Please, Cambry . . .

Give me a sign.

———————

SHE HEARD THE COP ROLL DOWN HIS WINDOW AND SHOUT: *Stop.*

She didn't. She couldn't.

He cut his engine, and in the heart-pounding silence, a sound caught Lena's attention. It was faint, tinny, warped by confined space. She halted. It sounded imaginary, illusory, like a ring in her ear.

Behind her, a car door creaked open. *Stop, now.*

Still, Lena focused only on that faraway sound, on that unreal echo. Barely there, lingering at the edge of her perception. She fought to believe in it, that it wasn't her imagination or the damaged cells inside her eardrums, that it was real and it *meant something*. It was coming from below. To her left. And there she saw a circle of old stones. A groundwater well.

Her blood turned to ice water.

Only now did she turn around, wobbling on weak knees to face the highway patrolman. He held one hand on his sidearm. But he was frozen, too, stunned midstride just like her, because he heard the same noise she did. *Oh, thank God*—he heard it, too. It was real. She blinked away tears and their eyes met. He already knew what it was, and in another awestruck heartbeat, so did Lena.

From the darkness of the Raycevics' well, the sound intensified. Hurt, hoarse with two days of thirst, begging to be found.

The cry of a little boy.

EPILOGUE

SHE DESCENDED THE NARROW SHAFT WITH HER HEELS AND shoulders arched against dry stone. Like wall-crawling down a chimney, knees pressed to her chest. Far too tight for the trooper, who fed her rope from above. The temperature chilled as she lowered into suffocating darkness, fifteen feet down, then twenty, then thirty, until she swore she was deep under the surface of the Yakima River again, reaching out with aching lungs, fearing her outstretched hand would find nothing, that Cambry was gone forever.

This time, Lena Nguyen was unafraid.

And at the bottom, she felt it—small fingers grasping hers.

She untied the rope from her belt loops and sat with him while help arrived, giving him water in small sips so he wouldn't vomit. Later, she would be unable to recall most of what she told the boy while they waited together—that he was safe; that good people were coming to help; that the loved ones we lose are always, *always* with us. All things that probably meant nothing at all to this dehydrated little boy with fractured legs. Sometimes all that matters is your voice in the dark.

But one thing, she would remember.

"Want to know a secret?"

Sure he did.

As firefighters and paramedics arrived in a swirl of echoed voices and flashlights lit them from above, Lena leaned in close for a whisper.

"My sister helped me find you."

ACKNOWLEDGMENTS

AS ALWAYS, I COULDN'T HAVE WRITTEN THIS BOOK WITHOUT the relentless support of my family. Thank you to my parents, for always believing in me and being my two biggest fans.

Thank you to Jaclyn—for putting up with all of my quirks and thousand-yard stares throughout the writing process, for urging me to slow the pace down from time to time, and for suggesting a story idea that quite possibly saved this novel.

Thank you to my amazing literary agent, David Hale Smith, who guided me out of a difficult situation to greener shores, and my additional gratitude to the expertise of Emma Linch and Martin Soames, and to the always-sage advice of manager Chad Snopek. I'm fortunate to have so many great people in my corner for this project, and hopefully many more to come.

Thank you to my incredible editor Jennifer Brehl at William Morrow, for your clear eyes and guidance as we made this story the best it could possibly be—right down to the formatting choices (and Peter Schneider, of course, for your always-on-point book and movie recommendations!). And a massive thank-you to the entire team at William Morrow for their wonderful work in polishing and delivering this story to readers.

Thank you, everyone.